LOVELACE AND BUTTON
(INTERNATIONAL INVESTIGATORS)
INC.

Also by James Hawkins

INSPECTOR BLISS MYSTERIES

Missing: Presumed Dead
The Fish Kisser
No Cherubs for Melanie
A Year Less a Day
The Dave Bliss Quintet

NON-FICTION

The Canadian Private Investigator's Manual

1001 Fundraising Ideas and Strategies for
Charities and Not-for-Profit Groups

LOVELACE & BUTTON (INTERNATIONAL INVESTIGATORS) INC.

A Chief Inspector Bliss Mystery

James Hawkins

A Castle Street Mystery

THE DUNDURN GROUP
TORONTO

Editor: Barry Jowett
Copy-editor: Lloyd Davis
Design: Andrew Roberts
Printer: Webcom

Library and Archives Canada Cataloguing in Publication

Hawkins, D. James (Derek James), 1947-
Lovelace and Button (International Investigators) Inc. / James Hawkins.

ISBN 1-55002-541-4

I. Title.

PS8565.A848L69 2004   C813'.6   C2004-905470-8

1   2   3   4   5   08   07   06   05   04

We acknowledge the support of the **Canada Council for the Arts** and the **Ontario Arts Council** for our publishing program. We also acknowledge the financial support of the **Government of Canada** through the **Book Publishing Industry Development Program** and **The Association for the Export of Canadian Books**, and the **Government of Ontario** through the **Ontario Book Publishers Tax Credit** program.

Care has been taken to trace the ownership of copyright material used in this book. The author and the publisher welcome any information enabling them to rectify any references or credits in subsequent editions.

J. Kirk Howard, President

Printed and bound in Canada
Printed on recycled paper ♼
www.dundurn.com

Dundurn Press
8 Market Street
Suite 200
Toronto, Ontario, Canada
M5E 1M6

Gazelle Book Services Limited
White Cross Mills
Hightown, Lancaster, England
LA1 4X5

Dundurn Press
2250 Military Road
Tonawanda, NY
U.S.A. 14150

For Nancy ... with love

chapter one

"Samantha Anne Bliss: do you take Peter Sebastian Bryan to be your lawful wedded husband, to have and to hold, from this day forward …"

"That's it, then," mutters David Bliss, Samantha's father, thinking that he is talking to himself. "The poor sucker hasn't got a clue what he's taking on. I just hope he doesn't blame me."

"Who's going to blame you?" whispers an enquirer, her voice barely audible above the rain hammering on the church's ancient copper roof.

"… till death ye both shall part?" continues the pastor.

Oh God! Was I talking aloud? "Sorry, Daphne," whispers Bliss.

"I do," replies Samantha, without hesitation.

No mention of honour or obey.

Did you expect there to be? She's a lawyer, not an office flunky. Anyway, when did she ever do what she was told?

There's a first time for everything.

"Peter Sebastian Bryan: do you take Samantha Anne Bliss ..."

David Bliss feels a slight tug and has to bend a long way to question the giant toadstool hat on his left.

"What is it, Daphne?"

"Don't they usually ask the man first?"

"Not the one who's marrying my daughter, apparently."

An indignant "Shush!" comes from the woman on Bliss's right and he briefly cranes around as if trying to locate the talkative culprit.

"I meant *you*, David," says Sarah, Bliss's ex-wife, as she digs him in the ribs.

"Sorry ..."

"In sickness and in health," drones the clergyman, "till death ye both shall part?"

"I do."

"I now pronounce you man and wife."

"I'm surprised Samantha didn't insist on changing that to, 'I now pronounce you woman and husband,'" Bliss mutters to Daphne as he shields his elderly friend against the deluge while leading her to the limousine.

"Weddings always make me so happy," snivels the grandmotherly figure under the hat, but Bliss's mind is on his ex-wife as he offers Daphne a Kleenex, saying, "That's 'cos you've never had one of your own, Daphne."

Daphne Lovelace, a lifelong spinster by sheer determination, haughtily waves off the proffered tissue with her own monogrammed silk handkerchief. "Well, it's never too late, David. 'Marry in haste, repent at leisure,' my mother always said. And you needn't look at me like that. I may not be a spring chicken but I've had offers.

Anyway, it couldn't have been too bad — aren't you planning on doing it again?"

"Whoever gave you that idea?" laughs Bliss, though he knows it would be easier to cart water in a sieve than keep a secret from Daphne.

"Samantha mentioned a certain little French hen," she replies cryptically, but Bliss refuses to play.

"Take off the umbrella, Daphne. You'll never get into the car wearing that."

"Huh. Cheek! Chief Inspector," she snorts, but complies, saying, "If Minnie had shown up you would have had someone else's hat to pick on. You should've seen the millinery creation I tarted up for her. I'm quite put out that she didn't even phone me to say she wasn't coming."

Bliss vaults into the car behind the aging woman and gazes intently through the windshield, questioning whether or not the chauffeur can see the road. "More suitable for a funeral?" he whistles, but it's an avoidance tactic immediately rumbled by Daphne as they drive off gingerly towards the Berkeley Hotel.

"I know you find Minnie a bit irritating at times, but we're going on a trip around the world together, you know."

"Yes. You've already told me — three times," he says testily, feeling he's heard sufficient eulogizing of Minnie Dennon, Daphne's overly amorous septuagenarian friend, to last a lifetime. "Though God knows how she can afford it."

Fifty miles away, in Daphne's hometown of Westchester, Minnie Dennon has a similar concern as she takes a contemplative look around her tacky little flat and spends a few moments thinking how different her life may have been without fate's malevolent hand.

"Some people have all the luck," she muses, as she checks that she has turned off the gas stove and the single-element electric fire, then quietly closes the front door behind her and listens for the latch to drop, before sliding the key under the doormat. "That's it, then," she mutters and, head down, pushes out into the rain. She has an important engagement — one of the most important in her life — and in veneration of the occasion she is wearing the drab olive suit she'd bought for her Alfred's funeral.

"Thirty-five years with the same man deserves some respect," she'd fumed at the time, nearly twenty years ago, when Daphne had suggested that the suit was perhaps a trifle sombre considering the flippancy with which she'd treated her marriage. "Anyway, it'll come in handy for your funeral," Minnie had added acerbically.

The smell of mothballs surrounds Minnie as she makes her way down Watson Street, then she takes a few moments to pause at the top of the High Street and compare it with the childhood view she fondly retains.

The picture in her mind may be faded and sepia-edged, but apart from some remodelling carried out by Hitler's flying circus, little has outwardly changed. A hotchpotch of wooden-framed Tudor buildings on one side of the street is mirrored in the windows of a few Victorian monstrosities, housing banks and a department store, on the other. The traffic is different; dozens of zippy little cars have replaced the monstrous traction engines that belched steam and smuts, though the gentle Clydesdales of the brewery's dray still clip-clop from pub to pub.

Minnie juggles a few coins in her coat pocket and eyes the sweetshop on the corner of Mansard Street. A KitKat or Mars bar, perhaps? But, knowing there is no point in recounting her cash, she shakes her head. Her path is set and she moves on past the butcher's, and the Mitre hotel, to a small café crushed under the insensitive shadow of a 1950s multi-storey car park.

Ye Olde Copper Kettle's front door leads Minnie into the past and, as she shakes off her coat, she winces at the huddle of youngsters crowding around the Internet terminals at the back of the room, so she closes her eyes and looks back. Stiffly starched white tablecloths match the aprons of the pink-faced young waitresses, their hair pleated up under lacy caps. The glow of a coal fire reflects warmly off the bone china crockery and polished silverware. Businessmen and bankers in blue mingle with tweedy farmers, and the town's Ladies sit in one corner poring over Paris chic in *Tatler* while they chat of Ascot and exotic holidays in Bournemouth or Brighton. But the depression of the late '20s has bitten deeply, and the genteel Edwardian tea-room is already fading.

A coarse voice shakes Minnie out of her memories. "Yeah. What-can-I-get-ya?"

"Just a cup of Earl Grey, please."

"Sorry, luv. We've only got regular."

"I remember coming here with my mother in the thirties," Minnie says, though it washes over the young woman.

"Nice … Did you want the regular, then?"

Minnie takes a deep breath; concerned that her plans are already unravelling.

"I suppose so," she says, resisting the temptation to run as she scans the plastic furniture and industrial china, "but please can I have a proper teapot, with a cup with a saucer."

The young counter assistant sees the despair in Minnie's eyes and softens. "Of course you can, dear. You just find a seat and I'll bring it over."

As Minnie pulls a chair from under a table, one of the teenage Web gamers, Ronnie Stapleton, sizes up the smartly dressed aging woman and tries to amuse his group of peers by snobbishly sneering, "Oh. I want a proper teapot like madam-f'kin' la-di-da over there."

"Cut it out, Ron," says Krysta, the fifteen-year-old love of his live, sensing Minnie's discomfort, but Stapleton's narcotic-addled brain blanks out his girl-friend as he continues to mock.

"Oh. Why don't you lick my f'kin boots?"

"Ron …" warns Krysta and he eases off.

"Aw'right; aw'right. Leave it out, girl; you ain't me muvver. Just get me some water will ya. I'm skint."

In London, in the elegant reception suite at the Berkeley Hotel on the south bank of the Thames, the father of the bride, Detective Chief Inspector David Bliss of London's Metropolitan Police, is about to make a similar request on behalf of Daphne Lovelace.

"I brought my own tea bag. It's Keemun — the Queen's favourite," Daphne explains conspiratorially as she squirrels it out of her bag while they wait for the remainder of the guests to arrive. "Would you mind asking one of the waiters to fetch me a pot of freshly boiled water and a nice china cup?"

"You can't do that here," explains Bliss, but her expression clearly says she can, and will, so he changes tack and starts, "There's champagne …" but he gets nowhere as Daphne fiercely points to her watch.

"It's four o'clock in the afternoon, David."

"Oh. Right," he says, and then collides with his previous boss, now his son-in-law, as he makes his way to the bar.

"David. A word ..." Peter Bryan begins as he drags Bliss aside and drops his tone. "Did you see Edwards at the church?"

"No. Don't worry, son. I don't think he showed up," laughs Bliss, knowing that while a general invitation went out to all the senior officers at the station, everyone was praying that Chief Superintendent Edwards would send his apologies. However, Edwards hasn't offered an apology — ever. He is an officer, with Brylcreemed hair and burnished boots, still marching in the past, who, on a good day, might apologize for being surrounded by incompetent idiots. He is a man whose pin-stuck effigy hangs in many junior officers' lockers. And he's a man who has stood on the gallows more than once, yet has always managed to somehow slip the noose and sling it around his accuser's neck just as the lever was pulled.

"Thank Christ ..." says Bryan, fearing that Edward's presence would curdle the champagne. Then he gives Bliss a quizzical look. "Hey! What's with the 'son' thing?"

"Serves you right for marrying my daughter, Detective Chief Inspector."

"You can cut that out, too, Dave," Bryan replies with mock shirtiness as he stalks off. "And don't expect me to call you 'Dad,' either."

"One pot of tea without the tea, please," Bliss orders nonchalantly as he turns to the barman, and he watches with amusement as the young man tries to work out whether or not he might be dangerous.

In Westchester, Minnie has scurried from the café, leaving the teapot half full, and is pushing on towards her goal when a Georgian mansion at the bottom end of the High Street solidly blocks her path. Westchester's old general hospital was her birthplace, at a time when few families could afford the luxury of a doctor-attended birth, but Minnie stops briefly and considers detouring to avoid painful recollections of the soot-encrusted stone building. There are no joy-filled births for her; only deaths. First her younger brother who never made it out of the aediculated front doors; solid lacquered doors fiercely barred with a sign declaring, "All accidents, admissions and enquiries *must* use side entrance." The double front doors were always kept well oiled, but were for the exclusive use of the Matron, together with consultant surgeons (not the riff-raff of general practitioners and interns) and mothers, with their perfect little newborns, who were ushered out through them and encouraged to pose for photos with the beaming sisters and nurses — like car builders touting their latest model to the press.

"They might let you into the world through the front door," the crusty ambulance driver had explained as he'd rushed Minnie's dying mother to the side entrance. "But Gawd help anyone who tries to get out through there."

Minnie's mother had been followed to the side door by various aunts, uncles and other family members, and finally Alfred, her husband. But apart from the time when she was first cradled in her mother's arms, a triumphal exit through the hospital's front doors has eluded Minnie and has been added to her lifelong list of unfulfilled dreams along with bridesmaid, ballerina and Princess Margaret.

After the opening of a new medical facility in 1970, the old hospital was converted into a home for the elderly infirm, and Minnie resolutely keeps her eyes on the pavement and sticks to the curbside as she passes. She pays a penalty as a car swishes by and douses her stockings and shoes.

She'd spent a long time choosing today's shoes; comfortable enough to carry her across town while stylish enough for her engagement. She would have preferred the stilettos of her fifties, when she'd still had Alfred to tango with, but age has whittled away her ankles and she had feared tripping and failing in her assignment. So she's settled for a clumpy pair of lace-ups with a heel low enough to make falling unlikely.

Bliss's ex-wife's wedding shoes have also been carefully selected, though not from her existing collection.

"Hah! Of course I have to have new shoes," she'd cried when George, Bliss's replacement, had timorously suggested that she might find something suitable amongst the fifty or so pairs already clogging several wardrobes.

Bliss is watching his ex-wife as she basks in the glow of their daughter, and he is weighing up the probable cost of her outfit when a familiar voice brings him back to earth.

"David ... Proud day ... How'r'ya feeling?"

"About as useful as a double-ended condom, to be honest, Mick," replies Bliss. "I wasn't even allowed to give Samantha away at the altar. She reckoned it was demeaning to be offered up like a sacrificial cow. So far, all I've had to do is get Daphne a pot for her tea."

"I dunno why we blokes bother with weddings," complains Inspector Williams, and Bliss is on the point of agreeing when he realizes that Daphne has found another reluctant ear.

"... and then we're going to Alice Springs and Ayers Rock."

"So how much is this little jaunt costing exactly?" asks Bliss, taking the spotlight and allowing a fellow chief inspector to escape.

· "Nearly thirty thousand pounds," replies Daphne smugly. "And Minnie insists on paying for everything. 'You can't do that,' I told her, but she's adamant. And it's hardly a jaunt, David. We're doing seven great rivers; the Zambezi, Niagara Falls, the Amazon ..."

Minnie gives a wide berth to Maplin's Travel on Market Street, where Sandra Piddock shuffles longingly through a large stack of tickets as she peers out into the October murk. "Hawaii, Bali, the Seychelles, the Pyramids and the Great Wall," she muses, then picks up the phone and listens to Minnie's recorded voice inviting her to leave a message.

"It's Sandra at Maplin's, Mrs. Dennon. Thursday afternoon. Just reminding you that we've got all the tickets ready for you and Ms. Lovelace. You'll have to collect them by tomorrow afternoon or we'll have to cancel them and you'll lose your deposit. If you have any queries ..."

Minnie has no queries. She has a meeting to attend and hurries on towards the city's Norman cathedral.

Detective Chief Inspector Peter Bryan is making the rounds alone as his new wife powders her nose, with the help of her mother and three of her bridesmaids.

"Gawd knows what they're doing in there," he says to his father-in-law with a nod to the washroom.

"Twenty-five years with her mother and I never worked it out," mumbles Bliss before changing the subject. "Young Daphne here is taking a trip around the world with her friend, Minnie."

"Wow! That's amazing," says Bryan with imprudent enthusiasm.

"Yes. First we're taking the Orient Express across Europe; then we're sailing the Aegean to Istanbul ..."

"That sounds absolutely fabulous. I'd love to hear about it sometime, but —" starts Bryan, with a couple of hundred guests waiting to congratulate him, though he can't escape so lightly.

"... then on to Cairo; we'll be cruising up the Nile to the Pyramids ..."

"I really ought to —"

"... then there's the safari in the Serengeti ..."

"Great, but —"

"... the Seychelles ..."

"Peter," cuts in Samantha, appearing from nowhere. "They're calling us to start the buffet — oh. Hi, Daphne."

"Hello, Samantha. I was just saying to your husband — oh! They've gone."

"Never mind, Daphne," comforts Bliss. "She completely ignored me, and I'm her father."

Daphne shakes her head knowingly, laughing, "Children," as if she's had a lifetime's experience.

The wet-dog smell of Minnie's saturated woollen overcoat mingles with the ecclesiastical mustiness of the ancient cathedral as she kneels and ponders what to say. Why did you let Dad die before I was old enough to know him? Where were you when Mum fell to pieces? Did you get a kick out of watching her shrivel into a lunatic? And how could you have let Alfred suffer the way he did? Did I ever miss a Christmas or Easter? "Believe," they said. "Have faith," they said. I believed; I had faith. Funeral after funeral, I stood with all the others, saying, "I know that my redeemer liveth." Well, where were you when I needed you?

"What choice have you left me? You've let me down," Minnie says aloud, her voice rising in a crescendo of anger. "I hate you now." She pauses and tries to rein in her feelings, but it's too late and she runs down the aisle with tears streaming down her face as she turns to shout at the altar, "I hate you! I hate you! I hate you!"

Ronnie Stapleton, forced out of the Copper Kettle by impecuniosity, is slouching past the cathedral in search of someone to scam for a fix, when the distraught old woman emerges into the rain. The young layabout sums up the situation in three strides and is already high on the proceeds of Minnie's purse when a spoiler steps in.

"Are you okay, ma'am?" asks a concerned young mother, sensing Minnie's distress, and Stapleton is forced to back off.

Minnie scurries away with a mumbled "Yes, I'll be all right." But the young woman puts Stapleton's rapid retreat in context, and takes careful note of the hand-painted swastika on the back of his jacket as he slinks away.

"Remind me to take Minnie a piece of wedding cake," says Daphne as the happy couple cross hands and slice into the multilayered confection at the Berkeley. "She'll be sorry she missed this."

"I doubt it," replies Bliss as he joins the applause for the newlyweds. "This is pretty small potatoes compared to the adventure you two have cooked up."

"Did I mention the Orinoco …" starts Daphne, but Bliss shushes her as the groom's brother coughs into the microphone and brings the room to silence.

"It is my duty as the best man at this wedding …" he begins and is met with a concerted groan from the floor. "All right … All I'm going to say is that when the

Commissioner called for better co-operation between
his senior officers and the legal profession, I don't think
he had bonking in mind."

The rain has intensified as Minnie sets her sights on her
final destination — Westchester's stately railway station
with its elegant glass canopy supported on cast-iron pillars
— and she is so focused on the journey ahead that she
takes no notice of Stapleton's shadowy figure lurking
behind her as she skirts the brightly illuminated main
entrance and heads for the goods yard.

"So ... Chief Inspector. Have I missed the best bits?"
asks an unwelcome voice as the speeches end, and Bliss
spins to find Chief Superintendent Michael Edwards on
his shoulder.

"Oh. You made it, sir," says Bliss, trying hard to
keep disappointment out of his tone.

"I thought I should show the flag, Dave. Esprit de
corps and all that. I just hope I'm not too late to toast
the happy couple."

"Esprit de corps," echoes Bliss sourly as Edwards
paints on a smile and makes his way towards the
newlyweds.

Inspector Williams creeps up behind Bliss, saying,
"He's gotta bloody nerve."

"Be nice, Mick," says Bliss. "You know — the way
we're supposed to treat villains nowadays."

"It's easy for you to say that, flying a desk at the
Yard. Anyway, you spend so much time out of the bloody
country you never have to deal with the bastard."

"Tut-tut, Mick," cautions Bliss, though he has no
intention of defending the senior officer. Neither is he

going to defend his cushy job liaising with Interpol, though he's conscious of the jaundiced eyes of some of his colleagues.

"So. How do you like shuffling papers, Dave?" asks Williams.

"It's okay," Bliss says with little enthusiasm, "but I think I'd rather be out chasing scum."

That's not true, Bliss acknowledges to himself as Williams wanders away. And he drains his Dom Pérignon, thinking, *The truth is you'd rather be back in France, dancing in the Mediterranean moonlight with a certain Provençal popsy named Daisy. She's still there, waiting for you.*

I know.

So, what's stopping you? You're forty-seven now. Your hair's beginning to slip south along with the flab.

It's not that bad.

Give it time.

It's impossible and you know it. She'll never leave there — what about her mother and grandmother?

Have you asked her?

"David ... David," a persistent voice breaks into his musings and he finds Daphne on his arm.

"The band's starting. How about the first dance?"

"Why not?" he says, though can't help wishing that it were Daisy.

In Westchester, at the railway station, Minnie has plotted her path, and she slips past the "Staff Only" sign at the goods entrance and onto the platform without looking back. Her slight figure registers hazily on the platform's rain-fogged security camera in the signalman's box just off the end of Platform One, but is unseen by Robert Mackellar, the duty signalman, as he fills his teapot from a boiling kettle, turns up the radio and auditions for a baritone part with the Merthyr Tydfil male voice choir.

"*Tonight ... Tonight ... Won't be just any night ...*" he sings to an audience of switches and monitors high above the station's platforms.

Minnie pauses for a second, the muffled tones of Mackellar's rich voice breaking into her thoughts, then, with her goal in sight, she puts her head down and presses onward against the rain. Behind her, Ronnie Stapleton briefly hesitates while deliberating on the wisdom of his chosen path, but he shakes off his unease and picks up Minnie's trail.

"*Tonight there will be no morning sun,*" continues Mackellar as a warning bell draws his attention to a flashing light on an indicator board.

Seventeen-fifty-seven non-stopper, he says to himself, and he doesn't need to refer to the schedules to know that the London-bound express has entered his section and will whistle past at a hundred miles an hour in just over two minutes.

The screech of the distant train's siren is lost in the maelstrom as Minnie heads for the platform's edge, while Stapleton keeps a careful eye on the surveillance camera and slips into the shadows of a giant billboard behind her.

Above Minnie, Mackellar sings along with his regular routine: "*Tonight ... Tonight ... I'll see my love tonight ... Pour a cup of tea; check line is clear ... And for us the stars will stop where they are ... and ensure the road crossing barriers are going down ... Today, the minutes seem like hours ... and make sure the signals are working and showing correct colour; confirm all points are properly set ... Oh moon ...*"

A minute to go — time to add the milk and sugar. But a closer look at the station monitor shows a misty figure at the edge of one of the platforms, so he hits a button to wake up an electronic announcer.

A tinny overhead speaker blares out a warning. "Attention all passengers on Platform One: please stand clear of the tracks." Minnie straightens herself, but doesn't back away.

"... *moon glow bright, and make this endless* ..."

Stapleton inwardly smiles at his luck; all he needs is the tornado of a passing train to cover his attack, and he measures the distance with the care of a footballer in the run-up to a penalty kick.

Minnie stands rigidly, her eyes focused on the past, and as she scans the faces of her childhood, she is deaf to the distant scream of the train's whistle and the singing of the rails.

Stapleton loosens his muscles, checks his timing and confirms the platform is free of potential witnesses.

A stream of urchins' faces play through Minnie's mind and she begins labelling them: Mark, Annie, Maureen ... but the picture quickly fades.

Signalman Mackellar's eyes are focused on Minnie's shadowy figure and his voice has a worried edge as he sings, "... *and make this endless day* ... *get away from the edge, lady. Please get away from the edge.*"

Minnie's handsome young father is with her now, giving her and her mother a final hug as his troop train readies to pull away from the same platform in 1939. "Bye-bye, Dad," she cries aloud, her sobs lost to the wind, and the tears continue as she mourns her childhood innocence shattered by the ugliness of war. "Missing. Presumed dead," was all the telegram had said, and she had cried alongside her mother for days until a sad-faced captain confirmed that her father's body had been identified.

Thirty seconds to go and Mackellar hits the warning again as his voice rises in crescendo. "… *endless night … Tonight … Tonight.*"

"Attention all passengers on Platform One: please stand clear of the tracks," repeats the ethereal messenger, but Minnie doesn't hear; she's dancing away her youth in the post-war euphoria, while her broken mother sits alone at home hoping the scars will heal.

Ten paces, Stapleton estimates, as he limbers up with a couple of gentle bunny hops. Overhead, the track's power wires begin to hum, drawing Minnie closer as she walks up the aisle to stand by the side of a youthful Alfred Dennon.

"I do," Minnie says aloud and inches forward as the siren of the approaching engine sends out a final warning.

Stapleton is running now, co-ordinating his arrival with that of the oncoming train, and Mackellar has stopped his singing and is heading for the window.

"Get back, lady. Get back!" screams Mackellar from his lofty perch, but his words are whisked into the wind.

Stapleton falters for a fraction of a second as he tries to process the sound, but his path is set; his mind made up.

The train's driver peers ahead through the murk, searching for the next signal, when Minnie and Stapleton come into view.

"What the hell?" he starts with one hand on the whistle and the other reaching for the brake.

Minnie is calm and is standing over Alfred's coffin now as the rush of the train's forward wind tears at her hair and the shriek of the whistle blasts her ears.

"Goodbye, Alfred," she cries and leaps just as Stapleton grabs for her handbag.

"Oh my God … Oh my God," screeches Mackellar as he throws all the signals to danger and races for the emergency phone.

chapter two

The Bluebottles, a six-piece combo of off-duty police officers, are hammering away on stage as Daphne Lovelace demonstrates the Twist to a handful of novitiates with more gusto than a sixties go-go dancer.

Peter Bryan keeps an eye on her as he puts on a serious mien and takes Bliss to one side.

"How the hell did they know where to find Daphne?" Bliss queries as soon as he's dispelled the notion that his son-in-law is pulling some sort of perverted joke.

"Apparently the killer ditched Mrs. Dennon's handbag in a dumpster outside the station. They found her wedding invitation in it and put two and two together."

"Oh my God," breathes Bliss, wondering how he's going to break the news. "Look at her. She's eighty-odd and she still thinks she's Ginger Rogers ..."

"Do you want me to —" starts Bryan, but Bliss cuts him off.

"No. It's your big day, Peter. Anyway, she knows me better."

"That doesn't necessarily make it easier," says Bryan sagely, but Bliss waves him away.

"Don't worry, Peter. Just get me a very large brandy ..."

"Aren't you going to drive her home then?"

"It's not for me, you idiot; it's for her."

Word spreads faster than cholera in a room filled with nearly eighty policemen, and a depression settles over the reception as Bliss gently leads Daphne from the dance floor. Samantha has heard the news and races to be at Daphne's side as her father edges the aging woman towards a distant chair.

"What's happening, David?" Daphne demands breathlessly, aware that she is suddenly the centre of attention.

"Just a minute," he says, and frantically signals the band to start up again.

"You're scaring me, David," Daphne continues, but Bliss needs her to be seated.

Daphne sits, crushed in her own private world, as Bliss forges through the downpour with his face pressed to the windshield. "There's no point in hurrying," he has told himself a dozen times since leaving the Berkeley, "it won't bring her back." But he can't keep his foot off the throttle. He turns on the radio to break the overbearing silence and catches the end of the hourly news.

"... reporting live from the scene of today's murder.

"In a bizarre attack in Westchester this afternoon an elderly pensioner was pushed into the path of a London-bound express."

"I don't think I want to hear," says Daphne quietly, and Bliss turns it off as the reporter confirms that the victim's name is being withheld while next-of-kin are informed.

"She doesn't have any — not close, anyway," says Daphne, before sinking back into her misery.

Detective Inspector Mike Mainsbridge of the British Transport Police is the officer in charge at the scene and is giving the same answer to the local radio reporter.

"What can you tell us then, Inspector?" demands the reporter.

"We've contacted a friend of the deceased and are awaiting her arrival, though we are fairly certain that we can positively identity her from articles found in her possession."

"Any suspects at this time?"

"We're looking for a white male, twenty to thirty years ..." Mainsbridge continues, while Ronnie Stapleton slumps on Krysta Curran's bed with his face buried in his hands as they listen to the report.

"Don't turn me in. I didn't do it, Krys, honest," he snivels. "The old bag just jumped."

Krysta swats ineffectually at her own tears. "They said she wuz shoved on the telly," she says, as if a picture of a police officer demands greater credence than mere words, and the tears continue to cascade down her cheeks. "You can't stay here ..." she is saying as the Inspector continues, "Fortunately we have a clear picture of the suspect from the station's surveillance camera ..."

Stapleton lashes out in frustration. "Switch it off!" he yells. "Switch it off." Then he sags in despair. "What am I gonna f'kin do, Krys?"

"You could turn yourself in."

"What — and tell 'em I didn't do it — yeah, right. They'll swallow that. I got form, remember. I'm on probation."

"Yeah. For a couple of ounces of dope — not for bumping someone off."

"D'ye think the filth'll care?"

"It'll be worse if they catch you."

"They ain't got no witnesses," spits Stapleton.

"You heard him, Ron — they got video."

"It was dark. They could be bluffing," he pleads, tears streaming down his face. "She f'kin jumped, honest." Then he brightens with an idea. "You could say I wuz 'ere all afternoon with you. We wuz playing on your computer — remember?"

Krysta's face falls. "I dunno …"

"I thought you loved me. I mean, it's not like it's gonna make any difference now. The old crumbly's gone."

"But, we wuz in the caff together. You wuz making fun of her. The others will know."

"Then we came right back 'ere afterwards, aw'right?"

Krysta keeps her eyes on the floor as she mumbles. "My mum and dad will be back soon."

"You're throwing me out?"

"Ron … I …"

"Oh. Screw you."

"Where'ya gonna go then?"

"Mind yer own f'kin business."

Daphne Lovelace has kept a stoic face since receiving the news, though she has loudly blown her nose on several occasions as Bliss drives her back to Westchester. "I'm afraid I rather spoiled Samantha's wedding," she starts, but Bliss rebukes her immediately.

"You most certainly did not. Hardly anyone noticed. In any case, it wasn't your fault."

"Well, I still feel responsible. Minnie was probably feeling miffed that I'd gone without her when she wasn't feeling well."

"In which case she wouldn't have been at the station?"

"Maybe she'd perked up and decided to come to the reception."

It seems unlikely, thinks Bliss, finding it difficult to imagine that someone of Minnie's age would venture to London alone. Then he chides himself for the thought; after all, she was just about to set out around the world.

"She was so thrilled about the trip," continues Daphne, reading Bliss's mind. "She's never really travelled anywhere before — not like me — and I was looking forward to showing her all the places I'd been ... Red Square in Moscow, Istanbul — the blue mosque — the Taj Mahal ..." Daphne's voice slowly fades in loss and sorrow and she blows her nose again.

The rain hasn't eased as Ronnie Stapleton slinks along the scruffy lane at the back of his parent's terraced house on the outskirts of Westchester. With his eyes focused steadfastly on the light from his mother's kitchen, Ronnie peers over the rotten lattice fence and sees her familiar figure fussing over the stove.

"I'm gonna chuck his dinner out if he doesn't show up soon," Dorothy Stapleton calls out to her husband, and she checks the clock on the microwave. "It's gone eight. I told him not to be later than six."

"I'll eat it," yells a child's voice in response, and the shadow of Ronnie's rambunctious ten-year-old brother, Marty, appears in the window.

"You will not, and it's time you were in bed," laughs his mother. "You've got school in the morning."

The muffled sounds and blurry images of his family tug at Stapleton, and the prospect of a hot meal and some warm, dry clothing drag him towards the backyard gate. They obviously don't know, he tells himself, and seriously considers walking in as if nothing has happened.

You're innocent, the voice in his mind says, though he hangs back, asking, How long before they see the news? How long before the knock on the door?

And how will they know it's you? The cop said it was a white male aged twenty to thirty. You're only eighteen.

What about the video?

They're lying. They always say they've got video.

And, what if they're not lying this time?

Ronnie Stapleton pauses with his hand on the gate latch and the memory of his father's final admonition ringing in his ears. "This is the last time, son. You only get one chance in my books," he'd said only three weeks earlier as he'd led his son out of court. "If the fuzz ever come looking for you again, you're out."

"Yes, Dad."

"Your mother and me won't stand for it — understand?"

"Sorry, Dad."

"You will be if you don't shape up.

"I'll have to do the honours, I suppose," says Daphne Lovelace, breaking a twenty-minute silence as she and Bliss approach Westchester. "It ought to be church, but my front room would probably be more fitting; I don't think God's been on Minnie's Christmas list for a few years now. And you'd be amazed what they charge for a service today."

"I wonder if she wanted to be buried or cremated," Bliss muses aloud, though Daphne's response holds no answer.

"I don't even know if she's got a will. I thought she was just like the rest of us, with a little rainy-day money tucked away somewhere, until a few weeks ago when she told me her plans."

The day that Minnie broke the news about her grand intentions had started inauspiciously for Daphne. Her kitten, Missie Rouge, had rounded up a couple of mice for recreation, but the young cat's natural boisterousness had overcome one of the terrified creatures as she'd enthusiastically batted it around the kitchen floor, whereas the other had gone to ground under the kitchen cabinet.

Minnie's unexpected arrival found Daphne sprawled on the kitchen floor with the vacuum cleaner's hose stuck under the cupboard.

"I did ring the bell ..." Minnie started, explaining why she had used her emergencies-only spare key on her friend's front door, but Daphne shushed her.

"Mouse," she whispered, then yelped joyfully as the little animal disappeared up the tube with a pronounced, "Plop!"

"That's put the wind up him," she cried triumphantly, and then she rushed into the garden to release the tiny rodent.

"Shakes 'em up a bit," she explained on her return, "but they usually survive." Then she turned quizzically to Minnie. "It's Wednesday. Isn't it your bingo day?"

"I thought it must be Alzheimer's or the gin bottle," Daphne continues to Bliss as they slow down in Westchester's suburbs. "I'd never seen her so flighty. And you know what she can be like when she gets excited. 'How about you and me taking a trip all the way around the world, Daph?' she said, out of the blue, so I started telling her all the places I'd like to go, just to humour her."

"But she was serious?"

"Absolutely. I even went with her to Maplin's when she booked. Then we had to go to London to get her a passport."

"Daphne …" Bliss pauses and puts a note of concern in his voice. "You do realize that the local police will probably want you to identify the body."

"Oh. Don't worry, David. I've seen more bodies than I care to remember. It's the least I can do for the poor old soul."

"I'll drop you home first and make some enquiries," says Bliss, knowing that he could just as easily pick up his cell phone and call Westchester's police control room, but preferring not to do so with Daphne sitting alongside him.

It is approaching nine o'clock when Daphne turns the key in her front door.

"I'll light the fire," she says, shuddering at the coolness of the empty house and the realization that she'll never be opening the door to her oldest friend again.

Bliss switches on the television and is surprised to discover that Minnie has become the poster child for Age Concern, and several other elderly-rights groups, and her demise has been catapulted to first place in the national news.

"With surveys just out showing that forty-seven percent of the general population, and a staggering seventy-eight percent of the elderly, are frightened to venture out after dark," begins the newscaster with a backdrop of a heavily dressed bag lady struggling along a dark street, "residents of the usually peaceful community of Westchester were shocked to learn today that a frail widow —"

"Turn it off, David. They make her seem like some friendless down and out," says Daphne. "I'll put the kettle on."

The sound of the front-door bell makes them jump.

"I'll go," says Bliss, and he is met at the door by Phil and Maggie Morgan, Daphne's elderly neighbours. Phil has armed himself with a large flashlight and the fire-place poker and is riding shotgun as he constantly sweeps the bushes while Maggie gushes, "Minnie's been murdered, David."

"I know ..."

"Pushed in front of an express."

"You'd better come in —"

"They say that bits of her were scattered halfway to Briddlestone," chimes in Phil, and Bliss changes his mind, eases himself out of the door and drops his voice.

"Look ... You can come in, but please don't upset Daphne. She doesn't want to talk about it at the moment, though it would be nice if you'd stay with her while I go to the station to find out what's happening."

Westchester's railway station is alive with uniforms when Bliss arrives ten minutes later. County police officers, together with specialists from the British Transport Police, shelter under the platform canopy, while a team of forensic scenes-of-crime technicians are scouring the track at the end of the platform in the daylight of a dozen halogen floodlights. But it's a lost cause. The driving rain has washed away all trace of the incident, and the speeding train has spread Minnie's remains for nearly a mile.

A cluster of officers gathered around a mobile control room in the station's parking lot fall silent as Bliss approaches, seeking the officer in command. He flashes his badge — "D.I. Bliss. Met. police C.I.D.," says Bliss, momentarily forgetting his recent promotion.

"Wow! God's squad," mutters the junior officer.

Detective Inspector Mainsbridge of the Transport Police introduces himself with a quizzical eye on Bliss's morning coat.

Bliss takes a mental look at himself and laughs, "It's my daughter's wedding. It's going back to the hire place tomorrow."

"National Crimes' Squad?" questions Mainsbridge, wondering why the heavy brigade would be involved in such a straightforward murder.

"Hardly — Interpol liaison officer, actually. I just knew Mrs. Dennon, that's all."

"Did you know her well?" asks Mainsbridge, angling for the significance of Bliss's presence.

"Just a friend of a friend — Daphne Lovelace. She was with me at the wedding. Have you established a motive?"

"Mugging. The surveillance camera caught him grabbing her bag. The tape's fuzzy, but we should be able to get the lab boys to clean it up."

"Cash?"

"Could be as much as ten grand in big ones, we think."

"Phew!" exclaims Bliss. "Ten thousand quid. That's a hefty bundle for an old woman to be carting around. How d'ye know?"

"We've got her bank book. It seems as though she's cleaned out her life savings over the past couple of weeks, two withdrawals totalling seven thousand. And it looks as though she took out a loan for another three."

"Hmm," hums Bliss. "You might want to check with the local travel agents on that. My info is that she's just spent thirty grand on a world trip."

Now it's Mainsbridge's turn to be surprised. "You're well informed."

"Inside information," Bliss says smugly, then asks, "Where's the body now, Mike?"

Mainsbridge takes a meaningful look along the tracks before replying. "We've found a couple of bucketfuls so far."

"Oh, shit," moans Bliss.

"Could you formally I.D. her for us, Dave?"

"Not in a bucket, I couldn't," replies Bliss seriously, and Mainsbridge gives him a wry smile.

"Well, if it isn't Chief Inspector Bliss of the Yard," says a familiar voice, and Bliss warms at the approach of a smiling face.

"As soon as I heard that Daphne Lovelace was involved I guessed you'd show up," laughs Superintendent Donaldson, slapping Bliss affectionately on the back. Then his face falls in concern. "How's the old bird taking it?"

"You know Daphne," starts Bliss, and Donaldson turns to Mainsbridge in explanation. "She was the charlady down at the Nick for years, but she cracked more cases than most of the brainless wonders in C.I.D. put together. 'I reckon old so-and-so did that,' she'd whisper in my ear whenever she brought my tea and biscuits, and I don't think she was wrong once."

"She's keeping her chin up," says Bliss, "but I'd better get back to her."

"Why don't you just get a permanent transfer here, Dave? We could do with a real live hero on the force."

"Hero?" queries Mainsbridge vaguely.

"Yes," says Donaldson, inviting Mainsbridge to search his memory banks. "This is *the* Detective Chief Inspector David Bliss."

"The Nazi gold case?" breathes Mainsbridge.

"The very same," says Donaldson, basking in his association with Bliss. "The man who uncovered a buried fortune off the coast of Corsica, and all he got was an extra pip on his shoulder."

"I'm surprised you didn't quit," says Mainsbridge. "You could make a mint if you wrote a book about it."

"Oh, I've definitely given it some thought," replies Bliss, though he doesn't add that the book he's planning is about an even greater mystery than the discovery of the missing Nazi treasure. Tell them you've discovered the identity of the man in the iron mask and watch them laugh their heads off, he tells himself, but lets it go. "Anyway," he continues. "If there's anything I can do to help."

Donaldson ticks off a completed task list on his fingers: "Forensics, witness appeal, coroner informed, murder squad are checking similar M.O.'s ... Not a lot more we can do till the morning. Mike's got everything under control here. I was just going for a bite to eat. There's a new steakhouse in the High Street; care to join me?"

"Any suspects?" asks Bliss, remaining focused.

Mainsbridge steps in, saying, "We've got a witness." And he pulls out his notebook to confirm the name. "A Janis Ng. She's pretty sure that she saw some young punk stalking the old lady outside the cathedral just before it happened. She didn't see his face, but he had a swastika painted on the back of his jacket."

"That should help ..."

"And the signalman saw him, though couldn't really give us much — talk about shaken up. The poor bastard knew exactly what was going to happen and couldn't do a thing to stop it — like watching a Hugh Grant movie. Then there's the surveillance tape, of course, though it's a bit murky."

"Right then, Dave. Let's eat," says Donaldson, but Bliss shakes him off.

"I really ought to get back to Daphne ..."

"Breakfast, then," continues Donaldson, undeterred. "Eight-thirty at the Mitre. We should have the whole thing sewn up by then. How long are you staying?"

"Couple of days, I expect. Just to keep Daphne company. I had tomorrow off anyway. My daughter was married today so I thought I'd take a long weekend. Though God knows what I thought I'd be doing. They obviously didn't need me."

"Always the same for us blokes," moans Mainsbridge. "Christmas, birthdays, weddings. I dunno why we even try. We might as well just hand over the chequebook and piss off to the pub until it's over."

"Sir," questions a sergeant. "The railway people are asking when they can reopen the line."

"Tell them we're still waiting for the engineers to examine the train's brakes, though it's a waste of bloody time. The poor bastard couldn't have stopped a bike that quick."

"How is the driver taking it?"

"Shock — completely confused. We've bundled him off to the hospital."

Ronnie Stapleton is also confused as he squats on the concrete floor of a phone booth, examining the contents of Minnie's purse while he tries to work out his future. "F'kin fourpence," he mutters in disbelief. "I ain't doin' life for that."

Stapleton's descent from mugger to murderer has left his mind racing faster than a rat in a maze. Escape ... but to where? And how? Thumbing a lift is a risky option, yet it's all he can afford. He would normally have jumped a train, but the sight of Minnie's body slamming into the front of the engine still runs and reruns in his mind like a cartoon character being whisked away at a hundred miles an hour. He closes his eyes, hoping it's just a crazy computer game and that when he comes out of it he'll be a winner, but the picture's even gloomier when he refocuses, and the tears start again. He'd like to be crying for the woman, but knows that he's not.

Krysta answers the phone at the first ring and accepts the charges.

"You shouldn't 'a called," she whispers. "Dad might have answered."

"You didn't tell 'em, did ya?"

"No. 'Course not. But everyone's talkin' about it."

"You gotta get me some dough, Krys. I gotta get away."

"I dunno ..."

"Please ..."

"I'll try. Call me back in half an hour, 'kay?"

Bliss is also wishing that it was simply a game as he views the station's surveillance video alongside D.I. Mainsbridge and sees Stapleton's shadowy figure racing across the platform towards Minnie's figure at the platform's edge.

"Try freezing it," Mainsbridge instructs the VCR operator, hoping to catch the moment of impact, but the technician has made several attempts already and is sceptical of his chances.

"It will be better when it's transferred onto a DVD, though I'm not promising," he says as he reruns the tape again and again, while grumbling about the inadequateness of the antiquated recording system.

"Sorry, guv," he says in exasperation as Minnie's body simply vanishes time and time again, leaving Stapleton holding her bag.

"I'd better get back to Ms. Lovelace," Bliss says eventually. "I'll have another look in the morning." And as he heads towards his car, he can't help hoping that if they play it enough times, Minnie will eventually not be whisked away like a magician's assistant.

Ronnie Stapleton is another player yearning for the immediate invention of time travel as he's forced out of the phone box by the evening's chill and he seeks some warmth from the window lights of a small street of dingy shops. A car slowly rounds the bend behind him. "Cops," he breathes, and he instantly turns to use the window as a mirror as he pretends to peer at the wigs in a hairdressing salon.

They must have changed the one-way system, Bliss is thinking, not recognizing the street, and then he is alerted by the loiterer's suspicious movement.

"Turn around ... let's see your face," mumbles Bliss, as he cruises slowly past, but Stapleton's face is frozen to the window display. Then Bliss's lights catch the offensive logo on the back of the boy's jean jacket.

"Got you," breathes Bliss in amazement, stepping on the brake pedal.

The car's brake lights bounce off the window and Stapleton hits the pavement at a run. Seconds later he is jinking down a side alley like a startled gopher.

Bliss is out of his car in a flash, but he wastes time as he ducks back inside to grab his cell phone. He should call for assistance, but he knows he'll lose his quarry if he does. And he still hasn't seen the youngster's face.

Stapleton is already racing down the littered alley, leaping boxes, abandoned bikes and rusty garbage bins, as Bliss takes up the chase. With his eyes firmly on the youth, Bliss lurches from obstacle to obstacle and curses the long tails of his morning coat as they snatch at passing junk and threaten to snag him.

A discarded supermarket buggy trips Bliss and sends him sprawling as Stapleton shoots from the lane into the High Street where the Odeon cinema is turning out.

"Police — stop!" yells Bliss, spurring his quarry on, and a group of youngsters neatly part to let the fleeing man through, then they jeer Bliss as he passes with shouts of "Let him go, Pig!"

The fleeing youth gains ground as a couple of drunks try playing catch with Bliss, and he's slowed further as he grapples with his cell phone.

"Which service do you require?" the emergency operator says for the third time before Bliss catches his breath sufficiently to screech, "Police!"

Encouraging yells from the cinema crowd still ring in Bliss's ears as Stapleton swings off the High Street and runs into the ancient stone perimeter wall of the cathedral grounds. "Got you," breathes Bliss, rounding the corner and finding himself in a blind alley, and he is just weighing up his chances of taking on the fit-looking youth when Stapleton, with age and adrenaline on his side, heaves himself up and over the wall with the aid of the iron spikes set into the top.

"Bugger," swears Bliss, and he scans unsuccessfully for an entrance or some kind of ladder before grappling for a toehold in the wall. His cell phone drops from his hand and lands in the scrub.

"Damn!" he mutters, scrabbling to retrieve it, and is considering giving up when he hears a groan from the other side of the wall and realizes that Stapleton hasn't yet escaped.

"Softlee, softlee, catchee monkey," Bliss tells himself as he gingerly scales the six-foot wall and quietly hauls himself up on one of the iron spikes.

Beneath him, Stapleton cowers under a small tree and massages an ankle.

"Just stay there, lad," calls Bliss firmly, and Stapleton leaps to his feet with a yelp and hobbles into the gloom of the cemetery.

"Oh, Christ!" exclaims Bliss as he struggles onto the wall and hears a rip as his tail catches in a spike. But now he's stuck. It's a six-foot drop either way and Stapleton is getting away.

"Police ... How can we help?" calls a desperate voice from his pocket and Bliss whips out his cell phone, but it's too late. A snivelling figure limps out of the graveyard's murk and stands under him at the base of the wall.

"I wanna give myself up," whimpers Stapleton.

"Hang on a minute," says Bliss into the phone, then questions his prisoner.

"What's your name, son?"

"Ronnie Stapleton," he mumbles, adding tearfully, "I didn't do it, honest. I wuz with my girlfriend all afternoon."

"Exactly what didn't you do?" asks Bliss, and he might have laughed if not for the seriousness of the situation.

"Talk about stitching himself up," says Bliss a few minutes later as Mainsbridge and twenty other officers help him down from the wall.

Ronnie Stapleton sits in a police car, tears still streaming down his face, while he is read his rights by a constable. "Let's see what's in your pockets, shall we?" says D.I. Mainsbridge once the officer has finished, and no one is surprised when a little old lady's purse is discovered.

A posse of press have arrived, flashbulbs popping, and Mainsbridge should be gloating over the successful arrest, but the look on his face says something is wrong as he begins to open the purse.

"Fourpence! Is that it?" he cries in disbelief. "Where's the rest of the money?"

"That's all there was, honest. I ain't spent any of it," replies Stapleton as the cameras click, not realizing that he's guaranteed himself a place in history as the country's most incompetent robber.

Also guaranteed are tomorrow's front pages in half a dozen dailies; a 1954 wedding picture of Minnie under the headline, "Murdered for a Widow's Mite."

Superintendent Donaldson has been hoisted out of the Feedlot Steakhouse with a phone call and he arrives, breathless, within minutes.

"Christ, David. You've only been back half an hour and you've already nailed a murderer — are you sure I can't interest you in a transfer?"

"No, thanks," says Bliss with a smile. "But I could do with something to eat now. All that exercise has given me an appetite."

Donaldson checks his watch and his stomach. "Well, most places are closing now, but we could probably get something at the bar of the Mitre Hotel; although you look as though you need something stronger than a sausage roll. And look at the state of your coat. I thought you said it was rented."

Phil and Maggie Morgan are still at Daphne's, both fast asleep on her settee in front of the fire. "I didn't like to wake them," Daphne tells Bliss as she lets him in and shushes him with a finger to her lips. "I think they were frightened of being alone with a murderer on the loose."

"He's not on the loose any longer," says Bliss, and Daphne seizes his meaning immediately.

"You've caught him already," she breathes and Bliss nods, underplaying his hand as he adds, "He was only a kid. He gave himself up."

"Oh, that's brilliant ..." she starts, but her face falls. "Not that it will bring Minnie back." Then her eye catches the jagged tear in the tail of his coat. "Oh my gosh! Look what you've done! And look at the mud on your trousers."

"It was raining," he says, childlike. "Don't worry. Mr. Donaldson says he'll pay for it out of petty cash. Talking of which, have you got a key to Minnie's place?"

A rough voice greets them as they open the street door to Minnie's building and triggers a shrill alarm. "Who-are-ya? I'm calling the cops."

"Mr. Ransom," yells Daphne, "it's me, Daphne. Minnie's friend." Then she whispers to Bliss. "He's deaf. I knew we should have left this to the morning."

"What d'ya want at this time o'night?"

"Oh God. He doesn't know," whispers Bliss, and is taken aback as the pyjama-clad old man shuffles out of his flat, saying, "She's been done in. The police and the newspapers was here earlier and I let them in."

"It's funny, but it's only just sunk in that she's gone," Daphne says as she opens Minnie's door. "I can feel the emptiness. It's as if Minnie took something with her."

Ten minutes later, Bliss has no choice but to agree with her. "Every single penny she owned, I'd say. So either young Mr. Stapleton is lying, or she was down to her last fourpence."

"But she paid for the trip," insists Daphne. "That was more than thirty thousand —"

"I just hope she took cancellation insurance," says Bliss, rechecking Minnie's bank book, "because according to this, she owes the bank three grand."

"Are you sure?" asks Daphne, peering over his shoulder and quizzing, "But why would she book a world tour if she couldn't afford a bus ticket to Bognor Regis, let alone a boat to Bombay?"

chapter three

The solidly constructed cathedral in Westchester is close to bursting with a volume of congregation rarely seen since its completion at the end of the eleventh century. Politicians, aristocrats and other show-offs vie for seats in the spotlight of the television cameras, while most of Minnie's elderly friends are lost in the crowd. However, Daphne Lovelace has muscled herself a front-row seat alongside David Bliss, though her earlier musings that she would have to take financial responsibility for Minnie's funeral have turned out to be entirely false. The cost should have been astronomical, but with the cameras and eyes of the nation on Minnie, several leading undertakers had tripped over each other on Daphne's doormat.

"I just hope someone chucks me in front of a train when my time comes," Daphne said, as she and Bliss pored over a pile of glossy brochures following pitches from a procession of salesmen offering their services for free.

"Minnie would have loved this," Daphne whispers to Bliss as they sit squeezed between the city's mayor and the chief constable. "She was born the same day as Princess Margaret, you know: August the twenty-first, nineteen-thirty."

"I noticed that in the program," admits Bliss. "But what difference does it make?"

"Well. She once told me that she was convinced there had been some sort of cosmological mix-up with their spirits at birth."

Bliss's guffaw brings a cautionary glance from the chief constable, and he turns it into a sneeze and covers his mouth with his handkerchief as Daphne continues, "That's why Minnie never used bad language or got drunk. She thought that would prove that she was rightfully the Queen's sister in place of Margaret."

"You'd better stop," laughs Bliss under his hand, "or I'm going to have to leave."

It's Wednesday, and in just five days Minnie Dennon has become the nation's best friend and everybody's feeble old granny, and her passing has pricked the conscience of an entire generation. Retirement centres and homes for the elderly across the country have been inundated with visitors. Florist's deliverymen and personal-alarm salespeople have lined up at the doors. Her gruesome death has been detailed, debated and discussed by a host of social activists in the press and has been held by every right-thinking media personality to signify the ills of today's society. Whilst, on the other hand, Ronnie Stapleton has been soundly vilified as a drug-addicted, Internet-obsessed freeloader who was more than happy to bump off some penniless old woman for the price of a box of matches to light his tokes.

However, the penniless part of the equation is a conundrum not easily resolved by Bliss, or any of the investigation team headed by Detective Inspector Mainsbridge. And Sandra Piddock, the travel agent holding Minnie's tickets, had been little help.

Sandra had spent the evening of Minnie's demise at the Odeon cinema with her boyfriend, Lenny, and when she arrived at work the next morning she was still inwardly chuckling about the crazy man in a wedding suit marauding his way down the High Street after the movie.

"Oh my God," her colleague laughed, shoving the *Daily Express* under Sandra's nose. "Was that him?"

While Ronnie Stapleton's face had been pixelled out of the front-page photo to protect his rights prior to him being charged, David Bliss, in his tattered tailcoat, was clearly identifiable. However, Sandra failed to connect the name of the murder victim with Minnie, the customer whose commission was going to buy her a diamond bracelet for Christmas, and had no idea that the sweet little old lady would not be collecting her tickets — until the man in the photograph, accompanied by Daphne Lovelace, walked into her office a few minutes later.

"Mrs. Dennon only paid the three thousand deposit," Sandra told them, once Daphne identified herself as Minnie's prospective travelling companion, then she took on a hopeful look. "Have you come to pay the balance, Mrs. Lovelace?"

"I'm afraid we won't be going," Daphne replied with the trace of a tear. "Mrs. Dennon's had a very serious accident."

"Accident" is a nice euphemism, thought Bliss, but it doesn't begin to explain the traumatic manner of Minnie's demise. Nor did their visit to the travel agency explain how Minnie had somehow eaten through nearly thirteen thousand pounds in the past few weeks.

"I'd like to know what she did with it," Bliss said to Mainsbridge the morning after Minnie's death, but the other officer still had Stapleton in his sights.

"I reckon the little tow-rag stashed it before you nabbed him. He had plenty of time."

"I'm not so sure ..." Bliss replied vaguely, having repeatedly watched the tape of Stapleton's initial interview, in which the young man blubbers continuously while denying that Minnie's purse contained anything more than the four pennies found in his possession.

"It was a bunch of bullshit. She didn't have squat," Stapleton whimpers as he massages his bloodshot eyes. "All that crap about proper teapots ... it was all bullshit."

"Are you trying to say that there was no money in Mrs. Dennon's bag?" Mainsbridge questions in disbelief.

"Fourpence, that's all. You know that already."

"I don't know that. In fact, I think there's a lot you're not telling me."

"It wouldn't have happened if she hadn't been so f'kin poncy."

"So, it was her own fault she died. Is that what you're saying?"

"I didn't push her, honest."

"Then why didn't you stay at the scene? Why didn't you phone the police?"

"With my form, who would've believed me?"

Stapleton's form — a year's probation for indiscreetly lighting up a reefer in a bus shelter occupied by a young constable aiming for a spot on the Drug Squad — has been kept from the press to ensure an unbiased jury, but his guilt has already been sealed. There is not a person in Westchester who doesn't claim to know the young villain, and there are few who believe that the gallows are too good for him.

Stapleton's shell-shocked parents have been besieged in their tomato-spattered home since the morning papers dropped the news on neighbour's doormats, and uniformed officers have been standing guard around the clock, though they have been unsuccessful in stopping the occasional missile. A tearful televised appeal by the accused teenager's father, Reginald, for his son to be given a fair trial was soundly booed by a lynch mob in his local pub, and the builder for whom he subcontracted had been on the phone, though not to offer support.

"I'm sure you understand, Reg," he said, without saying anything. "If it was up to me. But the clients won't like it. I've had calls already."

"Are you firing me?"

"Let's just say we're giving you time to sort out a little domestic problem."

The feeding frenzy had become insatiable by mid-afternoon on the day following Stapleton's arrest, when a raucous throng had lined the route from the police station to the courthouse as he was transferred for his first appearance. Thousands of keening women threw eggs and hammered their fists on the armoured truck carrying the young prisoner. Reporters, rushing out of the crowd with cameras held high, attempted to scoop a candid picture, and several television stations had cut into regular programming to show the event.

"I am the resurrection and the life ..." begins the mitred bishop solemnly, and the cameras home in on him as he proselytizes to Minnie over her flag-shrouded coffin.

The Union Flag, normally reserved for the high and mighty, symbolizes the extent of public feeling and the shrewdness of the church in aligning itself with the proletariat. But the nationwide television coverage has more to do with speculation that a low-grade Royal will put in an appearance rather than any need to appeal to the masses.

"... He that believeth in me, thou he were dead, yet shall he live," continues the bishop, leaving Daphne muttering under her breath, "Minnie's got a problem, then. She gave up on him years ago."

The tumultuous public gnashing of teeth that has swept the country since Minnie's death has been driven by the persistent press coverage. For the first few days following the incident, the sight of Minnie being physically sucked off the end of the platform by a two-hundred-ton monster proved infinitely more captivating than the inert body of some eighty-year-old who'd been splattered to death in her bed by a lunatic with a cricket bat.

The digitally enhanced moment of Minnie's spectacular evaporation would certainly win a prize in any competition for the world's funniest video, were it not so macabre, and most television presenters have done their best to make sure that the majority of people watched, by warning them not to. "Viewers may find the following pictures disturbing," they say in apparent seriousness, and macho teens, inured to video violence, email and text their friends — "Hey. Did you see the old biddy get zapped by a train?"

The major television news networks capitalized on Minnie's spectacular demise ad nauseam, until public indignation eventually shut them down. But the contentious decision to show the video in the first place, as much as the sight of Minnie being whipped away on the front of the express, has galvanized public opinion. The storm over the bootlegging and leaking of the video has given the government a headache which, by the morning of Minnie's funeral, has become a full-blown depression for the chief constables of the two police forces involved. Yet, despite exhaustive enquiries by both the Hampshire and British Transport Police, the culprit has not been found.

Another government headache, though less agonizing, has arisen over Ronnie Stapleton's treatment in the remand wing of the local prison. The televised image of Minnie's sensational downfall incensed many of the more respectable prisoners. Burglars, bank robbers and everyday car thieves bandied together in their revulsion — deciding that Stapleton's crime was on a par with diddling little children — and arranged a welcome party for him in the prison's shower room.

By Monday morning, when Stapleton had been due to appear in Magistrate's Court for a further remand hearing, Bliss was at Westchester Police Station conferring with Inspector Mainsbridge.

"I've just heard that your prisoner's had a very nasty accident in jail," said Mainsbridge, meeting his colleague in the foyer.

"Oh God! I feared that might happen," admitted Bliss as they made their way to Mainsbridge's office. "I bet every old lag in the country has a granny like Minnie, or they'd like to have one. The screws should have realized that was a possibility. They should have put him in segregation, or on the hospital wing."

"The trouble is that the guards have all got grannies as well, Dave," Mainsbridge said as he motioned Bliss to a chair, adding, "I thought you would have been glad to be back at the Yard this morning,"

"I'd cleared my desk to make way for Samantha's wedding," Bliss explained, "so a few extra days won't make a great deal of difference. And I can't help feeling we've missed something, Mick," he continued. "It just doesn't make sense for Stapleton to have legged it with that much money and then wander the streets in the rain. Why wasn't he getting pissed with his mates or beetling off to Paris for the weekend?"

Bliss and Mainsbridge got an answer, of sorts, a few minutes later when Stapleton's lawyer raised himself to a lofty five-foot-three in front of the cameras outside the empty courtroom.

"My client saw the deceased, Mrs. Minnie Elizabeth Dennon, in a very distressed state," Goldsmith meticulously explained. "He was concerned about her, so, in a spirit of altruism rarely seen in young people today, he followed her to the railway station to simply make sure she was all right. When he realized that she was standing too close to the edge of the platform for safety, he rushed to restrain her, to save her life, but unfortunately he only managed to grab hold of her bag."

"What a load of twaddle," Mainsbridge whispered in Bliss's ear as they watched on one of the station's sets.

"As a result of precipitous action by the police," Goldsmith continued smarmily, "and before they had established the full facts of this case, my client had been arrested and incarcerated in a penal establishment where he was seriously assaulted and sodomized."

"Serves the little bugger right," muttered Mainsbridge, and seemed unconcerned as Goldsmith had wrapped up his address by saying, "It is my client's intention to take action against the officers involved for unlawful arrest and unreasonable detention, and to demand a public enquiry into the laxity of the prison service."

"The Lord gave ..." continues the bishop with reverence, "... and the Lord hath taken away." Though Bliss can't help wondering if it might not be more appropriate to hold the railway company responsible for that.

"Ashes to ashes. Dust to dust," concludes the bishop, and Daphne sniffs loudly as the coffin containing a substantial amount of Minnie is slowly wheeled past them on her way to her final resting place.

"I hate to say it, David," says Daphne, as she takes Bliss's arm to escort the entourage out of the cathedral to the waiting hearse, "but I can't help feeling that young Master Stapleton got exactly what he deserved. Poor Minnie was so looking forward to that trip."

"Obviously," responds Bliss, and for that reason he hunts out D.I. Mainsbridge from amongst the throng of mourners.

"Let's have another look at that tape from the railway station, Mike," says Bliss. "It's not that I buy Stapleton's mouthpiece's story, but something doesn't add up here."

"What?"

"Well," starts Bliss, "we have the remains of the deceased's coat, her handbag and her purse. Yet we don't have a railway ticket."

"And ...?"

"I've checked at the station. There is no record of anyone buying a ticket around that time."

"So ...?"

"So, what was she doing there without a ticket?"

"Meeting someone, perhaps."

"Then they should have shown up on the next train."

"Stapleton could have stolen the ticket with the money ..."

"*If* he stole the money."

"But, if he didn't, who did?"

The missing money is still plaguing Bliss an hour later as he and Mainsbridge rerun the digitalized version of the surveillance tape for the *n*th time.

"It doesn't look as though her bag's particularly stuffed," says Bliss, peering closely as a smudgy figure moves across the platform one frame at a time.

"Ten grand in big bills doesn't take much space, Dave."

"True," agrees Bliss, then he follows Stapleton's progress as the shadowy teenager creeps out of the darkness and begins his run.

"See," explains Mainsbridge, pausing the image. "She starts to turn just as he reaches for her bag, then, 'Bang!'"

"He reckoned she jumped."

"I s'pose it's possible," admits Mainsbridge. "It's dark, foggy. The old bird is miles away in Kathmandu or Kuala Lumpur. He sneaks up behind her at a run and scares the crap out of her — 'Boom!' — she leaps like a rabbit with a shotgun shell up its bum."

"So, you think he might not have planned it."

"Hey, Dave. Don't worry. It's still manslaughter, even if he gets away with murder, and it won't matter a monkey's fart how much steam his mouthpiece blows."

A phone call cuts into their conversation, and Mainsbridge hands the receiver to Bliss. "It's a Chief Superintendent Edwards for you, Dave."

Bliss's face falls as he briefly cups his hand over the mouthpiece and mutters, "Damn!"

"Dave, old chap ..." explodes Edwards with uncharacteristic bonhomie. "Congratulations — that was a good collar, well done."

"Thank you ..."

"What's all this crap from his lawyer? Is he smoking something, or is he talking out of his backside?"

"Well, there are a few —"

"Rubbish, Dave. I've seen the video. Christ! The whole damn world's seen the video. It's cut and dried — nail the nasty little bastard's bollocks to the floor."

"It's just that —"

"Like I said, Dave, nice one." Then his tone takes on a sarcastic edge. "By the way, are you still working for us, or have you joined the turnip crunchers permanently?"

"I was just waiting for the funeral ..."

"Okay. I'll expect to see you first thing tomorrow morning, then."

"Yes —" Bliss starts, but the line is dead and he's still shaking his head as he replaces the receiver.

"Who the hell was that?" queries Mainsbridge.

"Edwards," replies Bliss. "Senior delegate of the sore-backside brigade at H.Q. He's bleating about me still being here. I've told Daphne that I'll go with her to the bank to sort out Minnie's affairs later this afternoon, but after that I'll have to get back to the big house."

"No sweat, Dave. They reckon it'll be weeks before Stapleton's fit to plead. Anyway, I've got all the evidence I need."

Mark Anderson, Minnie's bank manager, is well aware of his customer's demise but, other than offering his condolences, he's unwilling to discuss her affairs with anyone, even a chief inspector from Scotland Yard, until

Daphne puts the bite on him. Staring him coldly in the eye, she queries, "Aren't you the Mark Anderson who grew up on Batsford Street?"

"Yes," he responds cagily.

"I thought I recognized you," says Daphne triumphantly, and then her face sours as she closely scrutinizes him. "That's the trouble with small towns, Mark. I'm sure we all do things when we're teenagers that we hope will be forgotten ... although I doubt that Detective Chief Inspector Bliss would be too interested in hearing about —"

"All right ... All right," steps in Anderson, smiling wryly as he turns puce. "I'm sure Mrs. Dennon wouldn't have minded me telling you that I spoke to her about her account. It was my duty when she applied for the overdraft. After all, she was asking for a lot of money for someone with only a state pension to sustain her."

"So, what did she want it for?" asks Bliss, wondering how Minnie had sold him on the idea of a world tour.

"She said it was some kind of business partnership," continues Anderson. "Something so big she couldn't tell anyone for risk of ruining the deal."

"And you didn't need a business plan or some kind of collateral?" asks Bliss in surprise.

"Some of our more senior customers can be very persuasive, Chief Inspector," Anderson admits, giving Daphne a poisonous glare. "Anyway, in view of the circumstances, the bank has written off the debt."

"I guess Minnie knew about his past as well," says Bliss as they leave the bank. "What on earth did he do as a teenager?"

"I've absolutely no idea, David," chortles Daphne, "though something certainly made him poop his pants."

"You are incorrigible, Miss Lovelace," laughs Bliss, taking her arm and leading her up the High Street towards Watson Street and Minnie's last known place of abode.

Nothing has changed in the flat since Bliss's previous visit. "There's no point in going through the cupboards again," he is saying as he takes a contemplative pull at a corner of carpet while Daphne scours the little sitting room and rechecks the cushions of the settee, saying, "God knows what she did with the money. She certainly didn't buy furniture. This lot wouldn't get ten quid at auction."

"What's going to happen to it?"

"I'll probably chuck it out for the dustmen," suggests Daphne, and Bliss looks up with a thought.

"Bingo," he yells a few minutes later as he squats on the floor of Minnie's kitchen next to a garbage bag he's dragged out of a bin in the backyard.

With one hand over his nose, Bliss is holding up a crumpled piece of paper to Daphne with the other.

"What is it?" she asks, keeping her hands in her overcoat pockets.

"This," he says, unfolding it and flattening it on the floor, "is a Western Union receipt for four thousand, nine hundred pounds. And I bet there's another in here if I dig deep enough. Thank God the garbage hadn't been collected."

"But, I don't understand ..."

"It's the missing money, Daphne. Stapleton didn't steal it. She sent it to ..." Bliss pauses while he deciphers the writing on the receipt. "She sent it to Canada."

"She didn't know anyone in Canada," spits Daphne indignantly. "Why on earth would she do that?"

"I think it's a company name," says Bliss, reading aloud. "'CNL Distribution, White Rock, British Columbia.'"

"Call Mike, your Mountie friend in Vancouver," says Daphne, indicating Bliss's cell phone. "He'll know."

chapter four

Mike Phillips is a recently promoted inspector with the Royal Canadian Mounted Police in Vancouver, and he is growing accustomed to becoming embroiled in murder cases involving his English counterpart, David Bliss.

"I could get shot for this," says Bliss as he opens his cell phone and flicks through the digital address book looking for his Canadian colleague's number. "It's my job to make sure that people don't short-circuit the system," he continues irritably as he taps in the number of the officer with whom he had once teamed up to trace a serial killer. "That's what Interpol's for," he carries on as he waits for the connection. "If everyone made their own enquiries with foreign forces there would be anarchy."

"Oh, you can be such a stuffed shirt sometimes," says Daphne snatching the phone. "The closest I've ever been to being on the force was cleaning the constables' toilet down at the police station. So unless you think that applies ..." She pauses, with the phone close to her ear, mouthing "Voice mail," then adds, "He's on leave — Hawaii for two weeks," as she waits to leave a message, but then she changes her mind and slowly closes the phone. "Minnie and I were planning on going to Hawaii," she tells Bliss, with a sniffle of unfulfilled nostalgia, and then she brightens with an idea. "What about Trina?" she says, pulling out her diary and searching for a number.

"I don't know ..." begins Bliss hesitantly, having mixed feelings about the zany Canadian woman who had become enmeshed in Phillips's mass murder case and had found a kindred spirit in Daphne.

"It can't do any harm," continues Daphne as she punches in the international code. "We only need the phone number of the company, and then we can ask them about Minnie's money ourselves."

"I still think I should do it officially through Ottawa," Bliss is saying as Daphne listens for the ringing tone.

"Don't you worry, David. I'll talk to her," says Daphne sarcastically. "I wouldn't want her getting into trouble with Interpol as well."

"Vancouver Zoo. Monkey House," answers the voice on the phone, and Daphne puts on a puzzled face.

"Is that you, Trina?"

"Oh. Hi, Daph. Yeah, it's me. Hang on. There's a guinea pig on the loose ..." Then she yells, "*Kids!*" with such force that Daphne ducks.

"Sorry, Daphne," says Trina, coming back on the phone. "It's a madhouse here. I was just making some curried banana cake."

Daphne grabs a pen from Bliss's breast pocket, enthusing, "It's one of Trina's recipes."

"Hold on a minute," complains Bliss, grabbing it back as Daphne begins writing in her diary. "And that's my personal cell phone you're using."

"Oh. Sorry, Trina, I'll get it later. David's worried about his bank account now he's a lowly chief inspector. Oh. Did you know Samantha, his daughter —"

"Daphne ... *please,*" implores Bliss.

"Oh. Hang on, Trina. He wants to talk to you himself."

"Trina, do you know a place called White Rock?" asks Bliss without wasting expensive seconds on pleasantries.

"Sure. Just south of here on the American border. Hey, have you got another murder for me?"

"No ... Well, yes, in a way. One of Daphne's friends has been killed, and for some strange reason she sent all her money there last week — more than twenty thousand dollars, judging by the receipts," explains Bliss, before giving Trina the details of the money transfers, each for a little under five thousand pounds.

"Ten-four," says Trina once she has the information.

"What does that mean?" queries Bliss.

"No idea, but the cops always say it on television ... or is it ten-ten?"

Trina Button puts down the phone as her husband, Rick, wanders in from the garage with grease-stained hands.

"Rick, you'd better put a padlock on the guinea pig cage. I've got another murder case."

"What ... What are you talking about, Trina?"

"Surely you remember? The last time I was on a case the mob tried to murder him."

"Trina," Rick reminds her gently, "you were never on a case. You are a homecare nurse who just got caught up in some nasty business, that's all. Anyway, you don't have time for this now. I've almost finished the machine and Norman is on his way over for the inaugural run."

"Great!" shrieks Trina. I'll be out in two minutes. Just gotta make a call."

CNL Distribution is a multimillion-dollar corporation with shareholders who prefer to remain unlisted — everywhere, and the phone book offers Trina no help. Neither does the directory enquiry operator. With Rick calling, "Hurry up, Trina," she quickly tries the Western Union office in White Rock, but draws a blank there as well.

"I've no idea," says the clerk tersely. "We don't ask our customers their business."

"Do you have a phone number, then?"

"Sorry, ma'am. Can't help."

"Come on, Trina! Norman's almost here," calls Rick, and a moment later Trina is joined by her two teenagers, Rob and Kylie, as she stands in the garage with tears of joy streaming down her face.

"It's beautiful, Rick … It's absolutely beautiful," she blubbers, then she turns to an elderly-looking man who has just wheeled himself into the garage in an electric wheelchair.

"Look, Norman," she says, pushing her children aside for the newcomer, "isn't it wonderful? Rick is so clever, isn't he?"

Norman Spinnaker is, like all of Trina's patients, facing a bleak outlook. Diabetes has blocked his blood vessels and robbed his legs of the strength to carry him, while nephropathy has destroyed his kidneys. Without constant dialysis, or a transplant, Norman is well aware that he is never more than few days away from meeting his maker. But thanks to Trina's unbounded optimism, he looks to his uncertain future with more confidence than a teen pop idol.

"I think it's … um … fabulous," says Norman, critically eyeing the machine that Trina insists will save his life. "But are you sure about the power-to-weight ratio?"

"Absolutely," says Rick. "C'mon Trina, climb aboard and we'll give it a trial run."

"Yes!" exclaims Trina, and she punches the air triumphantly.

The machine is a two-person quadricycle which has been fashioned from a kidney-shaped fibreglass bathtub complete with faucets, shower and soap rack. Wheels, and a nautical steering wheel from a marine junkyard in West Vancouver, have been added by Rick, along with a brass bulb horn that he had liberated from a vintage Model T Ford in his college days. A limp Canadian maple leaf flag hanging from the top of the ten-foot shower pole caps off the bizarre-looking machine, and Rick gives the pole a shake as he explains in a mad-inventor's voice, "Shipmates and shipbrats … Note that this apparently standard shower unit is, in actual fact, the mainmast, from which a shower-curtain sail can be suspended. And this," he carries on as he triumphantly pulls a large yellow plastic duck from a bag, "this is the figurehead which I shall now fasten to the plughole puller while naming this vessel … " He turns to Trina with a questioning look.

"The *Kidney Queen*," suggests Trina regally.

"Absolutely," agrees Rick. "The *Kidney Queen*. God bless her and all who pedal in her."

"She's terrific," says Trina, running her hand over the canvas lawn-chair seats. "What d'ye think, kids?"

"You're crazy," spits Kylie. "Like, you really think you can pedal that all the way to New York?"

"No problem," says Trina as she hops in and tests the pedals. "It's all downhill from here. Check out a map."

"Mum," questions Rob, "why are you doing this?"

"To raise money for kidney transplants —" she begins, but her fourteen-year-old son cuts her off.

"No, I meant, why are you making me look such a dweeb?"

"A dweeb?" questions Trina, and she looks to Rick for support, but he's busy watching a spider on the ceiling.

"Yeah, Mum," carries on Kylie. "It's kind'a embarrassing. My friends all say you're weird."

"Hold on a minute, you two," says Norman, coming to Trina's side. "I think your friends must be weird. You're lucky to have a mother — what's that smell?"

"Oh — oh," cries Trina, leaping out of the machine and racing for the kitchen. "Flaming banana curry cake."

"You were saying, Mr. Spinnaker?" questions Kylie.

Trina's intended Kidney Run to New York is seven months away, but her goal to raise a million dollars for kidney transplants is already looking shaky. Her primary problem is that she lacks the wholehearted backing of the local Kidney Society. Indeed, the president and members of the steering committee have been frantically distancing themselves from the scheme from the moment Trina announced her plans.

Until Trina's arrival, the Society's fundraising committee had been both inoffensive and ineffective due to the advanced years of most of its members. And how Trina, in her late thirties, was elected to the chair of the committee at her very first meeting is still a matter of some debate, although some of the blame has been laid at the feet of Maureen Stuckenberg, the Society's perennial president.

"We need someone with bright new ideas," Ms. Stuckenberg insisted, and the group unanimously voted for Trina, knowing that any event requiring most forms of physical activity, financial input or personal solicitations by members could easily be discussed to oblivion within a year or so.

"Just propose a few of your best ideas," the president had told Trina a few weeks before the annual committee meeting, not knowing of Trina's passionate nature and unswerving doggedness in her desire to do good, and Trina arrived at the meeting weighed down with graphs, sketches and a slew of fundraising manuals, and quickly set the stage.

"You have to personalize the plea to open purses," she explained poetically to the group. "I mean, look at the opposition —"

"We don't think it's helpful to characterize other charities in that manner, Trina," Maureen Stuckenberg admonished. "We are all in the same boat when it comes to raising money."

"Okay. But we haven't got a bunch of goggle-eyed pot-bellied orphans on our side," Trina continued, undeterred. "To really squeeze the pips you need something zappy, like a kid with no legs or a hole in his face you can get your fist into."

"Trina ..." the President warned.

"Well, let's face it. Most of our people are just ugly, fat old fogies with nothing to show for their complaint but a dodgy urine sample. I mean, all they do is sleep."

"Trina. We are not in the business of exploiting the suffering of our patients."

Trina's mumbled retort — "Everyone else does" — didn't sat well with the executive, and she found herself with an increasingly hostile audience as she worked her way through her presentation.

Dances, duck races and fashion shows were all shrugged off without debate; lawn mower marathons, telemarketing and pet shows were given the cold shoulder; and Trina was getting down to the wire when she suggested inviting Martha Stewart to design a commemorative kidney-shaped teapot.

"Okay," she told the committee in desperation. "Idea number twenty-seven. We could do the same as the Women's Institute in northern England. They made a mint selling their own Christmas calendars."

"At last," Maureen Stuckenberg muttered under her breath, and immediately garnered nods of support from around the table.

"Shall we take a vote on that, ladies?" she proposed loudly, and had a full show of hands, until a spoilsport — Trina's geriatric predecessor — demanded details. "What kind of calendar was it? Recipes? Knitwear? Cute little cuddly animals?"

"No. Just portraits of the president and all the members," Trina responded imperturbably.

"Well, that sounds very sensible, Trina," Maureen Stuckenberg carried on, primping herself up and slicking back her eyebrows. But the spoiler had a cautious eye on Trina and insisted on specifics.

"Well, actually," Trina mumbled, with her head in her papers, "they all posed in the nude."

Ms. Stuckenberg came close to meltdown, but Trina was running out of options and persisted. "You needn't worry, Maureen. I mean, most of *them* weren't particularly good-looking, either."

"Trina. Our Christmas fundraising event has been very successful for the past twenty-seven years without smutty ideas like that," the president fumed indignantly, and bristled still further when Trina pointed out the obvious irony in the Kidney Society's seasonally appropriate sales of cholesterol-loaded Christmas cakes, giant chocolate bars and sugar-coated butter shortcake to a diabetes-prone, overweight populace with a forty-percent chance of developing kidney failure.

"It's like the Cancer Society selling cigarettes," Trina complained, but she was immediately shot down by Ms. Stuckenberg.

"Don't be so foolish."

"Or Alcoholics Anonymous pushing booze."

"Trina …"

"Or Gamblers Anonymous running bingos."

"This is ridiculous."

"Or Girl Guides selling chocolate cookies."

"Trina … the Girl Guides *do* sell chocolate cookies," Ms. Stuckenberg shot back.

"Well, they shouldn't. What kind of message does that send to impressionable young girls with weight issues and zits? No wonder teen suicides are on the rise. Maybe I should help them with their fundraising as well."

"I wish you would," Ms. Stuckenberg muttered through clenched teeth, adding, loudly, "Have you got any other bright ideas?"

Idea number twenty-eight, "the guinea pig Olympics," was dismissed without debate, and the twenty-ninth, "the Kidneymobile international marathon," was only adopted because it was already seven-thirty in the evening and several of the members were dozing off.

"As long as you're prepared to do all the work," Ms. Stuckenberg opined without troubling the group, "I don't see why we shouldn't adopt this idea."

"Thank goodness," Trina muttered, knowing that her thirtieth and final idea — totally naked ballroom dancing — was unlikely to get much applause.

By the time Daphne closes the door to Minnie's flat and walks with Bliss back to his car with her head down, it has started raining again in Westchester.

"I wonder if it will ever brighten," she says with an eye towards the leaden sky, but Bliss knows where her mind really is, and she confirms it a second later as she climbs into the passenger seat. "I still can't really take it in, David. It's a bit like getting a lump of coal in your Christmas stocking."

"Superintendent Donaldson has invited us to dinner ..." starts Bliss, hoping to cheer her, but she shakes her head.

"You go. I think I'd rather have a bit of time to myself if you don't mind."

"Okay. I'll drop you at home, and I'll try not to be too late. I have to get back to the office first thing; if I know Edwards he's already interviewing my replacement."

Dinner with Superintendent Donaldson at the Mitre Hotel is, like all meals with the great man, akin to culinary mountaineering, a point emphasized by the senior officer himself when he polishes off the entire bowl of bar nuts while awaiting the menu. "If it's there, eat it. That's what I say."

Mike Mainsbridge of the Transport Police has joined his fellow officers with the apparent aim of discussing tactics in the ongoing investigation, but he shows more interest in picking up tips on treasure hunting as he quizzes Bliss over his celebrated discovery of treasure in the Mediterranean Sea.

"What's the chance of finding more of the stuff?" he asks with an air of indifference that fails to disguise the fact that he may be planning an early retirement. "I mean, how did it get there, and how would someone actually go about searching for more? Where would someone start?"

"Personally, I think I'll start with the deep-fried double-cream Brie," interjects Donaldson, and Bliss is also working on his choices as he deliberates whether or not to reveal details, to explain that a bunch of renegade Nazi officers had fooled the world near the end of the war by pretending to dump several tons of stolen Jewish gold into Lake Toplitz in the Austrian Alps, when in fact they had loaded their loot into ancient Roman wine amphorae and sunk them off the craggy coast of a Corsican island.

"The breeze just happened to be blowing my way, I guess," says Bliss cryptically, knowing that his discovery had been predicated on the direction of the notoriously fickle Mediterranean winds. But Mainsbridge wants specifics. "Yeah. But how did you work it out?"

"Ah. You'll just have to wait for the book to come out," laughs Bliss, and refuses to be drawn further as he scans the menu.

"So you *are* going to write it, then?" Donaldson queries, but Bliss shrouds his plans with vagueness. "Who knows? I'll probably get around to it one day."

"Why not now?" asks Mainsbridge doggedly.

Because, though Bliss is loath to admit it publicly, a certain female by the name of Daisy LeBlanc would rather he keep her family's skeletons in a securely locked armoire. And Daisy, pronounced "Dizzy" in her Gallic tongue, is one person in the world whom Bliss would rather not disappoint at present.

"I hear you've got something going with a little French ..." says Donaldson with a wink, leaving the sentence in the air.

"How the hell ..." Bliss shoots back, then realizes that Daphne has been at work. "Go on," he laughs heartily, "call her a frog. Yes, if you must know. As Daphne said to me recently, I may not be a spring chicken, but I've had an offer."

Daisy's very tempting offer, to throw up her life as a French real estate agent to become Mrs. Chief Inspector Bliss, has been on the table for more than a month, but any delaying tactics on Bliss's part have been more to do with his contemplation of becoming Mr. Provençal Real Estate than a desire to fob her off.

Since his celebrated discovery he could leave the police force, and England, at any time and find fortune in his fame by chronicling his adventures, or so he is told. But first he has an obligation to redeem himself in the eyes of his colleagues by putting the skids under the universally despised Chief Superintendent Edwards.

Bliss's promotion to Chief Inspector, touted as a reward for his discovery of the missing treasure, had, he knows, roots that reached much deeper into the murky political underworld of the police force, and he is well aware that Chief Superintendent Edwards had a hand in the decision. "Always keep a dangerous dog on a very short leash," Edwards once told him, and he was convinced he had drawn Bliss's teeth by giving him a plum job with an office down the hall from his own.

"Interpol Liaison Officer," said the freshly painted sign on Bliss's door, and he was well aware of the jealous scuttlebutt amongst some of those in the junior ranks who weren't privy to his motives. "So Edwards walked, then," one of his colleagues said sourly after Bliss failed to show up at the disciplinary hearing that should have got the megalomaniacal Chief Superintendent off everyone's back.

"Just give it time, Bill," Bliss replied, knowing that, while Edwards might have escaped on this occasion, he was still firmly attached to the other end of the leash.

Daphne's house lights are spilling onto the darkened street as Bliss arrives after midnight. *That's very unusual,* he is thinking, having expected her to be in bed, but as he steps out of his car he's almost flattened by a musical din.

The third movement of Elgar's "Enigma Variations" is playing so loudly on Daphne's record player that she fails to hear Bliss at the door, and he's finally forced to bang on the window. It takes her almost a minute to answer, and he immediately senses a problem as she leans heavily on the door jamb.

"David ... I maybe ... What? What is it?" she asks, seeing his look of concern. "What ... What're you looking at me like that for?"

"Are you all right, Daphne?" he wants to know as he escorts her to the living room and turns down the music.

"Yes. Well, let's just ... um ... Well, there's a letter from Minnie."

"Perhaps you should sit down," he says, and reaches out to guide her.

"I'm all right ... I can manage. Thank you," she says curtly, and firmly throws off his hand.

"I know."

"Well, don't push, then ... You don't need to push... I'm perfectly capable ..."

"Just come over here and sit down," he tries again.

"You're pushing. Don't push ... D'ye wanna scotch?"

"No ..."

"There's some gin," she starts, then exclaims, "Oops!" as she loses her balance while reaching for the empty bottle. "Hold tight, Chief Inspector!" she yells as she falls against him. "Lower the gangplank — I'm coming aboard."

Daphne and Bliss crash together on the settee, and Daphne giggles for more than a minute while Bliss extricates himself and props her against the settee's arm.

"What's this about a letter from Minnie?" Bliss asks, and her laughter turns to tears.

"The stupid fucking — oops, sorry, Chief Inspector, sir," starts Daphne, then she pulls herself together and sits upright. "S'cuse me ... Little Miss Potty Mouth ...Where was I? Oh, yes. Silly billy — hah-hah, Minnie's a silly billy."

She looks to Bliss, pleading for sympathy as her eyes fill up, and she sniffs loudly as she says, "She's a — She's a dead silly billy, David."

"I know."

"D'ye know ... D'ye know ... D'ye know what she did?"

"No."

"She's a silly — oops, I already said that ... She ... Are you sure you don't want a scotch?"

"No, honestly —"

"I think I'll have another."

"Are you certain?"

"No ... No ... Well, all right, just a teensy-weensy — hah-hah, teensy-weensy, teensy-weensy. Hah-hah, that's funny — teensy-weensy, teensy-weensy, teensy-weensy ... That's funny, isn't it, Chief Constable? ... Oops, now I've insulted you."

"Daphne, love, what about Minnie?"

"Stupid fuck — oh, I already said that. Look ..." then she slides onto the floor and crawls towards the coffee table on all fours. Missie Rouge rises from the carpet, her red-haired hackles rising, and backs away warily as Daphne barks at the confused creature. "Woof-woof ... woof-woof ... hah-hah ..."

"Daphne ..."

"Oh, yes ..." she says, raising herself onto her knees and saluting firmly. "Daphne Ophee ... Ophee ... Daphne Ophelia Lovelace, number 7311281 reporting, Mr. Chief Constable, sir."

"What about Minnie?" demands Bliss.

Daphne falls back to the floor and grasps a letter from the coffee table. "Wrong address," she says clearly as she holds the letter triumphantly aloft for a second, then she crashes headlong onto the carpet.

"Oh, shit!" mutters Bliss as he rushes to her aid.

Five minutes later, Daphne is in her bed, snoring loudly, and Bliss leaves her door wide open so that he can listen to the reassuring sound as he returns to the living room and Minnie's letter.

My dear friend, starts the letter, as Bliss helps himself to a large scotch and carries on reading. *I don't know how to tell you the bad news. I was so looking forward to seeing all those lovely places you're always talking about — you've been so lucky, but I'm afraid I just got carried away and I don't think I can afford it now. I know I've let you down, but please try to forgive me. You're the only friend I have and I can't bear the thought that I've hurt you. Please forgive me.*

"'Ms. D. Lovelace, 27 Stonebridge Road,'" says Bliss aloud as he reads Minnie's handwriting off the envelope, and he sees the problem immediately. It's Stone*bank,* he says to himself, then he checks the postmark and realizes that the letter has been bouncing around the sorting office for over a week.

"It sounds suspiciously like a suicide note," Bliss is telling Donaldson by phone a few minutes later, as he relays the letter's contents. *Which leaves us with something of an embarrassment,* he thinks, though he doesn't say it, realizing that Donaldson is quite capable of working out the ramifications for himself.

"Why the hell did she book that trip if she knew she couldn't afford it?" soliloquizes Donaldson as he looks for a scapegoat while Bliss is wondering who is going to tell the media, the coroner and Stapleton's lawyer that the young man may not only be innocent but may actually be a hero, that Minnie Dennon may well have jumped?

"The media will bloody love this, Dave," fumes Donaldson, on the same page as Bliss. "I can see the headlines now. I mean, they've made such a big deal about her death, they'll look more stupid than us if they have to admit that Stapleton's innocent." Then he perks up and grasps at straws. "Of course, we don't know for sure that she planned it. And the boy certainly stole her purse."

"Or simply kept hold of it because he was traumatized," adds Bliss, snapping the straw.

"Thanks, Dave. I needed that," says Donaldson. "Can we discuss this over breakfast?"

"Sorry, guv. I have to leave at seven-thirty, assuming Daphne's slept it off by then. I'll call you from the office."

Seven-thirty sees the early-morning sun streaming into Daphne's living room, but if Daphne is awake, she's not co-operating. She had slipped to the bathroom at seven o'clock, and Bliss had put the kettle on with a sigh of relief, but her bedroom door had gently closed a few minutes later, and she still hasn't resurfaced.

I bet she's waiting for me to leave, thinks Bliss, and he is tempted to do so, but the morning television news changes his mind when it is revealed that thirteen pensioners have killed themselves overnight in different parts of the country. "This brings to twenty-seven the number of seniors who have taken their own lives in the past three days alone," the newscaster says as she introduces a spokeswoman for Age Concern, saying, "I understand agencies like yours are becoming disturbed at this apparent epidemic ..."

This is just synchronicity, he tries telling himself, though can't shake off the feeling that Minnie's death may have somehow sparked a series of suicides by elderly people.

By nine o'clock he's pacing. Daphne has obviously been awake for some time and he's beginning to wonder how long she can hide.

I could take her a cup of tea, he thinks, but he convinces himself that it might be better if she were to deal with her grief in her own way. In any case, he has his own grief to deal with in the form of Chief Superintendent Edwards.

"Good morning, sir," he says brightly as Edwards answers his phone at first ring.

"Ah, the hero's return."

"Actually —"

"Just give me five minutes, then pop along and see me, will you, David. I've got something that I think you're going to enjoy."

"Bad news, I'm afraid, sir," says Bliss, bracing for the explosion. "I didn't quite make it back last night."

"David," calls a pathetic voice from the top of the stairs, "are you on the telephone?"

"Can I call you back?" whispers Bliss, not wanting Daphne to overhear, but Edwards is seething.

"No, you f'kin well can't —" he's shouting as Bliss mutters, "Sorry — battery's dead," and hits the "off" button.

The degree of Daphne's degeneration is alarming. Without her false teeth and her customary blush of makeup, she has gained thirty years, and her puffy bloodshot eyes merely add to her age.

"You should stay in bed," says Bliss, guiding her back to the bedroom. "I'll bring you a cup of Keemun tea."

"I'll be all right," she says, but her tone lacks conviction. "Maybe an Aspirin."

"I'll find some," he tells her as she slumps onto the bed.

"You *do* know what that letter means, don't you?" she says, focusing on him for the first time and expecting a response.

"Well, I don't know ..." he waffles, but she's clearly reached her own conclusion and doesn't want to be contradicted.

"David. You've no idea how many deaths I've had to deal with," she says, her wounded conscience dragging her down. "I've lurched from funeral to funeral my whole life, and I've arranged quite a few of them in one way or another."

The metaphor isn't lost on Bliss, who is well aware of Daphne's exploits with a shadowy government unit during, and after, the Second World War, and he doesn't like the direction she's headed, but he can't stop her, as she continues: "The poor woman was just too frightened to tell me that she couldn't afford the trip. But what does that say about *me*, David? What kind of best friend does that make me? I might as well have been the one who pushed —"

"Oh. You can't blame yourself ..." he starts, but realizes he's wasting his breath.

"Of course I can," she says fiercely. "She could never have planned this trip on her own. She'd never even heard of Ulaanbaatar or Vanuatu."

"But you didn't know she couldn't pay."

"David, I've been Minnie's friend for nearly fifty years. I knew very well that she didn't have much money. Oh, she always had fur coats, and she could fork out for a pair of pricey boots from Merryweather's if they took her fancy, but you'd never want to delve too deeply into her underwear drawer."

"Well, she's not alone in that."

"You do realize that she was just waiting for me to pick up the phone and say, 'Never mind, Minnie. It doesn't matter,'" Daphne carries on. "That's why she didn't come to the wedding. She thought I didn't care."

"But you do care, Daphne."

"Caring is doing, David. Otherwise it's like a dead tree falling in an uninhabited forest."

"I'll get you that tea," says Bliss, heading for the kitchen with the intention of slipping in a call to Edwards, but he is not surprised when his plea for a few days' compassionate leave doesn't go over well.

"You were off most of last week," shoots back Edwards.

"I know, but I spent all weekend on this case."

"Not my problem, Chief Inspector. You should leave it to Hampshire and the Transport Police."

"I realize —"

"David," Edwards sighs in apparent exasperation. "You collared the kid for them based on the evidence to hand at the time. They're big boys down there. They don't need the Yard to wipe their asses."

I get the picture, thinks Bliss. Now the case looks as though it's going down the toilet, Edwards doesn't want anyone in his department with poop on their hands in case some of it rubs off on him.

"True, sir. It's just that Daphne needs —"

"Chief Inspector," says Edwards, hardening, "I'm trying to run a police force, not a granny-sitter's. Get her a do-gooder from social services if she needs help, but I expect you back here by midday."

"Yes, sir. Three bags full, sir," says Bliss, knowing that the line is already dead.

chapter five

The sound of Elgar follows Bliss down Daphne Lovelace's front path a couple of hours later. "I'll be perfectly all right," she repeatedly assures him, and he finally accedes to her request for some solitude. But the mournful music is still beating into his brain as he joins the motorway back to London, so he turns on the radio to change the tune.

"I'd hardly describe it as an epidemic," the minister of health is saying, and Bliss knows immediately that the man is being questioned on the current rash of suicides.

"Then, how would you categorize it, Minister?" demands the interviewer.

"There is no doubt that the figures confirm a slightly increased rate over the past week or so," admits the minister.

And that doesn't include Minnie, Bliss tells himself, while wondering if other unexpected deaths may have been similarly misdiagnosed.

"It's being suggested by certain elderly support groups that the government is actually encouraging seniors to kill themselves to alleviate pressures on over-burdened medical facilities."

"Nonsense!" exclaims the minister, but he is immediately ambushed by an irate welfare advocate.

"Minister," explodes the crusty-voiced woman, "your own figures suggest that as many as sixty percent of the elderly are unable to access care facilities; and with the increasing number of baby boomers ..."

Muttering, "I'm surprised she didn't accuse him of pumping out do-it-yourself euthanasia kits," Bliss changes the channel and focuses on the road.

Ten miles ahead, where the motorway cuts a swath though the ancient village of Nettlebrook, a soaring footbridge swoops over the six-lane highway and carries gaggles of schoolchildren to and from the village school. But it's eleven-forty in the morning, a time when, apart from a harried housewife hustling to the village store or the occasional hiker trekking across the South Downs, the footbridge is usually deserted. This morning is an exception: James Edward Temple, an eighty-five-year-old army veteran who has been a genial bar fixture at the local pub for the past fifty years, stands on the approach ramp in the heavy drizzle, looking down at the torrent of traffic and sees a gloomy future.

"I'll never make it by twelve," Bliss tells himself as he peers anxiously ahead through the spray, and he's forced to call Edwards.

"One o'clock. My office. And no more excuses," snaps the chief superintendent.

The signed resignation letter in his jacket pocket tempts Bliss — it only needs today's date — but he's unwilling to abandon his mission. "I'll do my best, sir," he responds as a traffic snarl ahead cuts his speed still further.

James Temple is also on a mission and, in Service tradition he's bulled his boots, polished the buttons of his British Legion jacket and pinned on his medals. Tobruk, El Alamein and Sicily laud the old Desert Rat's battle honours, proclaiming that he had shown his mettle alongside Monty in 1942 and had shipped across the Mediterranean in July of 1943 to be with Eisenhower at the start of the European liberation.

At his present speed, Bliss is nearly ten minutes away from the lofty footbridge in Nettlebrook, but he's in no hurry. If Edwards craps all over him for being late, he can always whip out his resignation letter. It sits, like a concealed weapon, in his pocket, and gives him considerable comfort.

Temple feels the same way about his maroon military beret. It's faded and battered now, and a moth has taken a bite out of one side, but it safely saw him through the war when so many of his colleagues' steel helmets proved to be soft targets, so he has put his faith in it again today as he straightens it on his balding head, squares his shoulders and readies himself for his final assault.

Two miles, just under four minutes, to the bridge for Bliss. The traffic has speeded somewhat and he's checking the car's clock. "Nearly twelve," he muses, and guesses that he'll easily make it to Edwards' door by one.

Temple checks his watch. "Three minutes to zero hour, Sergeant Major," he barks loudly and pulls himself to attention. "Once more unto the breach, dear friends," he says, then orders, "By the left ... wait for it ... wait for it ... Quick march."

On the bridge ahead of Temple, the dreary English day slowly turns to a dark Sicilian night, and the sky is suddenly lit by a thousand flares as the Germans and Italians prepare to defend the Mediterranean island; but the howitzers and machine guns aren't for him this day. "Left, right, left, right," he sings out with his head high, and he marches towards the far side where a cheering throng of Sicilian girls are waving and throwing flowers. "Hello, Johnny," they yell, and urge him onwards as he crosses in the sky over the motorway.

A giant gravel truck ploughing through the surface water is blocking Bliss with a cascade of spray, and he decides to sit back while others race blindly ahead.

"Parade halt!" orders Temple as he reaches the northern side of the bridge to find that the crowd has evaporated into the past. "About turn!" he bellows, and pirouettes neatly. "By the left ... Quick march!" he yells again, and the steel decking sings as Temple marches back to the zenith of the bridge high above the London-bound traffic.

The sweep of the bridge is directly ahead of Bliss now, though it's hazy in the wash of the enormous truck, but the figure of the lone soldier is clearly visible as he stands erect with his lips formed into a bugle, trumpeting "The Last Post" to the wind.

"What on earth is he doing?" Bliss wonders as he races towards the bridge.

"Parade ... dismiss," commands Temple, then he spins smartly to his left and stamps his right boot so solidly into the decking that it sets the metal bridge shivering from end to end. "One, two, three," he counts before snapping the sharpest salute of his entire career, then he takes four quick steps and dives head-first over the balustrade.

"What the hell ..." screeches Bliss, and he is instantly on his brakes as the old soldier plummets directly into the path of the gravel truck ahead of him. But the truck driver is too close to the plunging man and is oblivious to the danger until his windshield explodes.

"Stop! Stop! Stop!" yells Bliss with his eyes in his mirrors, willing himself into the psyches of the following drivers, while around him other drivers are chatting idly to their passengers as they forge unsuspectingly into the murk.

Einstein's law of relativity kicks in and slows Bliss's world, and he watches in amazement as the dozing driver behind him suddenly wakes up, slams on his brakes and slews violently into the path of a speeding BMW in the next lane.

Bliss is rapidly decelerating as the gravel truck looms large in his path, and he watches a ballet of the doomed in his mirror as car after car veers sharply to avoid him and smash into others. But the driver of a giant low-loader, laden with steel girders, knows that he can't risk swerving and losing control so he brakes, though not soon enough, and the sky behind Bliss blackens. He desperately searches for a way out but, with speeding vehicles crashing either side and the slowing gravel truck ahead, he finds no escape.

"This is it," sighs Bliss in resignation, and he is bracing for the crushing impact when the driver of the gravel truck abruptly loses his grip on life and leaves forty tons of rock in control.

"Oh, no," Bliss yells as the truck swerves towards the central barrier. But suddenly the road ahead of him is completely deserted, and with the words of the bishop at Minnie's funeral — "Yea, though I shall walk through the valley of the shadow of death" — in mind, he squeezes the throttle and leaves the carnage behind.

The wreckage is piling up on the London-bound carriageway as Bliss checks that he is clear of danger before sliding to a halt on the hard shoulder. But the mayhem is just beginning on the Westchester-bound side, where the gravel truck's remains, and most of its load, are sending cars, trucks and vans fishtailing along the wet road and crashing into each other.

A motor coach, crammed to the roof with elderly gamblers on a pilgrimage to a golden shrine, slams into the hurtling cab of the runaway truck and bursts into flames, then vehicle after vehicle smash into the inferno.

Bliss leaps out of his car, unscathed, and looks around in disbelief. "Oh my God!" he breathes and reaches for his cell phone.

"Eleven dead and sixteen seriously injured, most of them seniors with severe burns," a BBC radio reporter is saying into his microphone three hours later, when Bliss eventually slips exhausted into a makeshift refreshment tent that a group of villagers has set up on the roadside. Police, fire and ambulance personnel jostle for space as the reporter continues, "A police spokesperson estimates that it will be several hours before the road is reopened," and Bliss asks for a tea.

"Are you all right, sir?" asks a straight-backed, bearded man with a degree of authority familiar to Bliss. "You look all done in."

"No, I'm fine," says Bliss as he flicks open his wallet. "Metropolitan Police."

"George Donaldson," says the oldtimer in a broad country brogue as he pours from a giant pot borrowed from the village hall. "I used to be the local bobby here, afore they took away our bikes and gave a bunch o' bloomin' schoolkids fancy panda cars," he explains, confirming Bliss's suspicion.

"Better not let Superintendent Donaldson hear ..." starts Bliss, then he pauses with a quizzical look as the old man's name rings a bell, and George Donaldson laughs. "That's my son, Ted, over at Westchester you'd be talking about."

"So I guess you know what happened, then."

"Oh. Yeah. Old Jimmy Temple jumped off the bridge," he replies nonchalantly, as if it's a regular occurrence.

"You knew him?"

"I told my missus that summit like this 'ud 'appen," George continues, then leans in to whisper, "Alzheimer's," as if he is afraid of the word.

"Oh, dear."

"It started a couple o' weeks ago when he slapped a thousand quid on the bar in the White Swan sayin', 'Drinks are on me 'til it runs out.'"

"A thousand pounds?" queries Bliss.

"Well, there were bloomin' chaos. Must 'a bin nigh on five 'undred people crammed in that ther' pub within ten minutes. An' when the money ran out, old Bert, the landlord, were on the phone to the police station, but that were a waste o' time. 'Leave it to me, Bert,' I said and I arrested Jimmy for causin' a breach of the peace. Not that I had the power to do it, mind you, but it were just a way o' getting' him outside afore he were lynched. 'What d'ye wanna do a daft thing like that fer?' I said to 'im, but he didn't care. 'Plenty more where that came from, George,' he laffed."

Bliss's cell phone rings — the tenth such occasion since lunchtime — and he checks the caller's I.D. It's Edwards again; his spirits sink, but now he has time to respond.

"David, it's Mike Edwards. Look, I've only just heard what happened. Are you injured?"

"No. Just pretty shaken up ..."

"Well, don't worry about a thing. Take as much time as you want. Have the rest of the week off. I hear you did a great job getting some oldies out of a burning bus."

"Well, it was —"

"I'm putting you in for a commendation."

"Thank —"

"And I've got a nice little jaunt lined up for you. How do you fancy a conference in Seattle next week? They want an expert to speak about the growing international problem of people trafficking and I thought you'd be ideal."

"That would be —"

"Fabulous ... By the way, I might have been a bit hasty when I called earlier. Sorry about that. Just wipe out the messages, will you."

That was short and smarmy, thinks Bliss, wondering if he'd heard correctly. *Did he actually say sorry?* he queries, then replays Edwards' previous messages and tut-tuts over the string of abusive expletives, but gleefully saves each one. *One more nail in your coffin, Mr. Edwards,* he is thinking to himself when he feels a tap on his shoulder.

"So you've met my old dad, have you?" says Superintendent Donaldson.

"Yes," laughs Bliss with an eye on the senior officer's stomach. "I should've spotted the likeness. Interesting man; he seems to have his finger on the pulse. He was telling me about the old boy suddenly splashing his dough around a few weeks ago."

"I heard about that, but he was always a bit loopy. That's what happens to men who spend too much time on their own without a good woman to keep them sane," says Donaldson with an expressive wink. "Anyway," he carries on, "we can manage now if you want to get off home."

"Actually, I'm going back to Daphne's. I wasn't at all happy leaving her this morning."

Elgar is still performing as Bliss rings Daphne's front-door bell, but it's at a normal level now. Daphne, on the other hand, is far from normal. She's still wearing her nightdress and dressing gown, and her teeth are lying in a tumbler by her bedside.

"I didn't expect you back," she says with apparent grumpiness.

"Obviously."

Then she takes in his dishevelled appearance. "Oh my God. You've ruined another coat."

"Bit of an accident," he mumbles, as he leads her to the kitchen, saying, "I could use a special cup of your Keemun." But she breaks into a flood of tears and slumps into a chair.

Bliss doesn't need to ask; the signs are all around him. Breakfast dishes still litter the kitchen table, Missie Rouge is begging at the fridge door, and another dead gin bottle has hit the floor.

"What is it?" he asks gently as he hands her one of several fallen handkerchiefs.

"It's Thursday, David. Minnie always came for tea."

"I'll light the fire," he says, heading for the sitting room, but Daphne has other ideas. "I'd rather be on my own, David," she says, rising determinedly and edging him towards the front door. "You've got plenty of work to do, I'm sure."

"Edwards has given me the rest of the week off."

"Then you should visit Daisy. You've wasted enough time on me," says Daphne, and he's immediately torn between spending a wet weekend in Westchester or flying to the Côte d'Azur for a few days in the sun with the current love of his life. It has been a month since he's seen her, and he's beginning to worry that his next phone bill might be delivered in a truck considering the number of nights he's lain in bed like a teenager, whispering, "*Je t'adore,"* into the phone, while listening to her quirky articulation and her inability to sound *th* without adding a zed. "I zhink you are so 'andsome, *Daavid,* and I love you also," she would say, and he'd chuckle in warm memory of the first time they had met in Provence, when she had asked, in all seriousness, "What can I do you for?"

"I think I will light the fire ..." Bliss starts again, but Daphne is determined and stands sentinel at the sitting-room door. Now what? he wonders, finding himself in a standoff with an aging toothless tiger. "Okay," he says with a deadpan face, and he makes a convincing feint for the front door before doubling back to the sitting room, muttering, "I think I left my pen ..."

If the state of the kitchen had taken Bliss by surprise, the sitting room sinks him. Incriminating evidence is strewn all over the table and floor. Daphne has turned her filing cabinet inside out and has obviously been putting her affairs in order; she has even labelled a few of her more treasured items with names of beneficiaries.

"What's this all about?" Bliss wants to know sternly.

Daphne employs another flood of tears to duck the question and he guides her gently back to the kitchen chair as she mumbles through snivels, "She did it for me, David."

"That's nonsense. She did it because she'd got herself into a tight spot and didn't know how to escape."

"But if I'd got that letter on time, none of this would have happened."

"That wasn't your fault," he protests, but Daphne doesn't want to hear, and rambles on. "That's the trouble with life's lottery, David. Everyone thinks you're the winner if you outlive all your peers, but actually you're the loser. Every death leaves a deeper wound, and every funeral is just another painful rehearsal for your own. Well, I think I've just about got the hang of it now."

"Daphne! You've got to snap out of this, now," Bliss insists firmly.

"Oh, don't worry. As silly as it may seem, I don't think I'm as brave as Minnie. Anyway, the thought of that poor train driver — he probably dreamt of being on the railways from his first train set and never imagined he'd end up pulverizing an old woman —"

"Okay," interrupts Bliss roughly. "Enough of this. I'm going to clear up the kitchen while you get washed and tidied. I am taking you somewhere really posh for dinner, so you'd better put on a decent hat or we'll get thrown out."

"But —"

"No buts or I'll have to arrest you for disobeying a lawful order."

A wry smile, the first in a week, puffs out Daphne's cheeks. "Roger, wilco, sir," she says, then she pauses as she heads for the stairs. "Oh, by the way, Trina called from Vancouver. No one seems to have heard of CNL Distribution."

In truth, Trina Button hasn't made any enquiries beyond the phone book and the Western Union office in White Rock. She has been too busy with her training schedule, and she spends much of each day raising eyebrows in the ritzy area of West Vancouver where she lives by puffing up the hills on a rattle-trap of a bicycle while wearing a stencilled T-shirt saying, "Wanted — Your Kidneys. Dead or Alive."

Daphne also wants kidneys an hour later at The Limes, but she chooses hers flambéed in cognac, to be followed by tenderloin of wild boar on a pear purée, while confessing to Bliss that she's been so down since Minnie's death that she's hardly eaten.

The fresh memory of a busload of burnt bodies is enough to put Bliss off charred flesh for a week, so he flip-flops between a Dover sole and the vegetarian's platter as he looks up to say, "But this isn't the Daphne Lovelace that I know."

"Sometimes I feel myself slipping," admits Daphne. "The crazy thing is that when you get to my age the only thing you have to look forward to is memories of the past. I mean, take Phil and Maggie next door; they've been dead for nearly twenty years, but they just can't afford a decent burial, so they carry on."

"I know what you mean," laughs Bliss, thinking of his own parents slowly mouldering in front of a television as they wait for the Reaper's knock.

"You've seen the poor old souls in senior's homes, David. Those places are just undertakers' waiting rooms. The Eskimos have the right idea: stick granny on an ice floe and wave her goodbye."

"I doubt if they still do that."

"Well, they should. It would save the Canadian health service a fortune."

The probable savings in geriatric care costs as the number of suicides mount has not been lost on the public or the media in England, neither has it been ignored by more than a few families who have watched their long-anticipated inheritances being gobbled up by nursing homes and pharmacies, and Bliss isn't the only person wondering how many old folks might be being pushed, in one way or another.

"Talking of money," he says as their entrées arrive, "I suppose I should put in a formal request through Interpol to find out why Minnie sent that money to Canada, although I'm going to be near there next week.

Edwards is trying to butter me up with a trip to Seattle, though God knows when he thinks I'll have time to write my speech."

"Trina invited me over to Vancouver for a break," continues Daphne lethargically, "but I don't have anyone to go with now that Minnie's passed on."

"You should go. I bet the Rockies in autumn are fabulous," Bliss begins, then pauses with an idea. "In fact, I could take you."

"Oh, you needn't —"

"No arguments. It's just as easy for me to fly into Vancouver, but can you afford it?"

"Well, I had put some spending money aside for the trip with Minnie."

"Good. Start packing. I'll arrange the flights for Monday."

Friday morning starts on Thursday night for Bliss as he takes advantage of the clear road and races back to London. The last of the late-night drunks are still being hauled off the streets as Bliss sets to work on the mountain of reports that a couple of clerks had spent the evening culling from central records.

"The illicit trafficking in human beings," he types onto a clean screen and works his way through a million miserable lives as he catalogues the tides of poverty-stricken Southeast Asians braving the Pacific in rust buckets to reach North America; Iraqis and Afghanis desperate to be anywhere but the ruins created for them by their supposed liberators; North Africans trekking across the Mediterranean to Turkey seeking a better life, while the Turks trudge northward to Germany for the same reason; Moroccans swimming the Strait of Gibraltar searching for Spanish gold, while Sub-Saharan Africans flee despotic rulers and the desertification of their land; and South Sea Islanders sailing away to an uncertain future as their homes sink under a slowly rising ocean.

"Christ! The whole bloody world is on the move," Bliss muses at one point as he reads of the millions of impoverished Mexicans flooding the United States to join the thousands of persecuted Cubans who've risked everything on the leaky boat of a trafficker or a rubber-tire raft, and he can't help but marvel at the roll of the dice that put him in a white skin in a safe, warm land.

After five hours he has ten pages of notes, but if the conference organizers are expecting him to come up with a solution they'll be disappointed. "As long as multinational corporations collaborate with a handful of powerful Western governments to maintain a thou-sand-fold disparity between the incomes of the rich and the poor for their own self-aggrandizement, there will always be a trade in people trafficking," he concludes, and is tempted to add that it might be a lot simpler to bump everyone off and start from scratch.

It's seven-thirty a.m. and Bliss heads to the canteen for a quick coffee, but he finds himself ensnared by the breakfast television show as the latest suicide figures are trotted out on hastily generated scoreboards.

"Here's the situation at a glance," says the presenter with the same tone he'd used to announce the results of the general election, and it's immediately apparent to Bliss that the railways have continued to bear the brunt of the crisis, with fourteen jumpers in the past twenty-four hours. However, when James Temple's busload of elderly victims is included in the equation, the roads take the top spot with twenty-three deaths, while household poisons, car exhausts and prescription drugs vie for third place and bring the total to a round fifty.

As with any new disease, the public and press are well ahead of the authorities, and numerous gerontologists and psychiatrists specializing in the elderly have warned that mass hysteria may cause an unstoppable tide of death.

"We're starting to see the lemming effect in action," one studious doomsayer reports, totally ignoring the fact that, over the years, numerous scientific studies have completely debunked the mass suicide theory of the arctic rodents.

"I think we are witnessing the first manifestations of the coming Armageddon," a freaky religious guru promulgates, and the idea is certainly picking up steam as more and more deaths are reported.

"Doctors are reporting a major increase in the number of people requesting prescriptions for tranquilizers," reads an editorial in the *Financial Times*, prompting an immediate run on the shares of certain drug companies. While the wives of stockbrokers with holdings in undertakers, funeral parlours, crematoriums, florists, limousines and law firms are already choosing colours for their new Porsches.

Chief Superintendent Edwards is surprised to find Bliss already at his desk when he arrives a little before nine.

"Ah, nice of you to come back, Chief Inspector," he starts with a smile, then he spots the pile of paperwork on Bliss's desk and puts on a darker face. "I hope you haven't started on that lot yet."

"Finished," announces Bliss triumphantly.

"Actually, David," begins Edwards, in a tone that Bliss immediately recognizes as a precursor to disenchantment, "I'm going to have to cancel your trip. The Home

Secretary has asked the Commissioner to set up a squad to look into this suicide nonsense, and I've recommended that you be appointed to head it."

"Well, thank you for your consideration, sir," says Bliss, sweeping his hand over the papers on his desk, "but I'm already prepared for Seattle."

"Chief Inspector, you know the score," continues Edwards with his ears closed. "Ten thousand snuff it in an earthquake in Turkmenistan or Timbuktu and nobody gives a toss, but if a few crumblies in Tower Hamlets are considerate enough to bump themselves off to save the taxpayers a few quid, the public expects a bloody special squad."

"But I've already booked the tickets," lies Bliss.

"Well, cancel them — what d'ye mean, 'tickets'?"

"I'm taking Daphne Lovelace," Bliss explains, careful not to mention that he'd also planned on inviting Daisy.

"You're not still granny-sitting that batty old bird, are you?" scoffs Edwards. "Christ, she was prancing around like a bloody head banger at Peter Bryan's wedding."

"Well, she's not prancing around now," Bliss protests. "She needs a bit of a change of scenery." But it gets him nowhere.

"Cancel, Bliss," orders Edwards as he stomps off. "And I'll expect a preliminary report on the suicide situation by nine Monday morning."

How quickly the veneer of niceness slips from the face of the insincere, thinks Bliss as he picks up his phone and hits the first number on his speed dial.

"*Allô?*" answers a familiar voice as a phone rings in a real-estate agent's in the quaint Provençal resort of St. Juan-sur-Mer.

"*Bonjour,* Daisy," replies Bliss, "*Comment allez-vous, ma petite pucelle?*"

"*Daavid*," she laughs, "you are still speaking zhe French like zhe Spanish cow — *Tu parles français comme une vache espagnole.*"

"Zhank you," mocks Bliss with a laugh before inviting her to join him for a week's holiday in Seattle.

chapter six

October is sliding towards winter in the mountains corralling Vancouver, and the grizzlies are stocking their caves. But down in the wide estuary of the Fraser Valley, where concrete blocks and blacktop ribbons sprawl across a dozen Pacific islands, the balmy sea breezes spread a warm blanket over the city and will continue to do so until the full sun returns with the coho salmon in spring.

"This is the scary part," whispers Bliss to Daphne as they aim for the airport on Sea Island, and he watches nervously as they skim ever lower over the Strait of Georgia until the undercarriage of their 747 seems certain to catch in the tall masts of yachts sailing the smooth waters.

"I love it," enthuses Daphne with her face stuck to the window. "And look at all those log rafts. They must be miles long; thousands of trees all pulled by those funny little tugboats — and look at all the trawlers."

Bliss smiles at his old friend's re-found bounce, and a few seconds later he's thankful for the reassuring jolt as the indigo water solidifies into tarmac and they glide to a standstill.

"I hope Trina's here to meet you," he murmurs worriedly as they taxi to the terminal. "I've got to be in Seattle in a couple of hours to meet Daisy."

"Oh, she'll be here," answers Daphne confidently, and she is correct. However, Trina is not actually in the arrivals building. The sparkly young woman is outside, in the loading zone, where she is verbally dancing with a blue-suited security guard who is attempting to give her a ticket for illegal parking.

"Where does it say 'No Bikes?'" demands Trina as she sits in the cockpit of the Kidneymobile with her arms folded, while bemused travellers crowd around.

"Madam — 'No Parking' means no parking. Look at the signs," he says as he finishes writing the ticket and fruitlessly searches for a licence plate.

"No. *You* look at the signs, young man," she ripostes. "There are pictures of vans, cars, buses and trucks, but where is there a picture of a four-wheeled kidney-shaped bathtub complete with shower unit and duck figurehead, eh?"

"Can I take a photo, Miss?" asks an intrigued passer-by, attracted by the gaily coloured nautical bunting strung from stem to stern.

"Sure," starts Trina, and she primps herself up, but the security guard needs to win at least one battle and spits, "Put the camera away, sir. This vehicle is breaking the law."

"Come and look at this," yells a teenage footballer to a busload of his buddies. "This is cool."

"Stand back!" cries the guard in desperation, and he tries to make a cordon with his outstretched arms, but he's instantly swarmed. "Stop that!" he screeches as the photographer flashes off a dozen shots. Then he gets serious and pulls out his radio.

"Watch this," says Trina to the growing crowd, and she stands up in her tub to unfurl the makeshift sail from the top of the mainmast. Splashed across the cerulean blue shower curtain dotted with frolicking dolphins is a banner in six-inch-high fluorescent yellow lettering which reads, "Canada welcomes Lady Daphne."

"Assistance needed arrivals concourse," a desperate voice is bleating into a walkie-talkie as a motor coach pulls up alongside the Kidneymobile and disgorges fifty home-bound Chinese tourists.

"I's a Lady Daphanee," calls one of the visitors, deciphering the sign, and out come more cameras.

"This is an emergency!" pleads the security guard as the burgeoning crowd blocks the traffic and motorists start abandoning vehicles to rubberneck.

"It's for charity," Trina announces loudly, and the Chinese party's interpreter translates to her superstitious flock that a substantial donation will guarantee a safe flight back to Beijing.

"Oh, my!" exclaims Trina as coins and bills begin flooding into the bathtub.

"You can't collect for charity without a permit," yells the guard, feeling on safer ground, but Trina shrugs. "I'm not collecting — it's the Kidneymobile, not me."

The crowd intensifies as Bliss and Daphne clear immigration and customs and unsuccessfully search the sea of faces in the arrivals hall for Trina, and five minutes later money from all corners of the globe is pouring into the bath as the English visitors emerge inquisitively onto the concourse. One tourist from Los Angeles wants to know if Trina can break a Canadian hundred-dollar bill, then changes his mind and hands it to her with a smile, saying, "It's only good for Monopoly back home."

"I could arrest you for taking that," warns the security guard as he threatens Trina with his pen, but he's elbowed aside by the throng as more and more travellers empty their pockets and purses.

"But who is Lady Daphne?" queries one of the bystanders as the same question is being asked upstairs in the airport's press office and a reporter is hastily despatched to the scene.

Daphne is wearing one of her hats, a hat of such proportion that it had caused a commotion at the check-in desk at Heathrow because, in its bag, its dimensions had far exceeded the permitted size for carry-on luggage. "No problem," Daphne had trilled, whipping it out of the bag and plonking it on her head, explaining, "There, dear. Now it's not luggage."

Trina spots the telltale polka-dot creation and stands in her bathtub to rise above the crowd while she furiously waves a giant Union Flag. "David ... Daphne ... Over here!" she shouts, and the crowd turns as one and parts.

Daphne takes the sight of a couple of dozen bowing Chinese men in her stride and reciprocates with a series of polite nods as she makes her way through the throng, while Bliss keeps his head down as he trails behind her with the baggage cart.

"What on earth?" exclaims Bliss as they reach the hybrid machine, but Daphne adores it. A few minutes later with Trina — and a fiercely protesting Bliss — pedalling, she is enthroned atop the suitcases in the back of the bathtub and is waving regally to the crowd as they slowly move off. Well-wishers continue pouring money into the tub as they pass, while eager young children push and try to clamber aboard as the vehicle processes slowly towards the parking lot where Trina's car and a trailer await.

"Isn't this fun, David?" screeches Daphne in delight as she keeps up her waving, but Bliss is clearly under strain as he scoffs to Trina, "You're not really intending to pedal this all the way to New York, are you?"

"Exciting, isn't it?" bubbles Trina, and she beams at a press photographer who is running alongside, snapping pictures and making notes. "And it's not too late to volunteer to come with me," she adds, digging Bliss enthusiastically in the ribs.

"Sorry, I'm busy at that time," says Bliss.

"But I didn't tell you when I'm going."

"Oh. Didn't you?" he replies straight-faced, as yet another flashbulb pops in his face.

Bliss is still laughing about Trina an hour later as he approaches the American border in his hired car. *At least she cheered Daphne up pretty fast,* he admits to himself as he slows behind a nondescript white van with Washington state licence plates — just one of a thousand vehicles heading home from British Columbia at the end of another working day — and he watches with a professional eye as the customs officer takes a cursory look at two of the occupants' documents before waving the vehicle through.

"They could be smuggling almost anything in the back of that van," Bliss muses, his mind on his upcoming presentation, and as he creeps forward with his passport in his hand, he can't possibly imagine how right he is.

"Visa," demands the pinch-faced officer as he snatches the passport, and Bliss can't resist a wisecrack. "I've only got MasterCard and American Express," he says with a broad grin.

But the officer is not smiling — has possibly never smiled — and Bliss quickly changes his tune. "Sorry," he says as he flashes his badge. "I didn't have time to get a visa, but I'm from Scotland Yard on my way to address a conference in Seattle."

"Just pull over there and report to the office."

"Do I have to —" starts Bliss, but the officer stares skywards.

"Thanks," mutters Bliss with a scowl.

Trina Button, on the other hand, is beaming as she and Daphne tip bucketfuls of coins and bills onto her kitchen table in West Vancouver. "Maybe I should just go to the airport every day instead of New York," she laughs as she picks out the larger bills. "Though it won't help Norman now."

"Norman?" queries Daphne.

"Yeah, my kidney patient. I was hoping you'd get to meet him, but he passed away over the weekend."

"Oh, dear. His kidneys finally gave out, did they?"

"No, it was suicide," whispers Trina, without adding that she's somewhat perturbed because he seemed so upbeat about his chances when he saw the Kidneymobile.

"There are plenty of suicides about in England at the moment," declares Daphne as she helps Trina sort the coins by denomination and nationality.

"I've heard," admits Trina. "It was on the news. They're dying like flies, apparently. What's happening?"

"David's got a theory," continues Daphne. "He thinks it's probably some freaky religious sect like the Branch Davidians, saying, 'Hand over all your lolly and God will grant you immortality at Armageddon.'"

"Minnie wouldn't have fallen for that, would she?"

"Maybe," answers Daphne as she dabs at a tear with the back of her hand. "She could be very flighty at times. Though that wouldn't explain why she was so determined to take me on a trip 'round the world."

"You were really looking forward to that, weren't you?" says Trina as she hands over a box of tissues, then screeches in delight. "I know — we could take a trip. Let's surprise David and Daisy. Let's ride the Kidneymobile to Seattle and visit them."

"I don't think so ..." starts Daphne, but Trina is already running for her road atlas. "Look," she says sympathetically as she finds the relevant map, "I know it's not quite the same as going around the world with Minnie, but the scenery is wonderful; there are mountains, forests, lakes and the ocean, and we can stay in a really plush hotel each night — maybe even a spa."

"I'm not sure," says Daphne, though there is sufficient waver in her voice to let Trina in.

"We could get Rick to drop us near the U.S. border, then we'd only need to do about forty kilometres a day," she says with her finger on the map. "We'll keep to the coast and the back roads so we won't have to worry about traffic."

"But, I'm not sure David would really appreciate visitors."

"Oh, rubbish, Daphne," laughs Trina. "He seems like the kind of person who just loves to be the centre of attention."

However, thirty-five miles south of them at the American border, Bliss is already the centre of attention, and he is certainly not loving it.

"Look, I'm supposed to be meeting someone at Seattle airport right now," he complains as a customs officer hands him a white gown, saying, "I'm sorry about this, sir. But since 9/11 we've gotten a lot tougher on visitors."

"This is ridiculous," insists Bliss. "What possible reason would I have for smuggling dope into your country?"

"Just change in that cubicle over there, sir," says the officer as he pulls on a pair of surgical gloves, explaining coldly, "The fact is that the drug dog clearly reacted positively to something in your car."

Bliss clenches his teeth and spits, "But I've told you a dozen times. I just hired the damn car. I'm a senior police officer, for Christ's sake."

"Swearing won't help you, sir."

"I'm not swearing, you moron," Bliss mutters under his breath, though not quietly enough.

"I heard that," begins the officer, but a knock at the door saves Bliss as a young female officer struggles in with his luggage, enquiring, "Is this your suitcase, sir?"

"Yes," says Bliss frostily.

"Then how do you explain the presence of this herbal substance?" she asks as she flips open the case and triumphantly extracts a large plastic bag.

"I'm so cross that I left my bag of Keemun tea in David's suitcase," Daphne is saying to Trina as they finish counting and stop for a drink. "It's the Queen's favourite, you know, and I so wanted you to try it. But what with all the excitement at the airport I quite forgot about it."

"Never mind. I'm sure he and Daisy are enjoying it," says Trina, adding, "Can you believe it? I raised over a thousand dollars, not counting all the funny money."

"I'd still like to know more about that place where Minnie sent her life savings," says Daphne, and Trina has an idea.

"It won't take a minute," she says re-finding the Western Union phone number for White Rock. Then she covers her phone's mouthpiece with a handkerchief, pinches her nose and says "Hi" in a Liza Minnelli voice, adding, "this is Lindi from CNL Distribution —"

"Oh dear," says the friendly clerk. "You've missed him today, Linda. He was here a couple of hours ago."

"It's Lindi with an *I*, not Linda," explains Trina, to give herself thinking space. Then she carries on, "Do you know where he was going?"

"To the bank, I'd guess. He nearly cleaned us out of greenbacks again."

"Bank ..." echoes Trina. "Look, I'm new here and I'm gonna get into a lot of trouble if I don't catch him. Do you know which bank?"

"That's interesting," says Trina as she puts down the phone. "Apparently they change it into American dollars, but she doesn't know where they take it."

"America, probably," suggests Daphne logically, and Trina nods her agreement before saying, "I know. Let's do a bit of sleuthing. We could stake the place out and follow him when he leaves with the stash."

"Trina," cautions Daphne, "how will we know who he is?"

"Umm ... Good point," mutters Trina, then she adds unconcernedly, "Don't worry, I'll think of something."

"Well, don't tell David," cautions Daphne. "He can be very touchy about the public investigating cases without getting permission from Interpol first."

"Roger, dodger," quips Trina with an English accent, and she keeps it up as she says, "Do you take milk and sugar with your tea, Lady Daphne?"

Daisy is also drinking tea, though it's certainly not Daphne's Keemun. She's on her third paper cup since arriving at Seattle's Sea-Tac airport and she's nervously eyeing the clock above the arrivals indicator board when Bliss runs up and throws his arms around her.

"I'm so sorry, Daisy. *Excusez-moi*," he mumbles as he muzzles into the soft folds of her bouncy auburn hair and feels her melting in relief.

"It is not a problem," she mutters, close to tears, and their lips lock and remain so until a couple of blue-rinsed matrons complain to a security guard.

"*Puritains,*" mutters Daisy as they head for the parking lot, and ten minutes later Bliss pulls into Lincoln Park, where the city meets the sea, and slips a CD into the car's player.

"Recognize it?" he asks as the music swells.

"*Oui, Daavid,*" says Daisy as she lights up. "It is Monsieur Dave Brubeck playing 'Love Walked In.'"

"What a memory," smiles Bliss, and the music spins them back a month, to a magical night under the Mediterranean moon, skimming across the silky indigo waters on the deck of a luxury yacht. A flight of seagulls and a school of dolphins escorted them northward that night as they sailed from Corsica to the Côte d'Azur, and their path was illuminated by the slender beam of light from Venus.

"Look," says Bliss as he cradles Daisy's head against his chest and points to the crystal-clear Washington sky above Puget Sound and Mount Olympus. "It's Venus again."

"*Daavid,*" explains Daisy, recalling the two spoilsports at the airport, "I zhink I know why zhe American women don't like love."

"Why is that?"

"Because, perhaps zhe men here are not *romantique.*"

"Not like zhe French men," he laughs, but she shudders at the thought.

"Zhe French men, zhey are like zhe frogs," she claims. "Zhey make a lot of noise, and zhey hop, hop, hop from one girl to zhe next, but zhen," she shrugs her shoulders dismissively, "zhey fall asleep. *C'est terrible.* How you say — it is terrible."

"*Oui* — it *is* terrible," agrees Bliss as he kisses her, murmuring suggestively, "the beach is just over there. Maybe we should see if there are any frogs."

"*Daavid,*" laughs Daisy. "I zhink zhat you want to make love under zhe stars again."

"*Oui,*" he agrees, without hesitating, and Venus is still in the sky as they walk hand in hand to the water's edge. But the northern Pacific, chilled by the meltwater of a thousand Alaskan glaciers, is not the balmy Mediterranean, and instead of cuddling for love, they are soon huddling for warmth.

"I zhink maybe we should go to zhe hotel, *Daavid,*" mutters Daisy with a shiver after a few minutes, and they race back to the car with more than sleep on their minds.

However, Bliss has a surprise in store for Daisy. In place of a hotel, he has rented a luxurious log cabin in a mountainside resort where they can make up for a missed month, while surfacing occasionally to marvel at the moonlit vistas of mountains and lakes and snack on local oysters and champagne.

"I thought this would be more *romantique,*" Bliss tells her, not untruthfully, as their maid shows them around the cozy love eyrie. But it's already eight the following morning according to Bliss's internal clock, nine according to Daisy's, and no sooner have they warmed themselves in front of the cottage's log fire than they begin to drift off in each other's arms.

"Never mind," says Bliss. "We have the rest of the week."

As David Bliss and Daisy finally fall asleep in America, the Tuesday-morning telecasts in England are reporting that there has been no abatement in the number of reported fatalities, and Chief Superintendent Edwards would happily add Bliss to the list of dead, if he could find him.

The irate senior officer has been searching since ten minutes past nine the previous morning, when he'd found Bliss's hastily typed report on his desk, and, somewhat predictably, Bliss's cell phone had rung just as he was shepherding Daphne aboard the Air Canada 747 at Heathrow. Bliss had casually turned his phone off, but Edwards has pulled strings and is in hot pursuit. A stinging message awaits Bliss at the conference hotel in downtown Seattle — which is precisely why he and Daisy are staying twenty miles away on the slopes of Mount Rainier.

"I specifically ordered him not to go," Edwards is bleating to anyone who'll listen Tuesday morning, but he knows that he's been end-run. Bliss is flavour of the year with the hierarchy since his spectacular discovery in Corsica, and his recent rescue of a bunch of oldies from the burning bus merely adds gloss.

"What's the latest on the suicide front?" the commissioner wants to know at the Tuesday-morning prayer session, and Edwards is forced to flourish Bliss's report and pretend that his disobedient junior is still on the case.

"He's got several good leads," Edwards bluffs, then bites his tongue as he adds, "I've sent him undercover for a few days, and knowing David Bliss he'll pull something out of the bag."

"Good," says the commissioner. "I'll put the Home secretary in the picture."

Tuesday comes eight hours later to Vancouver and, as the morning sun lights up the snow-capped peaks, Trina drags Daphne to her favourite coffee house where she regularly antagonizes a group of serious crossworders by beating them to the easy clues.

"Hi, Trina," yells Cindy the manageress as they enter. "I see you've hit the headlines again."

"I know," squeals Trina as Darcey folds her arms over the partially completed crossword in the *Vancouver Sun* and tries to look enthusiastic about Trina's arrival, while Matt, Dot and Maureen, her fellow puzzlers, huddle closer.

"Look!" shrieks Trina, wrenching the paper from under them and flourishing the front-page photo in which she sits, beaming, alongside a fierce-faced Bliss. "This is David Bliss, the famous Scotland Yard detective who found all the Nazi gold. And this is Lady Daph, from the old country."

"But you're not naked this time," complains Matt, his mind on a previous occasion when Trina had posed topless in a publicity stunt.

"You'll go blind if you're not careful," laughs Trina as she tousles a few strands of the old man's hair, then adds, "Isn't it wonderful? My phone hasn't stopped ringing. I've already done two radio interviews, and we're on local television at lunchtime."

"I guess you won't have time for the crossword, then," says Dot hopefully, but Trina is already pulling up chairs for herself and Daphne.

The lunchtime TV appearance is scheduled to take place at the Canada–U.S. border and is timed to coincide with the intrepid duo's departure to Seattle, but Maureen Stuckenberg is also in on the act, and with several geriatric gang members from the Kidney Society in support, she is already being interviewed for the CBC's national television news as Rick, Trina and Daphne arrive at the Canadian side of the border with the Kidneymobile in tow.

"Yes. The Society thought it would be a wonderful way to raise public awareness of the urgent need for kidney donations," Ms. Stuckenberg says straight-faced, though she is reticent when asked if she will personally be riding the machine to New York.

"Maybe," she laughs, "though I think I'm getting a bit old for that sort of thing."

Daphne Lovelace has lied about her age so often she would have to check her birth certificate for an honest answer, though there is no doubt that she is considerably older than Maureen Stuckenberg, so it's not surprising that Rick Button is hesitant about their planned trip.

"Are you sure this is a good idea?" he asks nervously as he helps unload the Kidneymobile from its trailer.

"Rick," Trina explains carefully as she strings bunting and balloons to the mast. "What could possibly go wrong? I've got my cell phone and a spare battery; maps; list of hotels and several credit cards; plus we've got smoked-salmon-and-banana sandwiches and two flasks of tea. We're going to America, not Antarctica."

"I know."

"Just make sure you feed the guinea pig," she continues to her husband as she hands Daphne a crash helmet and helps her into the passenger seat.

"Right."

"And don't forget the kids."

"I won't."

"That's about it, then," says Trina as she prepares for her turn at the mic.

"What about passports?" Rick asks, and she rushes, red-faced, back to the car.

"Just don't let her talk you into doing anything silly," Rick cautions Daphne as Trina bounces in front of the reporter with a five-year-old's enthusiasm. "I know what she can be like."

"Of course not," Daphne replies, though as she and Trina slowly pedal away from the border crossing under the spotlight of the cameras a few minutes later, the Englishwoman is still concerned about the kind of reception they are likely to receive from Bliss should they actually reach Seattle.

A couple of hundred kilometres south of the border in Seattle, David Bliss has no worries as he slips into a back-row seat in the elegant auditorium of Washington State University for the opening address. He's not due to speak until Thursday and had whispered, "Don't go anywhere," in Daisy's ear as he'd slipped out of bed an hour earlier. "I'll just put in an appearance, then I'll be back. Nobody will notice whether or not I'm there."

"Is Chief Inspector Bliss of Scotland Yard here?" questions an amplified voice, immediately proving him wrong, and he reluctantly raises a hand. "There's a phone call for you at reception, sir," explains the speaker from the stage, and as Bliss makes his way towards the exit, muttering "I bet it's Edwards" under his breath, he's aware of a stir of recognition amongst the crowd.

"One moment, sir," says the receptionist as she connects the caller to the desk phone, and Bliss finds himself looking at a familiar face as he idly scans the front page of the *Seattle Times*.

"Scotland Yard Man in Town for Conference," screams the headline above a picture of him sitting next to Trina in the Kidneymobile. "Detective Bliss, who recently shot to fame around the world by unearthing a cache of Nazi gold, was spotted pedalling a kidney away from Vancouver ..." continues the article and Bliss yelps, "Oh, that's bloody marvellous," as he answers the phone to a reporter from the BBC in London and curses the marvels of global communication.

"I'm a very big supporter of charities," he's forced to say, thinking, *I'll strangle that damn Button woman* when the receptionist tells him that he has another call waiting.

"Bliss — it's Edwards," spits the chief superintendent. "I thought I told you to cancel that conference."

"Shit," mutters Bliss under his breath, wondering how much lower his day can sink. "Sorry, sir. I must've misheard. But I did the report you requested."

"I know that," shouts Edwards, "and you'd better come up with something damn good, because I just lied to the commissioner to save your ass."

"Up yours," mutters Bliss as he replaces the handset and turns to find himself face to face with the governor of Washington.

"Honour to have you here, Commander Bliss," says the governor with an outstretched hand. "So looking forward to your speech on Thursday. I must say we're rather counting on Scotland Yard to come up with something special to deal with this people-trafficking problem. I'm fed up with listening to lefties and commies continually knocking the decadence of America and the West without offering any sensible solutions."

"Right, sir," gulps Bliss.

"Oh. By the way," carries on the governor, pointing to the front page of the *Times*. "Nice touch, that. Very clever ... You can't buy that kind'a advertising. You boys certainly know how to milk the media. You sure must have some PR department over there."

Bliss's PR department is currently headed at full speed for the United States side of the border, with bunting and balloons flying, as Trina whoops, "Hold tight, Daphne. America, here we come."

"America sounds mighty fine to me," responds Daphne in a passable Texan drawl as she clutches the giant polka dot hat to her head. "This takes me back fifty years," she sings out as she pumps the pedals with the enthusiasm of a thirty-year-old. "We used to ride everywhere during the war, you know," she carries on as they approach the border at little more than walking pace while passing motorists "beep" and wave, and others pull alongside, yelling, "Saw you in the paper — good luck!" as they toss handfuls of coins into the back of the bathtub.

"Wow!" exclaims Trina as she gaily waves her thanks. "This is really going to work."

"Just take a look at this," blares the American immigration officer to his colleague as the Kidneymobile slowly pulls up at the control box. "And where are you two ladies off to today?" he asks as he tries desperately to keep his face straight.

"We're going all the way to Seattle," answers Daphne with aplomb.

"Well, I just hope you've got a licence to drive that," he jokes, and he's laughing so much that he signals them through without checking their passports. "Don't go breaking any speed limits," he calls after them. "The Highway Patrol is pretty hot around here."

"Thank you, officer."

"And don't go poppin' no wheelies, either."

"We'll remember that," laughs Trina as she gives him a friendly wave, but it's not their own speed that concerns them as they head south on the verge of the multilane freeway.

"This is just a little scary," shouts Daphne above the roar of passing juggernauts that whoosh past and pluck at her hat as they threaten to sweep the frail craft into their slipstreams.

"Time to hit the path less travelled," concurs Trina and she turns off the freeway at the first interchange. "This is better," they agree, as a cedar-lined lane leads them gently down to a flotsam-strewn beach where they stop for a sandwich and tea as the waves gently swish on the sand.

"We'll stick to side roads and stay close to the coast from now on," says Trina as she checks her map, "although we'll have to go inland a bit at first. Anyway, Rick can always come and get us if we run out of steam."

"The fresh air certainly gives me an appetite," admits Daphne as she tucks into a sandwich; then she pulls a face.

"What d'ya think?" asks Trina.

"It's certainly different," admits Daphne, surprised to find that Trina has creamed the smoked salmon and bananas together into a sandwich spread.

A bald eagle has caught Daphne's eye as it circles overhead, and she has trained her binoculars on it when Trina spots a surfacing whale in the blue bay and nearly wrenches her companion's head off in a grab for the binoculars. "And there's another, and another, and another," Trina carries on as orcas surface one after another.

"This is absolutely heavenly," whispers Daphne, and so the afternoon continues as they soar along peaceful side roads lined with tall pines and twisted arbutus trees, while porcupines, chipmunks and squirrels barely stir at their silent approach.

"It reminds me of gliding," whispers Daphne delightedly as they skim along under the cloudless sky with ravens, gulls and eagles as company overhead and their tires swishing along the smooth tarmac beneath them.

A half-dozen cars and a couple of vans pass them in an hour but, as the sun starts its slow descent over the Pacific Ocean, Trina is beginning to worry that they haven't seen anything resembling a hotel since leaving the beach. "There's a town up ahead," she calls out confidently as the pedals keep revolving, though it turns out to be nothing more than a signboard and a dozen abandoned shacks.

"It looks a lot bigger on the map," Trina complains, scratching her head; then, with an eye on the disappearing sun, she decides it's time to call Rick.

"Oh, damn," she says despondently as she checks the tiny screen on her phone. "We're out of range."

"We could flag down the next car and get a tow," suggests Daphne, and that remains their plan for nearly half an hour, until the sky turns progressively pink and the tall trees start to crowd in on them.

"It's a lovely clear sky," says Daphne as Venus begins to glow, but the evening's chill is already starting to nip.

"Perhaps we should have brought flashlights," mutters Trina with growing concern, though Daphne is less worried as she rummages in her handbag and announces, "I've got matches. A Girl Guide is never without matches for lighting signal fires."

"We only ever used them for lighting cigarettes when I was in the Guides," admits Trina sheepishly. "What else have you got in there?"

"Let's see," says Daphne, still rummaging, "a little candle, nail file, some string, safety pins, a small mirror for signalling, and a penknife with one of those things for getting stones out of horse's hooves."

"Well, that should come in handy," laughs Trina, though she's somewhat heartened. "Okay, let's push on," she says picking up the pace. "At least we'll stay warmer if we're pedalling and we're bound to get somewhere eventually. There should be a main road up ahead, I think."

If there is a main road, its traffic doesn't disturb the forest creatures, and in the deepening gloom the nocturnal predators begin another night of foraging. Cougars, coyotes and wolves are already on the prowl as a small herd of mule deer cross the road ahead of the two women and pause, mid-carriageway, mesmerized by the unusual sight.

"Get-out-the-way! The *Kidney Queen*'s coming through," shouts Trina and, as the animals scatter into the bush, the surrounding silence takes on an eeriness broken only by the whooshing of the breeze as they skim along in the growing darkness. Then a full moon starts to rise above the eastern horizon and startles them.

"It's absolutely crimson," breathes Daphne and they stop pedalling to watch its fiery ascent.

"I've never seen such an incredibly red moon," admits Trina.

But a full moon offers them some hope as they pick up the pace again. "At least it won't be totally dark," reasons Daphne, then she yelps excitedly, "House up ahead!" as she spots lights through the trees.

"Thank God for that," sighs Trina. "I was just beginning to worry about the bears and mountain lions."

"Oh, how exciting," gushes Daphne, though Trina is clearly relieved to see the set of double gates at the end of a driveway.

Mission of Mercy Monastery, announces an elaborately engraved wooden sign, though less encouraging is the addendum: "No visitors, solicitors or salesmen under any circumstances." However, there is an entryphone attached to the one of the gate pillars and Trina grabs it.

"Hi," says Trina breezily. "I'm really sorry to disturb you, but we're lost and need a phone."

"Sorry. We have no phone," answers the static-laden voice.

"Oh. Well, it's getting dark," pleads Trina. "Can you just let us in until we can get someone to help?"

"Sorry, ma'am. We have no guest facilities. It's only five miles to the main road."

"Five miles!" exclaims Trina as Daphne gazes to the top of one of the gate pillars and muses to herself, "That's strange. That looks like a surveillance camera up there."

"You don't understand," continues Trina. "We're riding in a bathtub."

"Madam, we are members of a strict religious order who have shunned all worldly goods, including bathtubs. I am sorry that we cannot help you. Good night."

"Wait," pleads Trina, then she sticks her mouth against the speaker and harshly whispers, "Look, I've got a ninety-year-old woman with me who is going to die of hypothermia if you don't let us in."

The static continues while the spokesman seeks advice, then the voice returns with a sympathetic edge. "You must understand, madam. We are a closed community. What you ask is impossible. However, I could perhaps send someone with a blanket and some hot soup."

"What kind'a mercy is that?" demands Trina, adding, "I've a good mind to report you to the Pope. There's bears and cougars out here, you know."

The surveillance camera still fascinates Daphne as she watches it sweep up and down the road, while another period of silence signals further debate. Then the ethereal voice asks, "Are you alone?"

"Of course we are," sighs Trina. "Otherwise we wouldn't need help."

"Wait there," commands the voice, and Trina turns to Daphne, muttering, "Like we could go anyplace else." But Daphne is still focused on the surveillance camera, and the immense electrified fence topped with razor wire which snakes off into the gloom, as she deliberates whether or not its intent is to keep infidels out or devotees in.

chapter seven

North of the border, in Trina Button's snazzy Vancouver kitchen, her husband's concern is growing as he stands at the window watching the red moon rising over the Rockies, and when the phone rings he races for it.

"Hello ..."

"Hi, Rick?" calls David Bliss breezily. "I was just checking up on Daphne — making sure she'd settled in all right."

"Oh, it's you, Dave," says Rick as he drops his tone and confesses, "Actually, I'm getting really worried about them."

"Christ! That's all I need," declares Bliss once he has been put in the picture; although initially he's more bothered about them showing up at the conference in the kidney contraption than not showing up at all. "So where the hell are they?"

"Dave, do you ever get that sinking feeling that something dreadful has happened?"

"Often with Daphne," laughs Bliss, "but she always manages to prove me wrong."

"Well, I suppose no news is good news," Rick carries on unconvincingly, though Bliss, with his recent experience with the media, would prefer no news of any kind involving Trina. "Oh, I'm sure they're all right," he blusters, adding, "I wouldn't worry about her knowing she's with Daphne. The old girl trained with the commandos during the war. She even parachuted behind the lines to help the resistance in France."

"But it's almost dark," carries on Rick as if he hasn't heard, "and Trina was supposed to call me as soon as they found a hotel for the night."

"Have you tried her cell phone?"

"They must be out of range. I just get her voice mail."

"What is zhe matter, *Daavid?*" asks Daisy as Bliss replaces the receiver and stares northwards across the darkening forests to the shadow of Mount Baker in the far distance.

"I wouldn't know where to start looking," he muses before explaining the two women's escapade to his companion. "They're like a pair of bloody schoolkids," he moans, still smarting over his embarrassment at the airport. "If she wasn't so flipping old I'd let her stew," he adds, though knows that he won't. "Sorry, Daisy," he says, with her coat in his hands. "They've probably got a puncture."

"I don't mind, *Daavid*. I zhink zhis is exciting, no?"

"No," he agrees, with far more force than intended.

By one a.m. the excitement is waning, even for Daisy, and their only lead has been a bar drunk whom they found regaling a saloon full of lumberjacks with his account of the happy pedallers heading for the boon-docks several hours earlier.

"They can't be far off," the denim-clad woodsman roared. "When I saw 'em, they wuz tryin' to outrun a porcupine."

But every tortuous lane in the area had taken Bliss and Daisy in circles, and many had petered out altogether or simply degenerated into the rutted tracks of logging roads. So, after three hours of vainly scouring the thickly forested foothills of northern Washington, they're ready to accept the comforting hypothesis that the two women have coddled themselves in the luxury of a ritzy mountain resort and are enjoying themselves so much that they've simply forgotten to phone.

"I'd better give Rick another call," says Bliss when they emerge onto the highway a few miles south of the Canadian border and spot a twenty-four-hour gas station with a phone booth. But Trina's husband has heard nothing and refuses to be mollified.

"Dave, believe me. She would have phoned. She *lives* on the phone. In fact, she's just waiting for the day when she can have one implanted."

"Maybe her batteries are dead?"

"Dave … She'd walk up to a complete stranger in the street and ask to use their phone."

"Really?"

"Yeah. She often does it. And she's so damn cheeky about it that they always say yes."

"I guess I'd better call the local police, then," concedes Bliss, before arranging a rendezvous with the anxious man in nearby Bellingham. A few minutes later he suffers a mild rebuke from the city's duty officer.

"Mebbe you should'a called us earlier," says Captain Prudenski of the Whatcom County force. "It's pretty damn cold out tonight."

"I know," says Bliss as he and Daisy stand shivering in the booth. "Though I still think they've probably snuck in somewhere toasty."

"Wait there," instructs Prudenski. "I'm on my way." Bliss uses the time to call his daughter in England, illogically persuading himself that Daphne might have phoned her. But his son-in-law answers and skips the pleasantries.

"Dave, what the hell's going on? Edwards has put me in charge of the suicide squad until you get back."

"At least he's keeping it in the family."

"You've really pissed him off this time. He told the commissioner you were on the case, and the next thing you're on the front page of this morning's *Daily Express* in a frickin' bathtub."

"Oh, no!"

"The old man wants blood — yours or Edwards'."

"As if I care," says Bliss, leaning on his letter of resignation and knowing that Edwards is no longer the only person with entries in a little black book. "But if Edwards drops me in it, I'll make sure he turns up as a villain in my novel."

"Anyway. What are you doing out of bed at this time? I thought you'd arranged to have a little French hen over there to keep your naughty bits warm."

"That's no way to talk to your father-in-law," jokes Bliss as he snuggles closer to Daisy, though his tone darkens as he adds, "Actually, Peter, we are waiting for the local law to show up. Daphne's gone missing."

"Missing?"

"Yeah. Though I'm sure she'll surface — she always does. Anyway, anything new on the suicide front?"

"Well it seems that at least half of the old dears sent their life savings to Canada in the weeks leading up to their deaths."

"CNL Distribution?" queries Bliss.

"Most, but a load of different companies as well, although they're all in British Columbia. And the money was always transferred through Western Union."

"Okay, Peter. Get me specifics — names, dates, amounts, et cetera — and I'll get hold of Mike Phillips in Vancouver. He should be back from Hawaii any day now. Do we know how much?"

"Probably half a million quid in total."

"Phew!"

"Mind, it could be more."

"Okay. Well, let me know. And tell Edwards that I'll deny any knowledge if he tries to claim that he pulled me out of the conference."

"I think you'd better tell him that yourself."

"So is zhat true, *Daavid?* Are you are going to write your book about zhe man in zhe iron mask — *l'homme au masque de fer?*" Daisy asks with alarm in her voice as he puts down the phone.

"I haven't decided."

"But you promised my mother zhat you would not."

"I know, Daisy. But sometimes you have to lift the veils from the past to move forward into the future," he says, recalling the torture that Daisy's family had suffered at the hands of the Nazis, and the fear that his exposé could reignite the torment. However, the look on Daisy's face suggests that he is close to sleeping on the settee for the rest of the week, so he quickly softens. "But I won't write it if she really doesn't want me to."

"Chief Inspector Bliss?" calls a voice from a police cruiser, and twenty minutes later Bliss is accompanied, with Daisy in tow, into the briefing room of Bellingham's police station by Captain Roddy Prudenski.

"Five foot two, blue eyes, grey hair ..." Bliss begins to a hastily assembled audience of thirty officers and state troopers, though he can't help feeling he's wasting his time, and theirs, thinking, *How many eccentric English geriatrics would you expect to find cycling the backwoods of Washington state in a kidney bathtub at two in the morning?* But he carries on: "She's accompanied by Trina Button ..."

"We've already checked all hospitals and hotels," says the captain once Bliss has completed his descriptions. "The last reliable sighting was a little after midday yesterday when they crossed the border from Canada. And they were apparently seen a few hours later heading inland towards the foothills of Mount Baker, though that's not confirmed."

"I can confirm that," says Bliss recounting the woodman's sighting, "though I've already checked the area where he says he saw them — nothing."

"There's that monastery place, sir," suggests one officer sharply from the back, and Bliss picks up a certain disdain in the man's expression which is immediately echoed by Prudenski.

"It's a bunch of aging hippies with a place up in the Cascades," snorts the captain. "They call themselves missionaries, though God knows what they do there. To be honest, we kind'a learned our lesson after the massacres at Jonestown and Waco, so we don't trouble them and they don't trouble us."

"It might be worth a look," suggests Bliss, though Prudenski is noncommittal. "Mebbe," he says, then continues with the briefing as officers make notes. "Current temperature is thirty degrees and considerably colder at higher elevations. The chopper is already up; highway patrols are on full alert." Then he turns to Bliss. "Anything else you can tell us about the ladies, sir?"

"Miss Lovelace has been missing on previous occasions," admits Bliss, adding, unnecessarily, "Though she's always shown up eventually."

"Let's hope that's the case this time," says the captain. "That's a mighty big chunk of real estate to get lost in up there."

However, the size of the search area is quickly whittled down once the sighting by the logger and the probable average speed of the Kidneymobile have been factored in. Large areas of virtually unscalable mountains and inaccessible forests have also been discounted so that, by the time Rick Button arrives from Vancouver, most of the possible terrain has already been covered.

"I checked with the immigration people at the border," says Rick, "and they definitely haven't slipped back into Canada. So it shouldn't be too difficult to find them."

But three hours later, as the first rays of dawn creep over the mountains in the east to sparkle on the blush of frost that dusts the treetops, there is still no sign of the missing women. Bliss and Daisy have aimlessly driven the back roads of Washington all night, and have repeatedly tripped over police cars doing the same thing, while a searchlight from the force helicopter has flashed across their path on more than one occasion.

"They certainly don't mess about here," Bliss says, speculating on how long it might take to get as many men on the ground in similar circumstances in rural England, and he looks to Daisy for a response. But she has reclined the passenger seat and is fast asleep.

"You poor thing," he breathes, and realizes that he too is close to exhaustion. *Perhaps I should stop for a snooze,* he is thinking, when he spots the Mission of Mercy's signboard.

"That must be the 'monastery place,'" he muses, and Daisy surfaces as he bumps onto the gravel shoulder to use the entryphone.

"Hi. I'm Chief Inspector Bliss of Scotland Yard," he says after waiting several minutes for the phone to be answered. "I'm sorry to bother you so early, but we're searching for a couple of missing women."

"There are no women here, sir."

"They were riding in a funny kind of bicycle thing ..."

"Like I said, sir, there are no women here."

"I just wondered if they might have stopped by here last night, seeking shelter."

"*Daavid*, look," says Daisy, slipping out of the car and tugging anxiously at his arm.

"What is it, Daisy?" he asks, as the voice from the entryphone is saying, "Sorry, sir. But we have no knowledge of any such women. Now if that is all ..."

It takes twenty minutes for Captain Prudenski and a posse to arrive at the scene, by which time Bliss has parked discreetly down the road, with the gates of the monastery some distance away in his rearview mirror.

"Look," says Bliss as he leaps from his car and holds out a mud-stained white handkerchief to his American colleague. "It's one of Miss Lovelace's," he adds with absolute certainty. "See the embroidered initials," he carries on, pointing out the *D.O.L.* neatly stitched into the corner. "It was right outside the missionary place back there."

"What do they say?" asks Prudenski with a nod to the monastery's gates.

"They deny any knowledge," says Bliss. "But I don't believe them."

"Let me try," says Prudenski. However, he gets a similarly polite cold shoulder from the man answering the entryphone a few minutes later, though when he requests a face-to-face meeting with someone in authority, the voice noticeably hardens.

"Do you have a search warrant, Captain Prudenski?"

"No."

"Then there is nothing to discuss. Please be good enough to leave us in peace."

"Now what?" questions Bliss, though with memories of the eighty-four deaths during the Branch Davidian debacle at Waco in 1993 in mind, Prudenski is backing off faster than a grizzly hunter with a jammed gun.

"She may have just dropped it as they passed," he suggests, and Bliss reluctantly admits to the possibility, though he questions, "So where were they going? Where does this road lead?"

The road leads nowhere, coming to an abrupt end just two miles further on, where it runs into a small mountainside lake.

"This doesn't look good, Captain," says Bliss a few minutes later, as he carefully scans the soft mud of the lakeshore but finds no trace of bicycle tires amongst the pad marks of bears and wolves. Then he turns worriedly to Prudenski. "If they'd doubled back towards the main highway we would have found them last night, and they most certainly didn't come this way."

"But there are no other roads," admits Prudenski, scratching his head as he checks his map.

"In that case; that only leaves the monastery," pronounces Bliss positively.

chapter eight

By the time Trina and Daphne have been escorted to an austere windowless room on the building's ground floor, the ecclesiastical aura of the Mission of Mercy Monastery has vanished.

"It smells more like a hospital," Trina whispers as soon as the door closes and an electronic bolt slides firmly into place.

"I know," Daphne whispers back. "But why are we whispering?"

Because, though neither will admit it for fear of spooking the other, they have both been rattled from the moment the giant double gates had swung open, revealing two deeply hooded men carrying a couple of burka-like shrouds which they insisted the women should wear.

"We wouldn't want to drive the monks crazy with desire," Trina giggled as she struggled into the shapeless gown, but then she shrieked in alarm. "Help! I can't see a thing."

"Neither can I," Daphne agreed, feeling such unease that she purposefully dropped her monogrammed handkerchief.

"We don't usually permit anyone to see our faces or hear our voices," one of the men explained in a gravelly tone, then informed the women that they would have to remain in the dark until they were ensconced inside the monastery. And thereafter, every attempt by Trina to garner information from their guide was silently rebuffed.

Several minutes of stumbling led them to the monastery, where doors opened and closed automatically as they processed through the building, until finally, following the hum of the electronic door lock, a metallic voice instructed them to remove their gowns, and continued, "Your presence has already greatly disturbed our community, and we now require you to remain in your room and fully respect our privacy."

"That's pretty snotty," Daphne mutters as she pulls off the robe, and she follows up with a half-hearted suggestion that the monks might ritually sacrifice young virgins.

"No fear for us, then," Trina laughs. However, her laughter rings hollowly a moment later when she spots a surveillance camera high up on the wall of the small bedroom. "Don't look," she cautions, but Daphne immediately spins to confront the device.

"There's something very funny going on here," Trina says a few minutes later, after unsuccessfully testing her shoulder against the solid steel door. "I heard a telephone ringing when we came in."

"I know," Daphne admits. "And he said they didn't have baths, but there's a bathroom right here."

"He lied. I didn't think they were supposed to lie," says Trina, slumping onto one of the hard beds and asking, "And did you notice the shoes they were wearing?"

"Well they certainly weren't rope-soled sandals," Daphne replies, going on to speculate that they had looked more like the gleaming shoes of army officers. But it was the sound of voices that had taken her most by surprise. Despite several rather obvious attempts by their escort to "shush" other inhabitants at their approach, Daphne had clearly picked up the high-pitched chattering of Chinese. "I knew a bit of Mandarin once," she tells Trina, and demonstrates with a few words before admitting that she had been unable to decipher what she'd heard.

"I'm sure I heard some pop music," Trina recalls excitedly as they continue piecing together the puzzle, like escaped hostages trying to lead the police back to their kidnappers.

"I'm sure I smelt perfume at one time."

"There was swimming pool — I definitely smelt chlorine."

"And a garage — there were petrol fumes."

"And somebody had been smoking outside the first door," Trina gabbles with the elation of a game winner. "I know because I can always tell when Rick's been to a bar."

"I smelt cigarette smoke on the hands of the bloke who gave me the robe," Daphne adds, before concluding, "I don't think this is a monastery at all."

"Are you sure?"

"Look around," she suggests with a sweep of her hand. "All this furniture looks like standard government issue, there's surveillance cameras and electronic door locks, and there's better security than Buckingham Palace."

"What're you saying, Daphne?"

"I think it's some sort of top-secret base where they carry out weird experiments on unsuspecting volunteers," the Englishwoman replies seriously, then adds a cautionary note: "Which means they are probably listening to everything we say."

"Oh, for Jesus Christ's sake. That's all we need," a man wearing headphones and a gleaming pair of military-issue shoes sighs, before yelling to his colleague, "Wally! Get in here!"

"Yeah, Steve?" responds Allan Wallace as he races into the surveillance room in the building's basement.

"You remember the two totally harmless old dames we let in just now cuz you wuz worried they wuz gonna freeze to death?"

"Of course."

"Well, you'd better start praying for divine intervention P.D.Q., cuz they've just rumbled the whole damn scene."

"What?!"

The raucous dawn chorus of ravens and crows is wasted on Bliss and Trina's anxious husband as Captain Prudenski and the night officers sign off watch at the main police station in Bellingham, leaving them in the hands of a more sanguine officer.

"It's almost daylight now," says Matt Larson, a straight-backed, no-nonsense captain, once he's paraded his officers and instructed them to keep a lookout for the missing women. "It won't be long before they show up, perky as sunflowers," he adds with a smile that's supposed to be comforting. "And they'll be asking what all the commotion was about."

But Rick Button is unconvinced and is becoming frantic. "Trina would not do this. Something's happened to her," he insists, though Larson is unmoved, and just two minutes later his optimism is vindicated when he's handed a communiqué by a clerk.

"Gentlemen," he says, beaming with good news. "The Kidneymobile has been found."

"Where?" demand Bliss and Rick Button simultaneously.

"Back in Canada. Just as I predicted."

You didn't predict that, Bliss muses to himself, but he is too thrilled to challenge the man.

"Is Trina okay?" asks Rick, but Larson has no specifics. "They must have recrossed the border last night when they couldn't find anywhere to stay," is all he can add as he hands Bliss the report. "You'd best check with the Canadian Mounties for more information."

But disappointment awaits. The machine has been discovered, dumped in a wooded area just north of the U.S. border, but there is no sign of the women.

"We'd better get back there quickly," Bliss tells Rick Button, and he catches Daisy's arm and drags her towards the parking lot. "They can't be far away."

Trina and Daphne are considerably closer than Bliss imagines, though they look more like wilted dandelions than perky sunflowers following a sleepless night spent worrying what the morning would bring.

"We're ready to leave now," Trina calls, as she jumps up and down in front of the surveillance camera, as she has done for the past twenty minutes. But she gets no response and is close to tears as she declares, "I wish I'd brought the guinea pig now."

"Why?" puzzles Daphne.

"Cuz he'd find a way out. He can escape from anywhere."

"This reminds me of when I was captured by an East German Stasi officer in Berlin after the war," Daphne muses as she assesses the situation.

"What happened?" breathes Trina.

"I had to sleep my way out," she admits sheepishly, without mentioning that she had actually fallen for the strapping *Kapitan*, though she refrains from suggesting a similar course as she ponders a possible escape plan. "I've got an idea," she says, and motions for Trina to follow her into the bathroom as she surreptitiously slips her penknife out of her handbag, telling herself, "I always knew this would come in handy one day."

"What're you doing?" Trina starts, but Daphne shushes her with a warning look as she turns on the bath taps and flushes the toilet as noisily as she is able. Then she whispers in Trina's ear, "Create a diversion. I want to see what's next door."

"Let us out, you bastards! We want to leave now," Trina rages a minute later as she furiously bangs on the handleless steel door with a metal chair, while behind her, Daphne has slipped under one of the beds and is busily working the pointed nose of the penknife's stone remover into the plaster wallboard.

"Please be quiet. You are disturbing our devotions," the tinny voice of the intercom cautions as Daphne furiously works at creating a hole.

"Let us out, then!" Trina continues shouting. "Let us out! Let us out!" Then she begins kicking.

"Stop that. You may leave in the morning," says the voice testily as the gravelly-voiced operative desperately scans the monitor looking for Daphne. "Please stop that noise."

"It's morning already. Let us out. Help! We've been abducted! I'm going to report you," Trina screeches as she continues kicking.

"Keep going," Daphne pushes. "I'm getting through." But although the first layer of wallboard gives easily enough, her digging tool is too short to penetrate beyond the cavity into the wall of the adjacent room. "Bugger," she mumbles, then she scuttles from under the bed just as the electronic bolt slides back and the door starts to open.

"What seems to be the problem, ladies?" asks a hooded one, pushing Trina roughly back onto the bed, while a bulky figure blocks the doorway behind him.

"We'd like to leave now, please," says Daphne as she picks up her handbag and stalwartly makes for the door with her head down, but he firmly grabs her as she passes.

"Sorry, ladies. No can do," he says. "In fact we're going have to ask for your co-operation for a little while longer."

"How long?" demands Trina, though she gets no answer as their captor holds out his hand and demands their passports.

Bliss and Daisy are also readying their passports as they follow Rick Button north at breakneck speed towards a small border crossing, and Bliss muses, "I hope they don't want to search me again." But his British passport carries him across unscathed this time, and a smiling face greets him on the Canadian side.

"As soon as I heard you were in town I knew there'd be trouble," laughs Inspector Mike Phillips with his hand out.

"Hi," calls Bliss, as he strolls up to the RCMP officer. "How was Hawaii?"

"Hot," replies Phillips, then his face drops and he spreads his empty hands in a gesture of despondency. "No sign of the women, Dave."

The Kidneymobile lies in a small woodland clearing just off the main highway, a few miles north of the border, but the sight of tracker dogs showing more interest in sniffing each others' genitals than following a scent tells Bliss a disappointing story.

"What ... No tracks at all?" he asks sceptically.

"Deer, elk and bear," answers one of the dog-handlers. "But nothing worth following."

"So where did they go?" Bliss asks, but he is faced with a dozen blank stares. "Look," he says, "Daphne may be a bit flighty, but she isn't Mary Poppins."

"So what are you suggesting?" asks Phillips, and Bliss looks back over his shoulder.

"I think that we're being given the runaround," he says, and his point is proven a short while later when he attempts to return, alone, to the States and is curtly informed by a blonde-haired shrimp of a border guard that his visa has been revoked.

"What do you mean?" he screeches in disbelief.

"Just carrying out orders, sir," says the diminutive woman.

"That's what the extermination camp guards always claimed," he mumbles under his breath as he uncurls himself from the car to confront her, demanding, "Why has my visa been cancelled?"

"Suspicion of importing illegal drugs, sir," says the officer, reading from a prepared script, but now she has a backup in the form of a heavyweight wrestler in uniform.

"It was just tea and you know it," fumes Bliss, refusing to back down. "It was a bag that Miss Lovelace, the missing woman, put into my suitcase because she'd already locked her own."

"I'm afraid it's not that simple, sir," the backup man says, and Bliss quickly gets the message as the female officer makes no attempt to disguise the fact that she's lying when she says, "You see, sir, according to this, it was found to contain a quantity of narcotic substance."

"In that case, arrest me and charge me with illegal possession," says Bliss, calling her bluff.

"We've considered that, sir, but in the interests of international diplomacy —"

"What do you know about diplomacy?" snorts Bliss, but the officer's impassive face tells him he's wasting his time.

"I want to speak to the British consul, right now," demands Bliss.

It takes Bliss three hours, some serious arm-twisting by the consul, and the intervention of the governor to get his visa reinstated, and he's grateful that he'd left Daisy holding Rick's hand in Canada while he's forced to suffer the obvious scorn of the immigration officers when they discover that they've been outweighed.

"You'll have to fill out a new application," the woman officer spits venomously, then she spends ten minutes checking and rechecking every point before announcing that his new visa will expire in just two days. "At midnight following your scheduled appearance at the conference tomorrow," she says firmly, and though no one says so directly, it's pretty clear that he can expect to be railroaded out of town immediately thereafter.

Trina and Daphne, on the other hand, are going nowhere and are back in the bathroom with the taps running.

"Did you see his face?" asks Trina, talking of the hooded guard. "He had terrible zits," she says as a voice calls from the intercom in the bedroom.

"Mrs. Button. Miss Lovelace. Please return to the bedroom."

"I think I'll call him Spotty Dick," laughs Daphne.

"Well, I'm calling the other one Bumface," giggles Trina. "He was all pinched and wrinkled, like some of my old patients. But what are we going to do, Daphne?"

"I did a course on captivity survival during the war," whispers Daphne, and as she sits on the toilet seat in the cramped bathroom she finds herself dusting off sixty-five years of memories to recall the little psychological warfare officer who'd scared the daylights out of her group of wartime volunteers as he'd swaggered his way around the classroom.

"The h'enemy takes comfort from the fact that they h'are h'in total control," the major had said, scattering aitches through his rapid staccato speech like a gunner firing tracers. "They'll tie you h'up, blindfold you and gag you. H'anything to stop you moving. Movement is a function of human behaviour. The h'idea is to prevent you from h'exhibiting normal human behaviour. It's h'all part of the dehumanization process."

"At least they haven't tied us up," says Daphne as the voice on the intercom becomes more belligerent.

"Mrs. Button. Will you please return to the room immediately."

"The golden rule is to start escaping from the moment you're captured," says Daphne, ignoring the voice. "Catch 'em off balance before they've decided what to do."

"But how?" Trina wants to know as the voice grows angrier.

"Mrs. Button. Return to the room, *now.*"

"It's all about control," Daphne continues unfazed as she zips through her memories of similar situations. "Once you roll over, they've got you."

"Mrs. Button. This is your last chance ..."

"And try to make eye contact with them whenever you can," continues Daphne quickly, as she remembers the final part of the officer's lecture.

"They'll avoid h'eye to h'eye contact whenh'ever possible because they 'ave to go 'ome to the wife and kiddies at the h'end of the day, and visit dear old granny h'at the weekend. So h'any action what makes you h'appear human makes it more difficult for them to take the final option." Then he'd dropped his voice to add, "Of course, there's always the vicious little bastard whose idea of fun is to poke out yer eyes with a knitting needle."

"What do you do in those circumstances, Major?" Daphne had enquired.

"You prays for an 'eart attack, luv."

The sound of the electronic bolt sliding back warns them that their time in the bathroom is up, and Spotty Dick wastes no time before thumping on the door.

"Mrs. Button. Come out now!" he shouts.

"What do we do?" whispers Trina.

"Just pretend everything is normal. It shouldn't take David long to find us," says Daphne as she coolly opens the door and stares directly at their captor, enquiring, "Can I help you, young man?" as if he's an encyclopaedia salesman.

However, nothing is turning out normal for Bliss at Bellingham's police station, where Captain Prudenski has been tipped off by the Customs Service and has no interest in becoming embroiled with a suspected drug dealer.

"I don't think there is anything else I can do for you, sir," Prudenski declares with a cold eye when Bliss says he wants to revisit the monastery. "The ladies' contraption was found in Canada, so I've no idea why you are even here. Why aren't you searching there?"

Looks as though I'm on my own, Bliss says to himself as he returns to his car and takes out his map.

"Would you like a cup of tea, Trina?" asks Daphne with utter seriousness as they sit at the small wooden table, and she continues prattling as if in a Monty Python sketch. "Whenever I have tea with Her Majesty we always have Keemun," she says, then she leans in conspiratorially. "It's her favourite, you know."

"I'd heard that," says Trina, playing along. But beneath them, in the basement's surveillance room, a hoot of laughter from Spotty Dick is quickly stifled by a newcomer who instantly takes in the scene and orders, "Wipe that stupid grin off your face, man, and get in there and stop them."

Daphne pours from an imaginary pot then she holds out a make-believe plate, asking, "Would you like a chocky bicky to go with that, dear?"

"Gosh, thanks ever so much," replies Trina as the door slams open.

"Just in time for tea," mutters Daphne, turning with an insouciant smile and asking, "Do you take milk and sugar?"

"Game's over," says Spotty Dick sourly.

"Oh, really. Does that mean we can go home now?" asks Daphne as a new face appears in the doorway, though this one is not shrouded by a hood.

"Leave us," the newcomer hisses to Spotty Dick, before he strolls into the room with the brashness of a corporate lawyer, pulls up a chair, and lets the tension build as his eyes hold steady on the two women.

"Ladies," he says eventually, making Trina jump, "I'm afraid that we have no choice but to keep you here as our guests until certain decisions have been made."

"But we wouldn't tell anyone what you do here — would we, Daphne?" tries Trina.

"You have no idea what we do here," continues John Dawson with polished authority. "But we are not prepared to take that risk. And you will be well cared for — providing you co-operate."

"But what about our families?" cries Trina.

"Ms. Lovelace has no family, but your husband and children will simply have to accept the fact that you are missing for the time being."

"You can't do this," spits Daphne. "I demand a lawyer. I demand my habeas corpus rights."

"Actually, ma'am," says Dawson, "I regret to inform you that you have no such rights under the president's anti-terrorism laws, and we can keep you incommunicado for as long as we deem you to be a threat to national security."

"And you seriously think that anyone would believe me to be a terrorist."

"Well, Ms. Lovelace, it seems that you entered the United States illegally by failing to obtain a visa at the border. So, yes, we do consider you a risk."

The Mission of Mercy Monastery doesn't appear on Bliss's map — in fact it doesn't appear on *any* map — and he's forced to drive blindly around the thickly forested foothills of the Cascade Mountains searching for landmarks until he spots a familiar bar.

A dozen pairs of eyes follow him into the saloon, but the surrounding forest is abuzz with the sound of chainsaws, so he's not surprised by the absence of the lumber-jack who'd spotted the missing women the previous evening. However, a paunch-bellied woodsman propping up the bar appears to be something of a fixture.

"I'm looking for the monastery place," says Bliss casually, once he's ordered a coffee, but he's surprised by the oldtimer's shrug of ignorance.

"Sorry, fella," says the gap-toothed senior. "I'm kind'a new round here."

A hoot of amusement from behind the bar leaves Bliss perplexed. "Do you know the place?" he asks, turning to the bartender.

"No, sir. Not me, sir. I don't know a damn thing," he replies, and as Bliss sweeps his eyes around the room, the other occupants snigger into their beers.

"I see," he says and changes his mind about the coffee.

"Hey — I've already made it!" the barman calls after him, then a gale of laughter follows him out the door.

Bumface and Spotty Dick are also finding amusement as they watch the surveillance monitors at the monastery and see Daphne and Trina scuttle back to the bathroom for another strategy session.

"God knows what the hell they do in there," laughs Bumface.

"That's one of life's little mysteries, Steve," says Spotty Dick, adding, "I even used to wonder if they had twin johns in the women's."

A cloud of concern suddenly darkens the other man's face. "They could be cooking something up," he warns, staring into the screen.

"Don't worry," chuckles Spotty Dick. "They ain't got a stove."

"Know thine enemy, Trina," says Daphne once the taps are running.

"What do you mean?"

"I've been thinking about the fence I saw when we arrived. It was designed to keep people out, not in. This is not a prison, and this isn't a cell."

"But what about the cameras?"

"Observation, not security," she says. "Otherwise they'd have one in here as well."

"Ladies ..." calls Spotty Dick on the intercom. "Come out of the bathroom, please."

"So what are we going to do?" whispers Trina.

"What would they expect of two middle-aged housewives?" asks Daphne, dropping thirty years without a moment's hesitation.

"Housework?" questions Trina.

"Precisely. And, just like good housewives, we'll put a lot of effort into it."

With his suspicions cemented, if not actually confirmed, by the occupants of the bar, Bliss finds the path to the monastery and makes his plans. There's clearly no point in knocking at the gate and asking politely again, he tells himself as he sits watching the road from a blind spot about a mile away from the monastery's gates. Courtesy is clearly not on their top-ten list of commandments.

Meanwhile, Trina and Daphne have plonked themselves onto one of the beds, with their backs to the camera, and have begun to knit.

"What the hell are they doing now?" asks Dawson with his eyes on the monitor.

"Knitting, John," laughs Bumface. "Her Majesty reckons they're making an escape rope."

Traffic is sparse as the afternoon wears on, and after more than thirty hours without sleep Bliss comes close to snoozing several times, but he needs something bulkier than an ordinary car to prise open the gates for him, so has no choice but to wait.

"Stop that!" orders Dawson's irritated voice on the intercom, and the two knitters redouble their efforts.

The door opens a minute later and Spotty Dick appears, asking, "And just what do you think you are doing?"

"Knitting, of course," says Daphne. "Here," she adds, holding out an imaginary skein of wool. "See if you can get the knots out of that, would you."

A mile away, a flash of white through the trees signals the approach of a vehicle larger than a sedan, and Bliss perks himself up and starts his engine.

"Ladies ... ladies," pleads Spotty Dick. "Would you please stop this nonsense."

"Nonsense?" retorts Daphne indignantly. "Didn't your mother ever tell you the story of the emperor's new clothes?" Then she holds up the make-believe rope and eyes it critically. "Not bad," she says, as she peers through the imaginary artefact and locks her gaze with his. "What do you think?" she asks with the calmness of a hypnotist, and the moment stretches and stretches until he finally breaks free. "By the way," she asks as he makes for the door with his head down, "what's your name?"

"That's interesting," she muses to Trina as the door gently closes.

A large white Ford delivery van passes Bliss's forested hideaway, and he waits for it to disappear before gingerly emerging onto the road. Ahead of him, the two men in the vehicle are trundling along the back road at a leisurely pace at the end of just another working day, north of the border in Canada, and have their sights set on a few beers and a game of pool or two in the monastery's bar.

"Wann'a smoke, Reggie?" asks the driver as he holds out a pack to the front-seat passenger.

"Sure. Why not, Buzzer," says the passenger, with a nod to the inert figure concealed under a large trough of dead salmon in the back of the van. "He ain't gonna complain."

However, in the monastery's surveillance room, Dawson is furious at the women's refusal to obey, and is screeching at Spotty Dick. "Can't you see what she's doing, you idiot? Get back in there right now and make them stop." Then he spins on Bumface, yelling, "Go with him and make sure he does."

Outside, Bliss is scorching after the Ford van, while anxiously searching ahead for the occasional flash of white through the trees; praying that he won't suddenly round a bend and find himself peering into their rear-view mirrors.

"Ladies ... ladies," repeats Spotty Dick, crashing back into the room while carefully avoiding Daphne's gaze. "You've got to stop this, now."

"Oh, hello," says Trina, picking up where Daphne left off. "Just hold the end of this, will you?"

"Stop it!" he yells, then unthinkingly gives them credence by snatching at the imaginary rope.

Bliss is still two hundred metres from the gates, and his pulse is racing as he nudges the car round bend after bend at breakneck speed.

"Now look what you've done," exclaims Daphne in mock anger as Trina starts to cry.

"Oh, for chrissakes ..." moans Bumface from the doorway.

Bliss's timing is perfect. He rounds the final bend just as the huge gates are swinging open, and without a moment's hesitation he guns his engine and flashes through the gap before the van driver has a chance to get his vehicle in gear.

"Terrific!" he exclaims as the giant gates flash past in a blur, and ahead of him, through the trees, he catches his first sight of the monastery. Then his whole world explodes.

chapter nine

Thirty minutes later, with the dust settled, Daphne and Trina are back in their room nursing their wounds after an abortive escape bid, while Bliss is back at Bellingham police station wondering how the hire-car company will react to their vehicle's shredded tires and the ragged line of bullet holes across the trunk lid.

"They sure as hell get touchy about trespassers up there," the desk officer explains as Bliss recounts the moment when a row of vicious spikes had sprung out of the roadway in front of him, a dozen sirens had screeched overhead, and a couple of hooded men had jumped from behind trees with sub-machine guns. "You're lucky to have got out alive."

"But what are you going to do about it?" demands Bliss angrily.

"I suppose I should give you a ticket for trespassing ..." the sergeant begins as he scratches his head, though is saved further deliberation by the appearance of Captain Prudenski.

"Chief Inspector Bliss, there's a couple of people who need to talk to you," he says without ceremony.

"People?" queries Bliss, but the captain clams up and ushers Bliss into a room where two smart-suited, smart-mouthed, executive types wait with painted-on smiles.

"Look, David — you don't mind if we call you David, do you?" asks one, his tone as clipped as his brush-cut hairstyle.

"Who are you?" queries Bliss.

"That's not important, David," starts the other, a beefier version.

"In that case, I think I'd prefer you to call me Detective Chief Inspector," says Bliss coldly, sensing that he holds the higher ground, guessing that their desire for anonymity means they are probably walking on quicksand.

"Dave ..."

"Detective Chief Inspector."

"Look, how long are you going to keep this up?"

"Until I start getting some straight answers."

"If that's the way you wann'a play it ..." says Brush-head. "In which case, we've come to tell you that the search has been officially called off. We're satisfied that the two ladies in question left the United States of their own free will sometime late yesterday evening."

"But that's not true," spits Bliss.

"Choose your words wisely, Chief Inspector. We do have the documents to prove what we're saying."

"Then how come the Canadians have no record?" demands Bliss.

"Sloppy record-keeping," continues Brush-head. "They're renowned for it."

"I don't believe this."

"Look, David — excuse me," says the muscular one, switching on a smile and putting a hand on Bliss's shoulder. "But you have to understand what you're dealing with here."

"I think I'm dealing with a couple of jerks who've been watching too much television," Bliss says as he shakes off the hand and heads to the door. "Now, if you'll excuse me, I have two women to find."

Brush-head beats him to the door and holds it shut with his back. "Sir. We're not asking. You should understand that you are only here as a guest. Your visitor's visa can be revoked immediately."

"You've already tried that once."

"We can do it again."

"And what do you think Her Majesty's government would say about that?"

"They'll say whatever we tell 'em to say, Davie boy," he scoffs. "Just like they always do."

Talk about Big Brother, Bliss is fuming as he steps outside and confronts Prudenski. "Who the hell are they?"

"Way above my pay scale," admits the captain, "but they've got more clout than the governor. He's called off all search efforts and put out a press release sayin' that the women were just fine and dandy when they crossed the border last night."

"But this is a load of nonsense," insists Bliss. "We checked all the border posts this morning. They did not leave the country."

"Dave, I hate to tell you this, but an immigration officer has remembered seeing them pedalling home."

"When? Where?" demands Bliss.

"Last night around ten. At the sleepy border crossing on the back road, near where the machine was found."

"This is ridiculous. They couldn't possibly have pedalled that far. What do the Canadians say?"

Prudenski shrugs. "Maybe they were asleep, Dave. Like I say, it's a dozy little place."

Doziness has also become a problem for Trina and Daphne after their break for freedom during the confusion caused by Bliss's unscheduled arrival, when Spotty Dick and Bumface raced to investigate the cacophony of sirens, gunfire and shouts of alarm and inadvertently left their door unlocked. The women were out of the room in a flash, but their flight came to grief at the end of the first corridor where Dawson had stood with his arms folded.

Soon after, Trina finally succumbed to more than thirty-six hours of wakefulness, and Daphne helped her onto a bed and covered her with a blanket before continuing her imaginary knitting.

"Is she all right?" Spotty Dick asks Daphne as he brings a tray of food early evening.

"She's worried about her poor little children. All alone, bawling their hearts out ..."

"Yes — cut that out."

"Have you got any little kiddies at home?"

"Leave it alone, will ya. I meant — she's not sick or anything?"

"Oh, no," says Daphne breezily. "She's Sleeping Beauty and I'm Snow White. And you could be one of the little dwarves. You can be Dopey if you want."

"Look, will you stop this nonsense," he says as Daphne picks up an imaginary broom.

"What are you doing now?" he demands in frustration.

"I'm sweeping, of course," she says as she nudges him roughly aside. "C'mon, out of the way. Got to get this place cleaned up. The wicked queen's coming for tea."

"This won't work, you know ..."

"Just move that chair, would you?" she asks as she keeps up her mime.

"No."

"Oh, you are a naughty boy."

"Shut up, you silly woman."

"Maybe you should be Grumpy, then," she says cheekily, and she catches the glimmer of amusement in his eyes before he slips out.

The day has also been long and sleepless for Bumface and his boss John Dawson, and as Spotty Dick shakes his head at Daphne's antics and returns to the surveillance room, the strain has them at each other's throats.

"Look," says Dawson, "we've got to do something. This is a situation that is not going away on its own."

"Take it easy, John," replies Bumface. "The heat's off as long as no one saw Buzzer dump the stupid bathtub thing north of the border this morning. I'd say we have a credible level of deniability."

"You aren't thinking straight here, Steve," replies Spotty Dick. "Those are two real live women in there who know damn well where they are. And the moment they get out and blab ..."

But Bumface is slowly shaking his head. "They ain't getting out, Allan. Not in the same state as they came in, anyway."

"Shit! You aren't serious?"

"Okay," says Bumface, "what the hell are we supposed to do? Let them blow ten years of hard graft? Not to mention my pension. And who's gonna tell them upstairs? Huh? Not me."

"Okay, okay. So who knows they're here?" steps in Dawson.

"No one who doesn't have to," replies Bumface. "Even Buzzer doesn't know where the damn machine came from. And no one knows officially. In fact, officially they left the country at ten last night. We couldn't bring them back now even if we wanted to."

"And what about the other patients?"

"They're hardly gonna say anything, are they?"

"Okay. But what about that British cop?"

"He's just blowing smoke. Anyhow, he's out'a here in twenty-four, sooner if he doesn't put a lid on it."

"It's not that easy," snorts the senior man, well aware that even a blast from a machine gun had failed to silence Bliss, and he storms around the room, seething, "You knew the rules: no one gets in."

"In that case, John," says Bumface with a wide-eyed expression of innocence, "no one got in."

"Can't you get one of the docs to pump 'em full of something to make 'em forget?" asks Dawson with a glimmer of hope.

"Oh, I could do that myself," says Bumface with his hand on his gun, but Spotty Dick is backing off, just saying, "Look, they're nothing but a couple of nut-bars —" when the deafening squeal of an alarm fills the room and they look up at the monitor to see the smudgy images of Trina and Daphne leaping up and down, screaming, "Fire! Fire!"

"Oh-my-God!" yells Spotty Dick and all three race for the women's room expecting a smoky inferno.

"Where's the fire?" questions Dawson as they rush in and find the two women casually reclining on their beds.

"What fire?" asks Daphne with blank-faced innocence.

"You pressed the fire alarm."

"Oh, yes," she says with an apologetic air. "So care-less of me. It was just smouldering. It must have been all that wool we left lying around. But it's out now."

"There is no wool," spits Bumface and, with a curi-ous eye on the surveillance camera, he climbs on a chair and wipes a finger across the clouded lens. "Hairspray," he announces as he sniffs the sticky translucent coating and gives Trina a poisonous stare.

"Ladies," sighs Dawson in desperation, "will you please stop this. We are trying to regularize the situation, but you're not making it easy for us."

"I wasn't aware that we were required to," says Daphne, then she leaps out of bed, puts on her polka-dot hat, and says to Trina, "Come along, Dorothy. We're off to see the wizard."

"Oh, for God's sake!" groans Dawson, and he ushers the other two men out, with Daphne's shout of "You can be the Tin Man if you like" echoing down the corridor after him.

"You are going to get us into a lot of trouble," laughs Trina as the door closes, but Daphne sloughs it off with a shrug. "They're a bunch of amateurs. Anyway, how much worse can it get?"

But the pain has only just started for Rick Button, and he already sees a long dark tunnel in his future. David Bliss isn't having a good day, either, and he is calling the Vancouverite from a pay phone in the lobby of a Bellingham hotel, fearing that the phone in his room might be tapped after several calls he'd made to the press in which he'd virtually accused the local police of a cover-up.

"They're scaling back the search, Dave," bleats Trina's husband with a mixture of desperation and despair, and Bliss allows the distraught man to carry on rambling mournfully about the meaningless of life without her. "Who cares how many cars are in the garage? What's my golf handicap, or how many stock options I get? I'd give up the whole damn lot right now to find her. I mean, take it — take it all, Dave. I'll start from scratch, live in a tent, eat garbage. I don't care."

"Rick —"

"Keep busy, they say. Keep your mind off it. But I don't want to keep my mind off it," he continues to blubber. "I don't want to stop thinking of her for a second. I'm scared, Dave; scared that if I stop thinking about her, it'll be like I've acknowledged that something's happened to her."

"I understand," says Bliss.

"How can you?" asks Button, forgetting in his self-pity that Bliss is also mourning a loss. "It's like nothing matters anymore. Like it was all for zilch. All those years we spent bringing up the kids, saving for houses, holidays and cars, all the times we laughed, and cried. It's all gone."

"You still have the memories, Rick ..." starts Bliss, then regrets it as the distressed man picks up on the finality of the words.

"That's it. That's all I have got left, Dave. It's not much to show for twenty years, is it? Just the memories and a bunch of old photos." Then he chokes up completely and hands the phone to Daisy.

"Hello, *Daavid*. Have you found anything?" she asks as Rick Button continues keening in the background, and Bliss has to admit that he's stumped.

"I zhink we all need some sleep," says Daisy, and Rick Button pulls himself together a tad and is back on the phone. "I've seen them on the TV, Dave. Snivelling wrecks barely able to hold their heads up after days without sleep. Pleading, begging, praying for the kidnappers to let their kids or their wife go. Well, that's me now. And they say I should keep strong for the children's sake — why? So they can look back later on and call me an insensitive bastard?"

"Where are the children?" asks Bliss, with no answer for the distraught man.

"Trina's mum's looking after them downstairs in the rec room," he replies before asking, "What's happening there?"

"Well, I've run into a few roadblocks," confesses Bliss, and he considers explaining his explosive imbroglio with the inhabitants of the monastery but changes his mind, saying only that he'd had an accident before taking a more pragmatic approach. "I've worked it all out," he explains. "From the time they were spotted by the lumberjack till ten p.m., when they were supposedly seen crossing into Canada, was less than three hours. It's forty-two miles — and that doesn't include the six miles that they would have gone in the wrong direction for Daphne to have dropped her handkerchief at the monastery."

"How fast —" begins Button, but Bliss already has the calculation to hand.

"Fourteen miles an hour — eighteen if we include the hanky. Could they have done that kind of speed?"

"You kidding? Not even if it was downhill all the way with a strong gale behind them."

"Quite. So where does that leave us?"

"You know where, Dave," says Rick Button, his voice cracking. "There's some real weirdos living up in the mountains."

"No. No. No. Don't even consider it," says Bliss. "Even if Daphne was dead I doubt if she'd lie down."

"So what are planning to do, now?"

"I've got a slight problem," he admits. "The hire-car people have dinged me five thousand dollars for the damage and they won't rent me another motor."

"You can borrow Trina's," starts Rick Button. Then he breaks down completely as he adds, "I don't think she'll ever be driving it again."

"Stop that," insists Bliss. "I'm sure it won't be long before we find them."

However, in the tangled rainforest close to the scene of the abandoned Kidneymobile, the Canadian searchers are losing hope as the moon rises for the second time without a sighting of the women. In any case, without witnesses, clues, trails or even the sniff of a scent, they've been stumbling around in the dark all day.

"We've had to call off the search for tonight, Dave," says Mike Phillips when Bliss phones him for news. "It's too risky to have people wandering about in the dark, especially with bears and cougars about. We'll go back at daybreak — though to be frank, I don't see them surviving a second night."

"I'm still convinced that monastery joint is involved," says Bliss, detailing his ill-fated incursion before scoffing, "They might call themselves monks, but that place is tighter than Fort Knox."

"So was Waco," Phillips reminds him, "but the Americans are adamant that the two women are in Canada."

"There's no way they could have got back, Mike."

"They could have hitched a ride —"

"No ..." interjects Bliss.

"Well, it's possible, Dave. Trina is certainly cheeky enough to have flagged down a trucker."

"So is Daphne," admits Bliss, "but U.S. Customs reckoned they'd pedalled back."

"Sure. No trucker would have risked carrying them over the border; too much red tape. He would have dropped them one side, then picked them up again on the other."

"Okay, so why didn't the dogs pick up a trail? And that still wouldn't explain why the authorities are on my back. According to the British consul I've trodden on some very tender toes."

And the extent of Bliss's clumsiness is brought home to him a minute later, when he phones his son-in-law England.

"Christ. It's four o'clock in the morning," moans Peter Bryan before adding, "Boy, are you in the khaki. Someone's tipped off the commissioner that you're running drugs into the States."

"Oh, that's brilliant."

"Edwards has pencilled you in for suspension."

"I bet he has," says Bliss, though he knows that his resignation letter will easily trump any hand that Edwards can draw.

"So, what's happened to Daphne?" asks Bryan, and Bliss takes a few minutes to vent his anger and irritation over his treatment by his American counterparts. "I don't know what they're playing at," he concludes, "but I'm going to keep believing she's alive until someone shows me a body."

"So, do you really think they're in that monastery place?" queries Bryan, and Bliss can only sigh in exasperation. "If they are, then the longer they keep them, the more difficulty they'll have letting them go."

John Dawson is facing that same dilemma as he paces the surveillance room with his eye on the clock. "Look, we gotta do something real soon," he tells Bumface and Spotty Dick. "That English cop, Bliss, ain't stupid. God knows how he knew where to find them, but he knew all right. And the chances are he'll try again."

"All we gotta do is deny it," insists Bumface as he lays back and confidently splays himself. "There's no photos, no inconvenient bodies — yet — and there's nothing in the press that we can't handle."

"And what're you gonna do — waste the pair of them? Cuz we sure as hell can't keep them forever," asks Dawson.

"It may come to that."

"You're crazy," says Spotty Dick. "Anyway, what about Bliss?"

"Maybe he'll have a nasty accident."

Bliss isn't planning anything accidental. In fact his motives are quite deliberate — to cause enough of a stench in Wednesday's press to stink out anyone with information about the women's disappearance. But at nine o'clock, when he answers a knock at his hotel room door, expecting a reporter from the *Seattle Times*, his face falls as he recognizes Brush-head and his sidekick from his morning encounter at the Bellingham police station.

"Oh, it's *you* again," he sighs, and he would have slammed the door if he'd been more alert.

"Dave —" says Brush-head as he saunters in.

"Chief Inspector."

"Okay, have it your way, *Chief Inspector*. Bottom line: we ain't askin'. We're tellin' ya: back off."

"Who are you?" Bliss demands with a quizzical eye, though he gets no answer and is forced to conjecture FBI, CIA, DEA, or some other group of testosterone-hyped college boys hiding behind a once-respectable set of initials. "You guys are a bunch of cowboys," he says dismissively.

"Dave, you don't understand."

"Oh, I think I do," replies Bliss venomously. "It might have been called fascism, Nazism, communism, Stalinism and various other *isms* at different times, but it all amounts to the same thing: Big Brother — the end justifies the means. It's sanctioned state terrorism and the suppression of any form of public dissension."

"Mighty big words, Dave."

"Well, I wouldn't expect you to understand them."

"Have you quite finished?"

"Yes, I think so."

"Good. Then I have great pleasure in informing you that unless you cease your attempts to make slanderous accusations in the media, you will be placed on our register of undesirable aliens and will never — I repeat, *never* — be permitted to enter the United States of America again."

"Suits me," says Bliss. "But what about Miss Lovelace and Mrs. Button?"

"Our position remains the same. The two women left the country of their own free will last night."

"That's a lie."

"Prove it."

The solidity of the two women in the monastery gives proof to the lie as they duck under a tent of bedclothes for a strategy session.

"I think Spotty Dick is starting to bend a little," whispers Daphne, and Trina lightens up a notch as she giggles, "Perhaps we should change his name to Wilting Willy."

"The snobby one talks as though this is official," carries on Daphne, "but it can't be, or the British consul would be banging on the gates."

"Which means?"

"That they're probably a lot more scared than we are," she suggests, not adding that it also makes them much more dangerous.

However, downstairs in the surveillance room, Spotty Dick and Bumface don't look particularly threatening as they slumber, exhausted, in front of the monitors.

"Keep an eye on those two," John Dawson had said, tapping the screen before leaving to get some sleep, and he made it clear that he expected a solution by the time he returned. "You two clowns started this circus. You'd better think of a way to stop it."

"So what are we going to do?" asks Trina, thinking Daphne has a plan.

"Hum," sighs Daphne, feeling herself sinking. "Maybe we should get some shut-eye and see what happens in the morning."

Meanwhile, in nearby Bellingham, Bliss finally succumbs to fatigue and unthinkingly uses the phone in his room to call the Button household to say good night to Daisy.

"I'm sorry about all this," he says, though she claims not to mind.

"It is exciting, no?"

"No," says Bliss positively. "It isn't. Well, certainly not the kind of excitement I'd had in mind when I invited you."

"Never mind, *Daavid*. I will see you in zhe morning and maybe we will find zhem."

"Maybe."

"That was *Daavid*," says Daisy, finding Rick Button in his office, struggling to keep his eyes open, fearing sleep to be an admission of the hopelessness of the situation.

"I zhink you should go to bed, no?" she says gently, but Rick has no such thoughts. In fact, he's determined to stay awake until Trina is found, and he has turned on almost every light in the house, emptied his briefcase, filing cabinet and car's glove compartment of business cards, and is frantically emailing Trina's photo and description to everyone he's ever met.

"Would you like a sandwich, perhaps?" asks Daisy, and he looks at her as though she is demented.

"How can I eat?" he asks through the tears, and she understands, saying, "I will see if zhe children are hungry."

"She would have called if she could," he sobs with total despondency as Daisy starts to leave.

"Oh, you should not worry. I zhink she will come back," she says, returning to place a comforting hand on his shoulder.

"No," he says positively. "Not alive, anyway."

John Dawson is close to accepting the same conclusion, but he lies awake praying for an alternative when his phone rings and a voice harshly whispers, "He's in Room 227, Bellingham Suites Hotel."

"You're good," says Dawson. "Thanks. I owe you."

Now what? he puzzles, and he wrestles with projected scenarios that all end nightmarishly in the electric chair, until his brain finally freezes and he falls unconscious.

Daphne wakes him at five in the morning as she tries to suffocate him with her giant polka-dot hat, and he surfaces, screaming, to fight off the sweat-soaked sheets. Then he reaches for the bedside phone and calls the surveillance room.

"Get up here, Steve. We need to talk."

"Okay, John."

"And bring some coffee."

"You know what we've got to do, don't you?" says Bumface a few minutes later, but Dawson is still reluctant.

"It's not like you can dig 'em up, brush 'em off and say sorry if the balloon goes up."

"Look, this is crazy, John. What the hell — we lose, what … two or three a week, *every* week."

"That's different. They never existed in the first place. We could lose the whole damn lot and no one would ask any awkward questions. But if someone starts digging and comes up with these two …" his voice trails off, his point made.

"We'll just have to make sure they're mighty deep."

"And what about him?" says Dawson, with an allusive nod to Bumface's colleague asleep in the basement. "He won't like it."

"It was his damn fault. He was the one who convinced me to let them in. Anyway, once they're gone there's not a lot he can do about it."

"When?"

"It'll be getting light soon. We'll have to leave it to tonight."

"Nothing messy, okay?"

"Sure, John."

"Get something from the pharmacy, so they won't feel anything."

" 'Kay."

"And what about that snoopy cop?"

"Leave him to me, John."

chapter ten

Wednesday morning begins before six for Bliss, with the insistent ringing of the hotel's automated wake-up service forcing him out of one nightmare into another, and he's on the phone to Mike Phillips by six-fifteen.

"Dave, there's absolutely nothing in the American papers," complains his Canadian colleague.

"I know," bleats Bliss despondently. "They were all over it yesterday. I did half a dozen interviews before a couple of heavies showed up and put the bite on me."

"So much for freedom of expression," breathes Phillips, "though God knows what their problem is."

"What's the Canadian press saying?" asks Bliss.

"They've rerun the photo of the pair of them in the Kidneymobile," he says, neglecting to add that Maureen Stuckenberg has backpedalled with more zeal than a trick cyclist and is now suggesting that the Kidney Society actually considered the whole scheme foolhardy from the beginning. "Rick's offering a reward for their safe return," Phillips continues, "though I don't see much point. From what I know of those two I should think that a kidnapper would be more than happy to get rid of them."

The second morning of captivity is also beginning early for Daphne, following a restless night spent dodging bullets and border guards as she slipped back and forth under the Iron Curtain with little more than a dubious diplomatic passport and a winning smile for protection, and she stirs to the sound of the electronic door lock.

"I've brought you something to eat," says Spotty Dick as he gently places a tray on the table. She slips out of bed, still fully clothed, and casts a wary eye over the bacon and eggs.

"I brought you tea as well as coffee," he adds, "and you can have more if you want."

This is a change, Daphne muses to herself, hesitating as she reruns her survival training course.

"H'eat when h'ever you get a chance," the expert had advised. "If they is gonna bump you off, they will. And arsenic h'aint 'alf as painful as having your fingernails ripped h'out one by one."

Spotty Dick senses Daphne's caginess and encourages her with a smile. "Don't worry," he assures her, "there's nothing wrong with it. Honestly."

"Thanks," she says, softly laying a hand on his arm and holding his gaze for a long second, before tucking in.

"What about Mrs. Button?" he asks with a nod to the sleeping woman.

"Goldilocks," corrects Daphne. "Oh, she's all right. She's found the baby bear's bed."

Bliss, on the other hand, slept on a bed of nails, and by the time Daisy delivers Trina's Volkswagen, a little after eight, he's fallen captive to a comfortable armchair in the hotel lobby.

"Did you have any trouble at the border?" he asks, once she's woken him and they are headed south towards Seattle. But Daisy has her eyes and mind on a black Cherokee a few cars behind them.

"*Daavid,* I zhink zhat we are being followed," she says worriedly. "I zhink zhat Jeep, he is behind us when we left zhe hotel also."

"I know," says Bliss with one eye on the mirror. "There's at least two cars on our tail, and I'm not sure about that white Ford ahead of us, either."

"What is it zhat zhey want?"

"Let's find out, shall we?" he says as he slams on his brakes and slides to a halt at the curbside.

"Now watch," he says as the driver of the first trailing car, a blue Honda, drives past with an air of apparent indifference, while in Bliss's rearview mirror the Jeep Cherokee makes a rapid turn onto the forecourt of a gas station.

"Now for the runaround," says Bliss as he waits for a gap in the approaching traffic and pulls a U-turn to neatly slot into the northbound lane.

The Jeep is already nosing back out of the forecourt, ready to pick up the northerly chase, when Bliss suddenly veers back across the road and dodges into the gas station behind it.

"Bastard," swears Bumface, at the wheel, as he is forced to continue north, while Bliss and Daisy pop out of the gas station's entry ramp and head south again at full speed.

"Now for the *coup de grâce,*" announces Bliss, and he resists the temptation to wave to the drivers of the white Ford and the blue Honda — now also headed in the wrong direction — as they zip past, while he makes a hard right into a side street and disappears into the underground parking garage of a hotel.

"Time for breakfast and a strategy session, I think," he says as he casually locks Trina's Jetta and guides Daisy to the restaurant.

Bumface is back at the monastery twenty minutes later, bemoaning his luck to Dawson. "Some damn woman picked him up and he gave me the slip," he complains, though Dawson seems unconcerned.

"Look, it's Thursday. You might as well leave him alone. He has to be out of the country by this evening."

"And you think he'll leave, knowing that we've got the dynamic duo in there?"

"He doesn't know that for certain," says Dawson. "All he knows is that the old buzzard dropped a handkerchief in the road outside. That doesn't prove squat."

"And what if he gets up at that conference and starts spouting off about this place?"

"Then someone will shut him up real quick."

"How?"

"I've taken care of it."

Bliss is also concerned about his upcoming speech as he sits with his back planted firmly against a wall.

"I'm due to speak at three," Bliss tells Daisy in French, as he keeps watch on the door while the waitress tops up their coffees. "But they're obviously trying to stop me."

"*Pourquoi célà?*" asks Daisy. "Why is zhat?"

"*J'ne sais pas.* I wish I knew," he says. "Although I'm not sure that I want to stand up there and talk about people trafficking when Daphne and Trina are missing.

I really should be in Canada helping to search for them, although I'm still convinced that they're here."

"In zhe monastery?"

"One of the basic rules of investigation, Daisy," he says, switching back to English as the waitress moves off, "is that when you have eliminated all other possibilities, the answer is whatever remains."

The look on Daisy's face suggests he's overstretched her linguistic ability, so he explains. "We know they were seen on the road to the monastery, and we know they were at the monastery gates. Now the Americans insist they left the country, but the Canadians didn't see them. Isn't that odd?"

"*Oui*," says Daisy, catching on. "Because zhey never care when you leave a country. It is only when you come."

"Quite."

"But the machine. It was in Canada, was it not?"

"It was," he agrees, "but nothing else was," and then he leaps up excitedly and heads for the pay phone in the lobby, muttering, "I've got to catch Mike Phillips before he leaves the station."

"Mike," Bliss asks, as soon as he is put through, "was Daphne wearing that stupid great polka-dot hat when she left Canada?"

"Yeah," laughs Phillips. "You can hardly see her face in the newspaper photos."

"So where is it, Mike? No one's suggesting that she tramped off through the forest wearing it, are they?"

"Their overnight bags are missing, too," Phillips reminds him, though Bliss doesn't find that strange.

"They wouldn't go far without makeup and stuff," he says, "But there's no way she would have stuck to that monstrous hat. And you know as well as I do that the absence of evidence is evidence itself. No scent, no tracks and no hat means only one thing: they were never there — full stop."

"What do you suggest?"

"Forget the search team. You're looking in the wrong place. Get a forensic squad to go over the contraption with a fine-tooth comb. Someone must have dropped it off from a truck; it's too big to fit in a car. Check it for fingerprints —"

"We're ahead of you there, Dave," interjects Phillips. "I had the fingerprint gal look at it yesterday. It was clean."

"Just the women's —"

"No. Clean — clean … Absolutely, totally clean."

"Well that's kind'a fishy for a start. Who would have wiped it? I mean, it's hardly a Jag or a souped-up Jetta. No one's gonna hot-wire it to pull off a heist or go for a joyride."

"I hear you, Dave," says Phillips. "I'll get the forensic boys on it right away."

"Check the tires, Mike. If it was wheeled off a truck there are bound to be some residues in the treads."

"Okay, Dave," Phillips is saying as Bliss responds to an insistent tug on his sleeve.

"*Daavid,*" whispers Daisy. "Quickly. Zhey are here looking for you."

The stakeout is tight. Double-manned cars — one at each end of the side street, plus a backup vehicle on the main road — while the driver of the blue Honda has slipped into the restaurant and is interrogating the waitress.

"Sure they wuz here," she says, nodding to the vacated table. "And they haven't paid yet."

"Thanks," says the burly man as he digs a twenty-dollar bill from his pocket. "Here. Keep the change," he adds, then he dashes off, sounding like a ventriloquist as he mutters into his lapel microphone, "Okay, guys. They're on the move."

However, in the nearby monastery, Daphne and Trina are clearly going nowhere, and the younger woman is rapidly falling apart under the strain as she snivels over her breakfast.

"All day yesterday I kept telling myself it was just a silly dream, and you just kept smiling and pretending it was a fairy tale. But it's not, is it?" Then she leaps up and screeches at the camera, "Why are you doing this? Why don't you let us go?" before flying across the room and viciously kicking at the door.

"Listen, Trina," says Daphne, as Trina limps back across the room and crumples into a blubbering ball onto the bed. "When Minnie died I looked into my future and all I saw was dementia, diapers and death. Then you and David gave me something to look forward to."

"But there's nothing to look forward to in here," Trina is saying as the door opens and Bumface scoots in, looking as though he's ready to strangle her before backing down and putting on a concerned look.

"Please stop shouting and kicking, Mrs. Button," he says gently. "We don't want you hurting yourself."

"I wann'a go home! I wann'a go home," howls Trina, and Daphne rushes to throw a comforting arm around her while appealing to Bumface.

"Why are you doing this? Can't you see she's frantic to see her family?"

"Well, she should behave herself then," says Bumface as he leaves.

The Bellingham back street is virtually clear of traffic by the time Daisy, alone, gingerly nudges Trina's car out of the underground garage.

"Just take it easy," Bliss told her. "Remember: they're after me, not you." But her hands are fiercely locked to the wheel as she emerges into the daylight and catches sight of the blue Honda.

"Don't be scared," Bliss had said, but Daisy's foot is shaking as she squeezes the throttle and eases the VW onto the quiet street.

The Honda driver is making a performance of folding his newspaper as Daisy passes, and she might have smiled at his ineptness if she weren't so terrified.

"Once they see I'm not with you they'll back off," Bliss assured her, but as she nears the main road the Honda is already creeping closer, and a black limousine with an official state licence plate is edging off a hotel's forecourt half a block away.

"Head north, back into the city centre," Bliss instructed, and as Daisy turns onto the main road she is so nervous that she misses the red light and nearly nails a speedy cyclist.

"*Oh! Pardon … Pardon,*" she cries as the cyclist glowers and swerves around her. Then she checks the mirror, spots the white Ford speeding towards her, and hits the gas in alarm.

"Don't race, whatever you do," Bliss warned, but with three cars on her tail she panics and reverts to her Gallic driving habits.

"Goddammit," spits the Honda driver as he realizes what's happening, and he yells into his radio's microphone, "Unit two — Unit two! Try to head her off."

"Ten-four," responds the driver of the black limo as he slams his foot to the floor. But Daisy is already gaining on her pursuers as she zips Trina's sporty little

Volkswagen around the streets — weaving from lane to lane with Mediterranean panache, leaving startled American drivers in her wake.

"Unit three!" yells the director. "Go north on Twentieth and try to get ahead of her."

"Ten-four," calls the driver of the white Ford, though he's barely finished speaking when Daisy slams her car broadside across the road and slips into a narrow service alley.

"She's trapped," muses the Honda driver, expecting the Volkswagen to grind to a halt amongst the garbage bins and discarded cardboard boxes, but the lane is wider than most highways in her native land, and Daisy screeches through without slowing. "Oh, man!" moans the lead driver, and he is quickly back on the radio. "All units: she's headed west on 55. I repeat — west."

"Whad'ya want me to do, boss?" queries the Ford driver, but the driver of the limousine cuts in. "I've got her. She's on 24 going north again."

Daisy spots the black limo pulling out of a junction ahead of her, and without slowing appreciably she flips the car sideways onto two wheels in the middle of an intersection, spins one hundred and eighty degrees, and takes off south again.

"Okay — back off! Back off all units!" yells the Honda driver, then he calls for reinforcements.

The siren and flashing lights of a police cruiser finally force Trina's Jetta to a halt a few minutes later, and as men come running from all directions, Daisy leaps out of the car and stands with her hands in the air, shouting, "Don't shoot! Don't shoot!"

"Boy, that was some fancy driving, ma'am," beams an officer as he lowers her arms and shakes her hand. Then another front-runner sticks his head into the car, asking worriedly, "But where is Chief Inspector Bliss?"

"*J'ne parle pas anglais,*" claims Daisy, as per Bliss's instructions, but one of the officers speaks French and steps forward to explain that he and his colleagues are a protection team sent to ensure Bliss's safety.

"It's just that the governor heard he'd had a few problems yesterday and wanted to make sure that he got to the conference all right," the man continues, before questioning, "So where is he?"

Daisy's eyes give the game away, and seconds later the lid of the Volkswagen's cramped trunk opens.

"Chief Inspector Bliss?" queries one of the officers as Bliss unwinds himself and groans in pain.

"Are you okay, sir?" asks one of the men helping him out of the back of the vehicle.

Bliss warily eyes the sharply dressed men surrounding him, demanding, "Who are you? What do you want?"

"Lieutenant Jewison at your service, sir," says the Honda driver, stepping forward.

"And …?" Bliss queries, expecting to find Brush-head and his sidekick amid the sea of faces with an order for his immediate deportation.

"And, I'm here to put this limousine and official escort at your disposal with the governor's compliments, sir," the officer continues, smiling proudly.

Ten minutes later, with Trina's car safely stored at the Bellingham police station, Bliss carefully checks the passing road signs through the limo's deeply tinted windows, still half-concerned that his escort might be whisking them to the Canadian border, while whispering to Daisy, "The trouble is, I've no idea who are good guys and bad guys anymore." But Daisy is more interested in a growing aroma that's permeating the air as they sink into the soft leather seats.

"What's that smell, *Daavid?*" she queries, turning her nose up at his jacket.

"Banana," he says sourly.

"*Banane?*"

"*Oui*," he says, cursing Trina for leaving a paper bag of the overripe fruit in the trunk of her car.

On any normal day, the owner of the Volkswagen might have laughed had she heard of Bliss's misfortune, though she is certainly not laughing today. Despite Daphne's repeated attempts to keep up the younger woman's morale, Trina is sapped by the constant anxiety over her husband and children, and by mid-morning she is close to crashing. "It's Thursday," she sobs. "I only made them food for three days, and I left the bananas in the back of the car."

"Oh, I'm sure they'll manage," says Daphne absently as her mind spins with implausible plans to break out of the room.

"Never, never, never, give h'up," the survival expert had repeatedly insisted. "There is no such thing as a totally h'escape-proof prison, h'and there never will be."

So what about this place? Daphne questions herself, then sets out to explore every conceivable escape route her mind can conjure.

"First: try to catch 'em h'off guard," the animated bantamweight officer had said as he'd pranced around, punching at an imaginary foe, but Daphne shakes her head at the prospect of taking on Spotty Dick and Bumface. And she similarly dismisses equally impractical notions involving tunnels, explosives and rooftop rescues. The idea of emulating a team of British officers, who had surreptitiously built a full-size glider in the attic of Colditz Castle during the Second

World War, holds her attention far longer than it warrants, and she is finally left with little beyond stealing a monk's habit and impersonating one of the guards. However, Spotty Dick and Bumface have given up their masquerade and now appear in T-shirts and jeans.

"They'll be pigging out at McDonald's on burgers and shakes," carries on Trina pessimistically, while Daphne is deliberating whether or not it will be possible to climb the razor-wire fence, or whether they should try to hack their way through it with her penknife.

"They're never gonna let us go, are they?" whines Trina, and Daphne finally decides that a serious talk is called for.

"Oh, for Christ's sake," says Spotty Dick, starting to rise as the two women scuttle back into the bathroom, but Bumface waves him back down.

"Hey, forget it. They might as well have one last fling if they want," he says and catches a critical look from his partner.

Daphne has picked up on the danger signals as well. "I don't like the way that Bumface is behaving," she admits with a worried frown. "He's lost his bolshiness. As if he doesn't care what we do anymore."

"What does that mean?" asks Trina in a whisper.

"It means he thinks he knows what's going to happen to us," replies Daphne as she recalls the captivity survival officer's warning to "watch h'out for any cold-hearted bastard who suddenly goes soft on you. It usually means he's getting ready to drop a bomb."

"Maybe they're going to let us go," suggests Trina, brightening.

"Maybe ..." says Daphne, appearing to agree, before adding, "But we've got to stay strong — all right?"

"All right, Daphne."

"Mustn't let them think we're weakening, okay?"

"Okay, Daphne. But what are we going to do if they don't let us out?"

"Come on, ladies," calls Bumface from the bedroom. "We've brought you some nice lunch."

"Thanks," mumbles Trina, and they emerge from the bathroom to find Bumface wearing something akin to a smile as he puts a laden tray on the table.

"There we are, ladies," he says as if he's prepared the meal himself, but Daphne has her eye on Spotty Dick, who is skulking nervously in the background, and she waits for a nod of approval that doesn't come.

"It's all my fault, Daphne. I'm always doing stupid things," says Trina as the two men leave, but Daphne is hardly listening and replies vaguely, "Trying to help Norman and the others wasn't stupid."

"Then why are we here?"

"Because —"

"I'm never going to see my kids again, am I?" keens Trina, unaware of the hiatus as Daphne struggles to get her thoughts together. "H'always watch for a change," the officer is saying in her mind. "H'especially if the greasy little bastards start treating you really nice."

"Listen," says Daphne, sidling up to Trina and stroking the heartbroken woman's hair reassuringly. "You mustn't give up. You've got so much to look forward to. But I've already lived my life — every day is a bonus. It's like being given extra time at the end of a hockey match with the chance to score the deciding goal."

"You can't. Not stuck in here," howls Trina.

"You're wrong, Trina. Maybe I've got the chance to score the most important goal ever."

"How?"

"By getting you safely back home to your family."

"And how are you going to do that? They're not going to let us go now. You know that."

"You've just got to follow the White Rabbit."

"What?"

"Trina. Surely you remember *Alice in Wonderland*?"

"Of course," she snivels.

"Well, then, all you have to do is drink the shrinking liquid to make yourself smaller and smaller until you can fit through the keyhole, and then you follow the White Rabbit to the Mad Hatter's Tea Party."

"That's stupid," she cries again. "There *is* no keyhole."

"Oh, yes, there is," says Daphne. "There's always a keyhole. It's just that you can't see it at the moment."

But Trina is unmoved and continues weeping, "I'm never going to see my kids again."

"Sure, you are," tries Daphne, though her tone lacks conviction and Trina buries her face in her pillow, crying the universal cry of the unjustly imprisoned. "But we didn't do anything wrong."

"*We* didn't," muses Daphne as she stares through the lens of the surveillance camera, seeking the faces behind it. "But someone obviously has."

"Trina," says Daphne quietly as she gently strokes the woman's hair, "don't eat or drink anything, all right?"

"Why?"

"I'm not sure," she replies, taking a close look at the meal, "but I smell something fishy."

"No problem. I don't feel like eating anyway."

"Good. So promise me."

"I promise," says Trina, her eyes drying a tad at the seriousness of Daphne's tone. "But what are you going to do?"

"I think it's time one of us got out," murmurs Daphne, and Trina screws up her face in confusion. "Leave it to me," whispers Daphne, then she heads for the bathroom, adding loudly, "I think it's time I had a long, hot soak."

"What the hell is the old bat on about now?" asks Bumface as he listens in.

"God knows," says Spotty Dick, having tuned the two women out while pondering his partner's sudden softening.

The road signs clearly indicate that Seattle is ahead of them, taking some of the pressure off Daisy and Bliss, if only temporarily, as they sample the comforts of nobility in the back of the governor's car.

"I zhink it is nice to have a limousine wiz a chauffeur," says Daisy as they snuggle together in the privacy of their tinted compartment while they watch passing motorists and pedestrians peering in for a glimpse.

"Maybe when I'm a famous author we'll have a chauffeur all the time."

"*Daavid,*" she cautions, "you promised my mother you would not write zhe book."

"Maybe if I hired a chauffeur for her as well — *peut-être?*" mollifies Bliss.

"*Oui* — perhaps," agrees Daisy, and Bliss demonstrates the advantages of the arrangement by kissing her warmly before picking up the phone to call Phillips in Vancouver.

"You were absolutely right about the kidney contraption, Dave," says the Canadian officer, "and it must have been brought over in a fish truck. There's a ton of salmon scales stuck in the tires."

"So it couldn't have been pedalled there."

"Correct. It's about twenty miles from the nearest salmon river."

"It's a long shot, Mike, but check with Canadian customs and see if they have any records of a large white van with Washington plates crossing the border in the early hours."

If Daphne has figured out an escape strategy by the time she returns from the steamy bathroom, her face gives nothing away as Bumface slides in to collect the lunch tray.

"You haven't eaten anything," he complains, spotting the untouched food.

"I'm not hungry," keens Trina as she sniffs back the tears.

"But you gotta eat, or you'll get sick."

"Breakfast was more than enough for me," chimes in Daphne heartily.

"All right," says Bumface, turning to Trina and cracking into a crooked smile. "Here's a deal: if you stop crying and eat your lunch, maybe you can go home tonight."

"Wonderful," shrieks Daphne delightedly, and she rushes across the room to hug Trina tightly, saying, "Come on. Chin up, Cinderella. We're going to the ball."

"Why did you tell them that?" demands Spotty Dick once the door has closed.

"I dunno," shrugs Bumface. "Cheer 'em up, I suppose."

"And what happens tomorrow morning when they wake up and they're still here?"

"*If* they wake up."

"What d'ya mean?"

"Look. They can't stay here and they can't go home. So work it out for yourself — okay?"

But Daphne has already worked it out. She's known the answer for more than sixty years — from the day of the escape officer's lecture.

"Never, h'ever, believe 'em h'if they says that they is going to let you go 'ome," the bubbly little man said, and then he had put a frown on his face and slowly shaken his head from side to side. "Believe me, the only 'ome that they 'ave in mind for you is with the 'eavenly father h'up above. If you get my drift."

"There just has to be a way out," muses Daphne, scrutinizing the sparsely furnished bedroom, the handle-less door and the surveillance camera.

"But he said he was going to let us go," Trina reminds her.

"I just hope that's what he meant," says Daphne, hiding her pessimism behind a smile, then adding gently, "but it never hurts to have a backup plan, Trina."

One plan that *has* worked is that of Washington's governor, and as three o'clock rolls around Bliss steps on stage at the conference to be welcomed by the American delegate of Interpol.

"Ladies and gentlemen," announces the Los Angeles officer, "it's my privilege to present from Scotland Yard — and I hope he'll excuse me for saying this — one of the world's most celebrated detectives since Sherlock Holmes: Chief Inspector David Bliss."

Bliss takes to the podium, and as the applause dies in Seattle, Daphne Lovelace is headed back to the bathroom with the germ of an idea.

"But you just had a bath," says Trina confusedly.

"I know," replies Daphne. "And I feel so much better. Maybe you should do the same."

"I don't —" starts Trina glumly, but Daphne cuts her

off, grabs a hand and hauls her out of bed. "Mary, Mary, quite contrary," she scolds as she pulls the younger woman to her feet. "Come along. It'll do you good."

But Trina's bath is short-lived, and a few minutes later, as they emerge together from the bathroom, she slips into bed and buries herself under Daphne's enormous hat. Daphne, on the other hand, muses, "I think it's time for a good clear-out," and begins a major housekeeping effort, muttering, "We can't leave the place in this state. What would the next people think?"

Fifteen minutes later she is still bustling around, sweeping, mopping and dusting, when Dawson enters the surveillance room and gives Bumface a quizzical look.

"What the hell is going on now?" he wants to know as the screen momentarily falls under the dark shadow of Daphne's mattress.

"She's trying to turn the mattress," laughs Bumface as Daphne lurches clumsily around the room with the springy beast, before it momentarily wavers in the air, apparently out of control, and collapses back onto her bed in the same state as it began. Then he shakes his head incredulously. "She reckons mattresses have to be turned every two days to get rid of bedbugs and evil spirits."

"Hah," snorts Dawson derisively, though when the picture clears he frowns at the untouched food on the table.

"They'll get hungry eventually," shrugs Bumface as he checks the clock.

It's four-thirty by the time Bliss wraps up with a warning to the conference: "If Western governments continue shoring up their flagging economies by subsidizing, and encouraging, rampant consumerism, then they risk being swamped by an unstoppable tide of the very refugees that their policies have created."

"You were wonderful," says Daisy as Bliss comes off stage and finds a crush of reporters waiting for him.

"Really?" he says. "To be honest, I don't remember a lot of what I said. I'd left my notes in the cabin."

"Hard-hitting words, Chief Inspector," says a reporter with a microphone in Bliss's face. "So you're actually suggesting that police crackdowns on trafficking merely provide greater incentives and increased incomes for the criminals and organizations that provide the service."

"Well, it's a strategy that's worked extremely effectively with alcohol, prostitution, gambling and drugs over the years," agrees Bliss. "Where would the Mafia and the Colombian drug cartels be without the demand for illegal products and services?"

"So you're advocating that we just open the borders?" asks another incredulously.

"I'm suggesting that you might take a different view if you lived in a tin hut and tried to survive on a dollar a day, while the guy in the country next door spends ten times that amount feeding his pet poodle. But what I'm really advocating is —"

"There's a phone call for you, sir," butts in Lieutenant Jewison as he tries to lead Bliss into a side office.

"I just wanted to mention the missing women ..." starts Bliss, but Jewison keeps up the pressure.

"He said it was urgent, sir."

"I bet it's Edwards," murmurs Bliss, guessing that it won't be long before the chief superintendent disembowels him for playing politics. But it's Mike Phillips with news of several vehicles fitting Bliss's description of the van he'd followed to the monastery. "And this is interesting, Dave," carries on Phillips. "One of them belongs to a fish dealer. Apparently he goes back and forth a lot. I've asked Washington police for a make on the licence plate."

"Fifty bucks says he delivers salmon to a certain monastery place."

"That's a stretch, Dave."

"We'll see."

"So what are your plans now?"

Bliss's plans are not for the ears of Lieutenant Jewison, or anyone else in the American administration, so he answers only that he and Daisy will collect their belongings from the cabin and then head back to Vancouver once they've picked up Trina's car from Bellingham.

"That reminds me," he says to Daisy as Jewison escorts them back to the limousine. "I'd better give Rick a call."

By early evening, when Bliss gets through to him from the limousine's phone, Rick Button is sinking rapidly. With no sleep since Tuesday morning, and no food since Tuesday night, Trina's husband is fighting to stay afloat on coffee and a fast-deflating bubble of hope.

"I've been on the Internet," he tells Bliss. "Do you know that the odds of finding someone alive are less than ten percent after the first twenty-four hours? Did you know that?"

"No," admits Bliss, "although I do know that Daphne has beaten those odds before." But Bliss catches the flatness of defeat in Rick Button's tone, and knows that the other man has made up his mind when he responds, "It'll soon be getting dark again, Dave."

By the time that the sun finally hits the western horizon, Captain Prudenski is back on duty in Bellingham, and he has a compassionate hand for Bliss when Jewison delivers the English officer to collect Trina's car. "I'm sure they'll show up sooner or later," says Prudenski, though Bliss knows that "later" only means one thing.

"Let's hope so."

"So. What are your intentions now?" asks Lieutenant Jewison, pointedly checking the office clock.

"I think we'll find somewhere in the city for a spot of dinner before heading back," says Bliss, fearful that someone has already planned an escort all the way to the Canadian border.

"No problem, sir," says Jewison with a farewell salute. "My mission is accomplished anyway."

But dinner is the last thing on Bliss's mind, and no sooner have they left the city centre than he U-turns and takes a fast spin down a deserted lane, with Daisy riding shotgun.

"Zhey are not following," says Daisy after a few minutes, and Bliss quickly heads for a now-familiar road out of town.

"It's about twenty miles," Bliss is telling Daisy, as Bumface finally gives up hope of the two women eating lunch and returns with Spotty Dick to collect the tray.

"Oh, look: here's the White Rabbit at last," mutters Daphne as Spotty Dick enters, then she turns with a scowl for Bumface, saying, "Which means you must be the Queen of Hearts," before laughing, "Off with his head. Off with his head."

"You haven't eaten your lunch," says Bumface with a little less bonhomie than he'd shown earlier.

"I was hoping for jam tarts," continues Daphne, keeping up her banter, but Bumface is ignoring her as he gives Trina's bed a curious look.

"What's up with her?" he demands, advancing on the bed with growing inquisitiveness. Then he snatches the giant hat off the bed and finds only a pillow and a rolled bundle of bedding underneath the sheet.

"Where's Mrs. Button?"

"You must mean Little Bo Peep," says Daphne gaily. "She slipped out earlier to look for her sheep."

"What're you talking about?"

"Oh, I'm sure they'll be back in a few minutes, dragging their tails ..." Daphne continues prattling as she makes a play of looking out of the door, and Bumface roughly pushes her aside to stick his head into the bathroom.

"Mrs. Button ..."

"I told you —" starts Daphne, but Bumface rounds on her, grabs her by the throat and stretches her onto her toes.

"Where is she?"

"Gone for a walk."

"John!" Bumface bellows at the camera. "Lock everything down." Then he returns to Daphne and ratchets up the pressure as Spotty Dick skulks in the background.

"I said, Where is she?"

"You're choking me."

"I know. Now, where is she?"

"What's up, Steve?" yells Dawson, crashing into the room.

"The Button woman's gone."

"How the —?"

"Someone must've left the f'kin door unlocked," he says, glowering at Spotty Dick.

"So, where is she?" Bumface tries again as he squeezes harder, but Daphne closes her eyes and lets herself go limp, forcing him to drop her to the floor.

"Christ! You've killed her!" says Spotty Dick, angrily stepping forward.

But Daphne is back in the wartime classroom, listening to the lecture on torture — psychological or physical. "The h'only truth what the h'enemy wants to hear is what suits them. It's like the old ducking chair for witches. You're only h'innocent if you drown."

"Wake up, you old bat!" screeches Bumface as he empties the cold contents of the teapot over Daphne, but Dawson drags him away.

"Leave her," spits Dawson. "The other one can't have gone far." Then he turns on Spotty Dick. "Tie her up and make sure you lock the door properly this time."

"I didn't leave it open ..." he starts to complain, but as the other two men race off in search of Trina, he quickly bends to the semiconscious woman and harshly whispers, "Can you hear me?"

"Yes," she mutters.

"You've got to escape. Do you understand?"

"Yes."

"I mean it ... You must get out *now*."

"I know. But how?"

chapter eleven

S torm clouds, ahead of a depression sweeping in from the Pacific, are forming over the mountains of northern Washington as Bliss races back towards the monastery, and the overburden of spruce and cedar further deepens the shadows along the twisty roads of the foothills.

"I've got nearly four hours before my visa expires," Bliss explains to Daisy, in the twilight, "and I'm damned if I'm leaving without them."

"But what are you going to do, *Daavid*?"

"Well, I've tried asking politely, and I've tried force. So now ..." he pauses, before confessing, "I've absolutely no idea. Maybe I'll look for a hole in the fence. Maybe the gates will be open."

But the gates aren't open. In fact, the gates haven't been opened for over an hour, which gives Dawson some comfort when he runs to the gatehouse and checks with the flak-jacketed security guards.

"No one is to get in or out!" he shouts to the two armed men, before looking to Bumface, asking breathlessly,

"How long has she been gone, Steve?"

"I dunno. I'd have to check the surveillance tapes," says Bumface, turning back towards the building. "But I haven't actually seen her move since lunchtime."

"Christ — that's six hours," says Dawson as he scans the fringes of the rapidly darkening forest. "If she's in there we'd never find her."

"Yeah. But she'd never get over the wire."

"Check that the fence power is on when you get back," says Dawson as he frantically searches the gloom for movement. "And give me some more lights — I can't see a damn thing."

"Okay, John."

"And tell Allan to get a move on. We need him searching out here right now."

But Allan Wallace, alias Spotty Dick, isn't planning on hunting far for Trina. In fact, as he stands frozen in the open doorway of the women's room with a length of rope in his hand, he too is seeking an escape route.

"What's going on?" queries Bumface, running up to his stupefied colleague.

"The old lady's gone as well," utters Spotty Dick, with all the surprise he can muster.

"What?!" shouts Bumface.

"I dunno how it happened," says Spotty Dick. "She was out cold, and I just went to get the rope like John said —"

"And you left the f'kin' door open again," yells Bumface, snatching the rope.

"Don't worry. They can't get far," says Spotty Dick.

"They f'kin' better not," warns Bumface as he heads to the surveillance room, calling over his shoulder, "You'd better go and tell John what's happened."

"I'll drop you at a bar a few miles from the place," Bliss tells Daisy as he drives the tortuous road on automatic pilot, while he grapples with his conscience over his failure to take on the American authorities. *You should have stood up at that conference and given them shit*, he thinks, and he takes out his frustration on the road as he slams the car round a bend at double the posted speed. But he slackens off, knowing that someone would have stood up, saying, "Surely all the evidence points to the women returning to Canada, Chief Inspector."

"No, *Daavid*. I will stay wiz you," replies Daisy, as he uses the hand brake to rally the car through a hairpin, but Bliss doesn't hear as he asks himself, *And wouldn't you have taken the same tack in a similar situation on your patch?*

No.

Are you sure?

Yes — all right, he admits as he fishtails his way out of a greasy mud slick, although it still doesn't explain why they're more concerned about upsetting a bunch of armed religious fanatics than the disappearance of a couple of women.

But you weren't at Waco, were you?

"Are you all right, *Daavid*?" asks Daisy as he misjudges a corner and scythes a path through a patch of bracken before regaining the road.

"This is like a really bad movie," he says without answering her question. "I should have put my foot down. I should've called a press conference, caused a scene — accused them of a cover-up. I should have done something."

"But zhey would have arrested you and sent you home."

"Why, Daisy? What are they afraid of? And who are 'they'? That's what I want to know."

John Dawson is also searching for answers as he scours the grounds for Trina, but he finds only deep shadows, and the occasional shuffling patient, until his worried-faced operative reappears.

"Where's Allan?" demands Dawson.

"He left the door open," squeals Bumface. "The other one's got out now."

"Shit! What's he doing?"

"I sent him out here to help you."

"Well, where the effin' hell is he?"

"What I'd like to know is why everyone is so damned determined to kick me out of the country," continues Bliss as he slips the near-side wheels onto the verge to avoid a suicidal rabbit, then spots the isolated woodsmen's bar and slides to a halt amid a hail of gravel.

"You'd better wait in here," he says, quickly climbing out.

"But why?" asks Daisy.

Because fresh memories of machine gun shells ripping into the trunk of his car leave Bliss wondering how far the inmates of the monastery are prepared to go, though he doesn't say so.

"If I'm not back in an hour, call the police," he carries on as he runs around to open her door.

But she sits back resolutely. "Why you say you not come back?"

Good question, he thinks, wondering if the mention of gun-toting guards will pry her out of the car or stick her to the seat.

"Because of the ..." he starts, with the words "machine guns" itching to get out, but then he backtracks, telling himself that it was nothing more than a warning shot across his stern. "Because it might be a little dangerous and I want you to stay here," he says lamely, causing her to firmly plant her backside on the seat. "In zhat case, I come wiz you."

"Women," he mutters in exasperation. "If it's not Daphne, it's you."

"But *Daavid*," says Daisy as she lightly strokes his cheek, "I come all zhis way and we have just one night together. Now you say you will never come back."

"Well, that makes me feel more a lot more confident, I must say."

"Zhat is good, no?"

"No — *Yes* ... I don't know," he fumes as he slumps back into the driver's seat. "I don't know anything anymore."

"Oh, *Daavid*," Daisy purrs reassuringly. "Maybe if you want to write zhe book about *l'homme au masque de fer*, you should let me come with you."

"That's blackmail."

"*Oui* — as we say, it is *la chantage*."

"Well you could at least deny it ..." he starts, but he gives in with an alternative idea. "Oh, never mind," he says, then dashes into the bar.

"Hey, man, you still owe for a coffee," calls the barman lightheartedly, but Bliss puts on a no-nonsense face. "Enough crap," he says, sticking his police I.D. under the man's nose. "Now, what the hell's going on up at the monastery?"

The bartender's eyes zip nervously around the room and catch some warning glances. "It ain't sensible asking questions like that around here," he says to Bliss, and he reaches to clear a dirty beer glass off the bar.

"Well, I'm asking," says Bliss, grabbing the glass and holding it hostage.

"Hey, man," he says with a shrug, "this is a small community — the trees have ears."

"Then you must know something about the people there?"

"Sorry, man," he says unapologetically. "We don't have no contact with them. None of them ever come in here — but they wouldn't, would they?"

"And no one is curious?"

The barman checks the faces of a dozen tired old loggers before shrugging again. "Don't look like it, do it?"

"But you must know *something* about them."

"Hey, they don't bother us."

"Can I make a call?" asks Bliss, though he doesn't wait for a response before lifting the receiver of the bar phone and dialling Mike Phillips's number. "What's the name of this joint?" he asks the barman while holding for the connection, and then he turns his back on the bar and cups his hands around the mouthpiece.

"Mike, I'm at a bar called Pete's Place," he says, then quickly explains his intention of returning to the monastery. "If I don't call you back in exactly one hour," he goes on to say, "then you better start some serious shit-stirring with the local force. Okay?"

"I don't know ..." begins Phillips worriedly, but Bliss's mind is firm.

"One hour, Mike," he says, and then he pulls the barman towards him with a crooked finger and hands him the phone, saying, "Give this police officer the address and directions to this place. And if I'm not back in an hour, expect an international invasion."

In the quickly fading dusk of the forest, Dawson and Bumface are running from the gatehouse towards the main building with growing desperation.

"I'll tell the staff to get all the others inside," yells Bumface as they reach the main doors. "We'll have to let the Rottweilers loose."

"Wait a minute," says Dawson, hanging back with concern. "What about Allan? He's gotta be out there as well."

"Okay, so what else do you suggest?" demands Bumface. "He's gonna get it one way or another. At least it'll be quick."

However, Allan Wallace has no plans to be caught in the open by the dogs, or any other way. He has slipped a spare key for Buzzer's van from the cabinet in the surveillance room and is headed for the gates at full tilt.

"Where's Buzzer going?" enquires Bumface as he spots the white van speeding along the driveway towards the gates.

"He can't get out," says Dawson confidently. "I told the guards to lock everything down."

But Wallace has another view and he roars up to the gatehouse, yelling, "Quick! Open the gates! I'll get them."

"I thought Mr. Dawson said I wasn't to open the gate for anyone," equivocates the guard.

"He didn't mean *me*, did he?" yells Wallace.

"I don't —"

"Quickly, man. Open the damn gates."

"I ought'a check ..." says the guard, still vacillating, but Wallace keeps up the pressure.

"Look. It'll be your fault if they get away."

Bliss's mind is tumbling with implausible machinations as he screeches around the familiar bends before the monastery's gateway, though with Daisy alongside him he has no intention of trying to ram his way in again.

"I think I've got a plan," he says, with less than a mile to go, though it's not a plan, merely a sketchy outline, and he warns her not to leave the vehicle under any circumstances.

"If anything happens to me, don't try to help. Don't stop for anything. Just drive back to the bar and scream for help."

"*Oui.*"

"Here's Mike's number," he adds, handing her his notebook. "And make sure they call the police in Bellingham."

"*Daavid.* Zhis is dangerous, no?"

"No," says Bliss, though he is still wondering if that means "yes" when the opening gates come into view. "Hold tight!" he yells, slams on the brakes and feels the adrenaline rush as he readies to run the final few yards.

Spotty Dick is someone else with pulsing veins, and he sits at the wheel of the van watching the gates slowly open as his foot taps the pedal.

"Hurry up. Hurry up," he breathes and is within inches of hitting the throttle when Dawson and Bumface run to the gateman breathlessly shouting, "Shut the fucking gate. Shut the fucking gate!"

"But Mr. Wallace said —"

"I don't give a shit ..." starts Dawson. "I told you ..." and then he spots the shadow of Bliss standing in the gap between the gates and he pales. Pulling himself together, and dropping his tone, Dawson cautiously advances, asking, "Can I help you, sir?"

"I was intrigued by your ecclesiastical pontification," starts Bliss conversationally as he walks forward into the light. "Was that Episcopalian or Catholic, Mr. — um, or should I address you as 'Father' or 'Brother' or —"

"Who are you? What do you want?" enquires Dawson with growing suspicion, while behind him Spotty Dick is being forced by Bumface to back the van off.

"That's what I like: a man who cuts to the chase," carries on Bliss in Oxbridge tones while extending a hand, but he finds his advance blocked by a wall of flesh as one of the gate guards joins Dawson, so he turns with a broad sweep of his hand to indicate that he too has backup. "My wife and I are members of the Church of England ourselves," he says, pointing to the indistinct figure of Daisy in the driver's seat of Trina's car.

"Sorry," says Dawson, using the weight of his presence in an effort to intimidate Bliss back out of the gates, "we're not open to the public."

"Oh, I quite understand," says Bliss, appearing conciliatory, though there is no retreat as he adds an edge to his voice. "But I believe two of my friends are here. Mrs. Button and Miss Lovelace —"

"I've never heard of them," cuts in Dawson, sharply. "Now, if you'll excuse us ..."

"What is your name, sir?" enquires Bliss, digging in his heels.

"We have no use for names here," says Dawson, advancing to within an inch. "Now, you've caused enough trouble here already, so get out before I —"

"Before you what?" challenges Bliss.

"Before I call the police and have you thrown out of the country again."

"Go ahead," says Bliss with his feet firmly planted just inside the gates.

The ten minutes that it takes Captain Prudenski and his officers to arrive drag one second at a time for Bliss, as he stands eye to eye with Dawson between the partially opened gates, and his natural craving to strangle the truth out of the man before him is only assuaged by the attendance of the armed guard. While, were it not for the presence of Daisy, Dawson's ferocious stare suggests that he would happily strong-arm the Englishman out onto the road. However, Bliss's impassive expression and rigid stance make it very clear that has no intention of going anywhere without the Misses Lovelace and Button.

Unfortunately, Prudenski takes a different view. "I'll have no choice but to arrest you and hand you over to immigration for deportation," says Prudenski on hearing Dawson's contention that Bliss is trespassing. Then he adds, "Please don't force me to do that."

"It's very tempting," says Bliss, wondering whether he can squeeze some press coverage out of the incident.

"You'll never be able to return to the States if that happens," warns Prudenski.

"But you've got to do something. The women are in there."

"Sir, if you have the evidence — and I'm talking *real* evidence here — then I'll be more than happy to apply for a search warrant."

Bliss knows he's sunk, but his feet are still firmly planted. "I'm warning you, Captain," he says with his teeth clenched, "if you don't take some action I will make sure that you are held accountable for aiding and abetting the abduction of the two women. Do I make myself understood?"

"Absolutely, sir. So, to put your mind at ease, and as a real special favour to you as a visiting officer all the way from the Old Country, I'm gonna do one more thing." Then he turns to Dawson with a serious mien. "Let me ask you real clear, sir. Do you have any idea of the whereabouts of the two ladies in question?"

"No, sir."

"None whatsoever?"

"That's correct, sir. They are not here."

"There you are, Chief Inspector," says Prudenski, turning back to Bliss. "You heard what the man said. Now, I wouldn't want you getting into trouble with the immigration people cuz they can be mighty mean. So I'll be happy to escort you to the border."

"This is preposterous," yells Bliss directly into Dawson's face.

"Sir ... Just one more time," asks Prudenski. "Do you have any evidence —"

"All right. All right," cuts in Bliss. "You've made your point." And giving Dawson a final poisonous glower, he walks back to Trina's car with his head down.

As the gates to the monastery quickly close behind Bliss, Dawson rounds on Bumface, spitting, "What the fuck's going on?"

"We've got a problem, John."

"I know that, you damn fool."

"No. I mean a real big problem," he carries on, and then he leads his supervisor to Buzzer's van, where Spotty Dick is frozen to the driver's seat on the end of a guard's pistol, while behind him, in a compartment partially concealed beneath a pile of salmon, lay Daphne and Trina.

"Allan, Allan, Allan," says Dawson, shaking his head in despair. "What the fuck am I gonna do with you?"

"Okay, ladies. Get out, and no talking," says Bumface, opening the rear doors and dragging salmon carcasses aside.

"Take 'em back and put 'em in separate rooms," says Dawson. "I'll deal with this mess here."

"Sometimes I think I'm going insane," muses Bliss as he drives away from the monastery with Prudenski on his tail. "Two weeks ago we were at Samantha's wedding, and then Minnie chucks herself in front of a train and look what happens. How can I just go back and face her friends? 'Where's Daphne?' they'll ask. What am I supposed to say? 'I lost her.' I mean, she's hardly a piece of luggage that Air Canada misplaced on the way over; she is not going to turn up in Honolulu or Buenos Aires. This just doesn't happen. Ordinary people don't just disappear."

"Never, *Daavid?*" queries Daisy.

"Not without good reason — the odd bored housewife who runs off with the postman or someone nabbed with their hands in the till — that sort of thing."

"Nabbed?" questions Daisy, but Bliss's mind is stuck on the conundrum of Daphne's disappearance.

"It's the fact that someone obviously wanted their mobile-thing to be found in Canada that makes me so certain they've been abducted."

"Abducted?" inquires Daisy, losing further ground in Bliss's ravings.

"Daphne had absolutely no reason to disappear. This is a nightmare," he rambles. "The depressing thing is that she was actually making final arrangements. Maybe she had a premonition."

"*Oui.* I understand zhat," says Daisy, briefly catching up. "It is zhe same word — *prémonition.*"

"But what about Trina?" continues Bliss, ignoring Daisy in his deliberations. "All the silly woman was thinking about was next year's trip." Then he pauses with a thought. "What if they've gone to New York?" he finds himself saying, before a pothole in the road jogs his brain and he shakes his head in disbelief. "Why am I even considering this? They were in that monastery place — which, by the way, is obviously not any kind of ecclesiastical establishment. And, even if it is, how the hell did they know that I'd been kicked out of their stupid damn country before?"

It's only ten p.m. when they reach the border, and Bliss is tempted to insist on staying until midnight just to be awkward, but realizes it will get him nowhere. Instead, he turns on Prudenski with a threatening finger. "If it transpires that those women are there, I'll make sure you get busted so far you'll have carpet burns on the underside of your chin."

"I'm sure that we all appreciate the advice, Chief Inspector," says Prudenski with a sickly smile as Bliss starts to drive away. "Now, you just mind those Canadian bears. They can give you a mighty powerful hug."

"Get stuffed," murmurs Bliss.

"And you have yourself a good night, too," calls Prudenski in his wake.

Mike Phillips is waiting for Bliss on the Canadian side, and his face is clouded in mock annoyance. "Hey! You didn't call," he says as Bliss drives up.

"Oh my God!" exclaims Bliss. "I'm so sorry, Mike. I forgot."

"No worries," says the Canadian officer, softening. "I phoned Bellingham police and they told me their captain had everything in hand."

"Oh, yes. He had everything in hand all right."

"Anyway, nice to have you back in one piece. I guess they didn't bring out the artillery this time."

"No, but they didn't bring out Trina and Daphne, either."

"I dunno what to suggest."

"Tell me where the hell we go from here," sighs Bliss in frustration.

"You need to go to bed," says Phillips. "You look as though you haven't slept in days. And what's that smell?"

"Bananas," grunts Bliss, then his voice cracks in annoyance as he looks back over the border. "They *are* there, Mike. I don't care what the Yanks say. They are in that monastery place."

"Well, you silly old fool," Daphne Lovelace says to herself as she scans the bare, windowless room from her new bed, "see if you can do a better job of getting out of this one."

But she is on her own now. Her co-escapee has been confiscated, together with her polka-dot hat, her penknife and the rest of her Girl Guides survival kit.

"And stay out of the bathroom this time," Bumface admonished as he shut the door, making it quite clear that the ruse to conceal Trina in the ductwork beside the shower unit would not work a second time. However, without her penknife and nail file to turn the screws, and without Trina's slender body to hide, there is no chance of Daphne repeating the exercise.

Thinking of Trina, Daphne puts her ear to the wall in the hope of hearing the younger woman, but there is nothing beyond the distant hum of exhaust fans and machinery.

"Some hospital this is," she muses as she contemplates the surveillance cameras and the lack of door handles, and she finds herself questioning the need for such security. A sanatorium for the mentally impaired, perhaps; yet the scattering of patients she'd seen when Bumface had escorted her and Trina from the gatehouse to the group of modern buildings had clearly undergone surgery — one in a wheelchair being pushed by a pretty young nurse wearing whites.

The patients had looked ordinary enough, although most appeared to be Chinese or Korean. But they had all averted their gaze and scuttled away at the approach of Bumface and the two women.

"Why won't they look at us?" Daphne had mused aloud, and had caught a vicious rebuke from Dawson.

"Shuddup, you old bat," he'd spat, before shooing the patients off as if they were prowling dogs.

"H'if you h'escape — don't get caught. And h'if you get caught — watch h'out. 'Cos things is going to get a lot worse," the little survival expert warned, and Daphne reruns those words as she stares at the blank walls and glumly assesses her prospects.

Allan Wallace is someone else facing a gloomy future. The bruises around his eyes are already blackening. And he would like to undo the lashings that bind him to the chair so that he could at least stem the blood pouring from his nose, but his right wrist is so badly smashed that his fingers droop uselessly. In any case, he has company.

"I'm sure you realize that your actions have jeopardized the entire operation," says a white-faced Dawson.

"What are you going to do?" snivels Wallace.

"Nothing," says Dawson after a thoughtful pause. "And you'd better pray that English cop doesn't do anything either. Then — maybe in a week or so, when things have quietened down — we can get back to normal and forget all about this unfortunate little incident."

"But what about the women?"

"Not your worry now, Allan. They'll be taken care of."

"Okay, John," he says in apparent resignation.

But there are two sides to John Dawson and, faced with the prospect of having to flay himself in front of his seniors, he chooses the darker of the two.

"Give it a couple of days 'til the heat's off," he tells Bumface once he's back in the surveillance room. "In the meantime, they are not here, and they never were here. Okay?"

"And what about Allan?"

"Shame. Nice guy — fancy him being crushed by a falling tree like that."

chapter twelve

"Now *this* is what we term a heavy mist in Vancouver," explains Sergeant Mike Phillips, showering rainwater out of his hair as he meets Bliss and Daisy for a pre-dawn breakfast at their hotel. "And this is for you," he adds, taking a soggy sheet of pink message-pad paper from a pocket of his drenched raincoat and handing it to Bliss as if it might explode.

"I guessed he'd track me down eventually," snorts Bliss once he has read the command to telephone Chief Superintendent Edwards — and it *is* a command.

"The operator reckoned your boss melted the transatlantic wires," continues Phillips while they take the elevator to the hotel's top-floor dining room from whence, according to the brochure, they will have unparalleled vistas of verdant islands swimming in a bright blue ocean, together with a grandstand view of pristine peaks as far away as the Washington Cascades.

"Oh, yes, he can be very pleasant at times," sneers Bliss when they emerge from the elevator to a drab scene of rain-cloaked windows.

"Wann'a use my cell phone?" offers Phillips, but the look on Bliss's face suggests he would rather stuff needles in his ears. "Oh, what the hell," he says finally, and tries unsuccessfully to peer through the miasma of darkness and rain as he taps in a number from memory.

"I hear you've been causing trouble for our American allies, now," complains Edwards as soon as they are connected.

"Really," says Bliss, giving up at the window and finding a seat next to Daisy. "And who would have told you that, sir?"

"Bliss. Stop pissing about and get back here while you still have a job to come back to."

"And what about the missing women?"

"Leave that to the Canadians."

"They are not in Canada," he seethes, and then he reaches forward for his coffee cup and lets out an anguished shriek.

"What is it, Chief Inspector?"

"I think I've just put my back out, sir," says Bliss with absolutely no attempt to hide the fact that he's lying.

"What?"

"I'm afraid I'm going to be off sick for quite awhile — oh!"

"What is zhe matter, *Daavid?*" asks Daisy, rising in concern as Bliss closes the phone and hands it back to Phillips.

"Nothing, Daisy, I'm fine," he laughs, waving her back down. "Although I do believe that Mr. Edwards has just smashed his telephone."

But Bliss's laughter is short-lived. "Come on, Mike. Some ideas, please. That place is no more a monastery than this is a brothel."

"I wish I knew," says Phillips, pouring himself a second coffee. "Rick Button is doing a nationwide appeal at ten this morning, though God knows how the poor guy's gonna manage. I can't picture what he's going through."

"I can. But it's the wrong nation he's appealing to," rages Bliss. "Why is no one listening to me? Have I become the invisible man?"

"I'm listening, Dave. But as long as the Americans maintain they're in Canada, what can we do?"

"Just 'cos they say it, doesn't make it so. Christ Almighty, they insisted the Iraqis had chemical weapons when anyone with half a brain knew they didn't."

"I've passed on all the information about the place through Interpol," continues Phillips as he adds milk and sugar, "and they're promising a full investigation."

"Or another whitewash," scoffs Bliss.

"Why?"

"Because there is obviously something very fishy going on there," says Bliss, and he makes another stab at peering through the darkness as if trying to see through the chimera surrounding the monastery and connect with Daphne. However, in the pre-dawn gloom he finds only the dreariness of another anxiety-filled day, where even the navigation lights of a trawler departing from the harbour under the nose of the waterside hotel are lost in the murk.

"I can't see a damn thing through this," admits Bliss, giving up, while beneath him at sea level, Vincent Kelly, the trawlerman, edges his boat forward with his eyes glued to the radar.

The muscular Kelly is still considered a greenhorn in the tradition of west coast trawling — a mere thirty-eight years of age, but unlike many of his peers who have given up their family's seafaring businesses in favour of more dependable work ashore, Kelly has apparently thrived. However, while he may have taken over the boat from his father, he did not inherit the ocean's abundance of salmon, cod and herring which had originally paid for it.

"You know, back in my day, son, I can remember when ..." bearded old men with whisky-veined noses and nicotined fingers often reminisce as they sit on Vancouver's fisherman's wharf watching their final years slip past. But if anyone ever did walk across the bay on the backs of salmon, capsize with the weight of his nets or sink under his catch, it was long before Vincent's time.

"Hah! Call them fish?" an oldtimer will grumble, surveying today's measly haul. "We wouldn't a' fed the cat with them in my time."

But today, somewhere off the southernmost tip of Vancouver Island, close to the entrance to Puget Sound, Vincent Kelly has a catch already lined up for him. So, despite the dense fog and the torrents of rain tattooing the ocean's surface that will keep most sailors in the bar, he'll allow satellites to guide him and radar to protect him as he steers a well-worn path.

However, the fish with Kelly's name on it is still a long way from being landed, and as soon as the trawler hits deep water, he kicks up the throttles and listens with satisfaction to the comforting sound of twin diesels burbling richly beneath his feet.

"Hey, Mick," he calls to the wiry deckhand who is making coffee in the cramped galley behind the wheelhouse. "Hurry up. I need you on lookout."

"Coming, Vince," says the hand.

"Don't forget your binoculars," continues Kelly as he jams his face to the windshield, searching worriedly for a glimpse of any of the semi-submerged logs that bedevil boaters off the forested shoreline of the Pacific northwest.

Thirty miles west, on the far edge of Kelly's radar's horizon, Captain Hwang of the South Asia Steamship Company has no such concerns as he stands on his bridge with his mind on Seattle's ritzy fish restaurants and dockside strip clubs. With nearly a hundred thousand tons of ship and cargo under his feet it would take an entire raft of floating logs to put a dent in his hull. However, before he can relax over a cold beer, a warm lobster and a hot hooker, he will have to navigate the narrow strait that separates Vancouver Island from the rugged coastline of northern Washington, then thread his way through a string of forested islands at the entrance to Puget Sound. He will also have to rendezvous with Vincent Kelly's little trawler without attracting the attention of the Coast Guard.

A third of the way around the globe, in London, it's already mid-afternoon, though it's not much brighter than Vancouver. "Thank God it's Friday," mumble millions of disheartened office and bank workers as they wish away the gloomy afternoon surfing the Internet for dreams in Barbados or Barcelona, while many others have already locked their desks and made a bolt for freedom.

Maurice Joliffe, a brittle eighty-two-year-old with little substance to show for his longevity, is also making a break for freedom, and he pedals his creaking bicycle along Kensington High Road, head down against the rain, with a loaded pistol in his pocket.

Joliffe and his steed are of similar age, both seeing their first daylight sometime between World War I and the Great Depression, and both suffer from arthritic joints and fatigued parts from which they are unlikely to recover without expensive surgery. The rusty springs of the pushbike's saddle squeak at every bump in the road, and the cracked leather seat bites into Joliffe's bony backside, but he willingly suffers the pain, telling himself that a new saddle now would be an unnecessary expense. It's not as though he's ever going to need the bicycle again after today, and he has already mentally pledged it to the Salvation Army.

Maurice Joliffe, "Jolly" to many who have known him as the man who empties ashtrays at the Lucky Seven Bingo Hall in Balham, stops obediently at a pedestrian light while a couple of zippier cyclists take it as an opportunity to get ahead of the traffic. But now is not the time to get hauled in by an inquisitive cop who might question the bulge in his mackintosh pocket, so Jolly takes the opportunity to re-evaluate his plan while he waits for a wet-footed bunch of office girls to struggle across the road in front of him.

It's the gun that concerns him most, and he continues to wonder whether there might not be a better way. But it's a question that's been torturing him for two days, and he already knows that no other weapon is as reliable or dependable for his purpose — no other weapon can be guaranteed to achieve his ultimate goal.

The handgun, an officer's service revolver dropped by a clumsy captain during a military exercise at the end of the Second World War, had become Joliffe's property in a barrack-room poker game, and he has polished and oiled it weekly ever since, though he has never once fired it. The heavy pistol, now with the initials MJ carved into its walnut stock, is the only souvenir of his two years' conscription as a national serviceman, and he has kept it squirreled away from his wife and kids for more than fifty years, somehow knowing that a day would come when his care would finally be repaid.

Today is that day, and as he pedals determinedly towards his objective with an entire tube of mentholated analgesic rubbed into his joints, his mind is finally at rest with his decision, and he can't help but feel that it was always destined to be this way.

"Just look at the rain," says Bliss gloomily, as torrents wash against the dining room's windows. "I just hope that they're not outside somewhere ..." Then he pauses in astonishment at his own words. "What am I saying? What am I saying?" he questions. "I'd love them to be outside."

"Well, we wouldn't be able to search much in this, even if we knew where to start looking," admits Phillips, although Daisy isn't letting anyone give up as she turns to Bliss. "But you must find zhem, *Daavid*. Poor Rick will have — how you say — a heart attack if he does not go to sleep soon."

"I wish I could put his mind at rest," admits Bliss, while Phillips continues to stare out of the window, musing, "I have this feeling that if I could focus my mind just a tiny bit more, I'd work out what happened."

Bliss has no such dilemma. "This is crazy," he says. "It's bloody obvious what happened. I bet they bumbled into that place late at night, and those trigger-happy jerks gunned them down thinking they were terrorists. Knowing those two, they were probably climbing the gates or trying to cut a hole in the fence."

"So, why not own up and just say it was the women's own fault?" asks Phillips.

"They can't. Not without giving away the nature of the place — whatever that might be."

"You could be right."

"Which explains the way they dumped the bathtub thing back in Canada, and why they were so keen to get shot of me."

"So. Where do we go from here? They obviously can't admit it now."

"Not unless someone turns up the heat in the press," agrees Bliss.

"Thank God there's nothing in the papers," says Bumface, as he and Dawson breakfast on large coffees in the surveillance room.

"I bet there is in Canada," moans Dawson sullenly. "And knowing our luck, somebody will see it."

"Deny, deny, deny," Bumface reminds him. "They wuz never here, remember?"

"Oh. Don't be so f'kin naïve," spits Dawson. "The guards saw them, half the friggin' patients saw them, and they're splattered all over the surveillance tapes."

"Maybe we should ... you know ... just get it over with right now," says Bumface, hanging himself with an imaginary noose.

"That's very clever, Steve. Then if someone really starts digging and we can't produce warm bodies, we can always say that they sprouted wings and did a Harry Potter over the fence."

"Just trying to be helpful, John."

"Well, you ain't," fumes Dawson. "This is your neck I'm trying to save here and don't forget it. You were the duty officer when that prick Wallace let 'em in."

"It's a bit late now, though, isn't it," cautions Bumface. "You're in it as deep as us."

Jolly Joliffe stops his bicycle a block short of his chosen destination to look at his watch. It's five minutes before four — five minutes to zero hour — time for final preparations. And without taking the revolver from his pocket, he clicks the chamber into place and checks that the safety catch is on, then reaches inside his jacket to ensure that the single page of his hand-printed will hasn't fallen from his wallet.

Hah! Won't they be surprised when they get the news? he says to himself with thoughts of his five children on his mind, then he waits until the minute hand of his watch shows three fifty-seven before pushing off the curb to continue painfully along his path.

It's two minutes to four by the time the old man's destination comes into view, and he's relieved to discover that everything looks as it should.

Ahead of him, at the top of a short hill, lies a solid Georgian building that has changed so little since its inception that only the illuminated sign over the doorway would have startled an eighteenth-century costermonger or his mule. "Barclay's Bank," proclaims the sign, although the words are illegible to Joliffe through his rain-fogged spectacles as he parks his bicycle against the curb.

Joliffe checks that the bank doors are still open before removing the trouser clips from his ankles and unhooking his backpack from the rear carrier. Then he gives his gun pocket a reassuring pat, straightens himself on the polished brass handrail and pulls himself up the short flight of stone steps.

"You only just made it," laughs the young assistant manager as he stands at the door with keys in his hand.

"Thanks, mate," mutters Joliffe, and he pauses momentarily to regain his breath before entering the old building.

The door closes with a solid "clunk" behind Joliffe, and the teak floor echoes with his footfalls as he makes his way towards the polished mahogany counter. Only two of the tellers' windows remain open, and the bevy of last-minute customers are punished for their tardiness by being forced to wait. But Joliffe is in no hurry, and he hovers for a few minutes at a rack of brochures promising lifelong financial stability to anyone who can afford it, while deciding which of the young clerks to approach.

Kim Kramer, a puppy-faced blonde with a dozen rings through her eyebrows, easily wins out over the uncompromising Janice Smith, who, with her thick-rimmed glasses and screwed-back hair, appears to have practised looking like a bank clerk from birth.

It is five after four. The last-minute customers have been as anxious to escape as the staff, and Joliffe is on his own as he shuffles towards Kim.

"Ah, my final customer of the week," she says with relief as she puts on a broad smile, though her nose turns up at the strong odour of mentholated rub commingled with the wet-dog stink of a sodden raincoat. "And what I can do for you today, sir?" she asks, quickly bringing back the smile.

Joliffe checks left and right, ensuring that the other clerks are busy cashing up and that the last of the customers have left. He wants no heroes, no interference, no one to wreck his moment, and he leans forward and places his sopping backpack on Kim's desk, calmly stating, "I want you to put ten thousand pounds in here please, Miss."

"What?" questions Kim as her smile morphs into a look of puzzlement. She knows the drill — knows she should nudge the panic button with her knee, knows that as soon as she pulls a wad of bills from a special compartment in her money drawer she will trigger an alarm. But she hesitates — surely this toothless geriatric is pulling her leg.

"Sorry?" she queries, still convinced that she has misheard the grandfatherly figure.

"I've got a gun," continues Joliffe, doing his very best to put on an "I-can-be-violent" face as he slowly pulls it from his pocket and draws her eyes to it. "But don't worry. I won't hurt you — not if you put ten thousand pounds in my bag."

Kim hits the alarm with a shaky knee, then opens her drawer and begins to count out the money. But she pauses, still questioning her senses, and looks up, desperately wanting to say, "Please don't be silly. Just leave and I won't tell anyone." But Joliffe's gun hand is shaking worse than her knee, and she's too terrified to speak.

"Hurry up. Hurry up," urges the old man as he nervously eyes the other tellers. But if anyone knows what's happening, they're not reacting. However, as Kim slowly fills the bag, in accordance with the bank's security policy a flurry of activity is taking place behind the scenes. The manager is on the phone to the police station, the safe is being locked, alarms are being rung at the bank's head office, and a supervisor is heading towards the front door to provide the assistant manager with backup.

"C'mon, luv. Get a move on," pleads Joliffe, guessing that his time is running out, and Kim speeds up a fraction.

"Sorry," she mutters, emptying her drawer and handing him the bag. But she hangs on as he starts to take it and steels herself to look into his tired grey eyes and question, "Are you really sure you want to do this?"

It's a question that Joliffe has asked himself time and again over the past few days, and as he takes the bag, he seeks to reassure her. "Don't worry. I'm going to bring it back, luv. I'm only borrowing it for a few days. And I'll pay the interest." Then he shoves the gun back in his pocket, pushes himself upright against the desk and hobbles towards the front door.

Despite the bank's policy of not interfering with armed robbers, the sight of a dishevelled renegade, apparently on the loose from a nursing home, shuffling his way out of the building with a bag of loot is so ludicrous that the two men at the door block Joliffe's path to freedom.

"Why don't you just put down the bag, sir?" suggests the supervisor gently, stepping forward as if to take it. Joliffe doesn't hesitate. He pulls the loaded pistol from his pocket and sticks it to his temple.

"Open the door or I'll kill myself."

"Don't be silly, sir," says the supervisor, uneasily backing off a notch.

"I mean it," continues Joliffe, releasing the safety catch. "I've got nothing to lose."

"Oh, come along, sir," chides the assistant manager with a dry laugh, but Joliffe isn't joking.

"Open the door," he shouts, cocking the trigger with a click that reverberates around the cavernous room with the force of a gunshot. Then he counts, "One ... two ...

"Okay — okay," says the supervisor, opening the door. "You go ahead."

"Armed robbery in progress" is the report that immediately electrifies the police airwaves, galvanizing every officer on duty into a state of alertness and sending a helicopter, six police cars and a vanload of heavies in body armour to the front line, while additional units are scrambling from across the city to provide backup.

The sound of sirens startles Joliffe as he hobbles down the bank's stone steps to his getaway bike. He hadn't anticipated such an immediate hue and cry and is rattled as he straps his bag of winnings to the carrier.

"C'mon, c'mon," he mutters, angry with himself for his clumsiness. But he finally gets it attached, and lifts his leg over the crossbar to find the pedals. However, in his panic, he's overlooked two crucial elements: the gun in his pocket is still cocked, and he's forgotten to put on his bicycle clips.

"Damn," mumbles Joliffe, remembering the clips, but it's too late. A police car, screeching out of an inter-section behind him and weaving quickly through the busy traffic, forces him to take flight. With adrenaline juicing life into his aged legs, he kicks off from the curb and spins the pedals with such vigour that, by the time the police car skids to a halt at the bank, he is pumping his way out of sight over the top of the hill. With rasping breaths and thudding heart, Joliffe fights to keep the pedals turning, but his break for freedom is short-lived. As he crests the rise and starts his descent, the flashing lights of police cars emerging from the murk at the bottom of the hill tell him he's trapped.

He hits the brakes, but the rain-slick rubber pads skid uselessly around the rim, so he decides to let go. The pedals of his ancient bicycle are exhilarated by the sudden freedom and take on their own life, spinning and shrieking like delighted kids on a merry-go-round. Joliffe, too, is elated, and despite his fear he drops fifty years as he looks to the bottom of the hill and plans to evade capture by leaping the curb and detouring through a pedestrian walkway. But fate takes a hand: Joliffe's flying chain grabs his flapping trouser leg and jams it into the cogwheel. The pedals stop with such jarring suddenness that he's almost overthrown, but he hangs on and flies headlong down the steep slope, wobbling errat-ically, while he frantically tugs at his wedged leg.

A couple of umbrella-wielding women step blindly onto a crosswalk in Joliffe's path and he frantically screeches, "Out of the way! Out of the way!" as he tugs furiously at his jammed leg.

The women leap back to the curb, but Joliffe has lost control and is heading into oncoming traffic, forcing drivers and pedestrians to clear a path. A speeding courier skids on the soaked roadway, ricochets his van off a bus and swerves into the path of an oncoming lorry. A woman police driver, screaming through the traffic with her siren, slams on her brakes and watches in horror as the truck veers across the road ahead of her.

"Oh my God," she breathes as the twenty-ton monster scythes through a central hurdle and barrels towards a crowded bus stop.

With only seconds to react and nowhere to run, a dozen startled pedestrians stand transfixed like store dummies.

Joliffe sees the disaster unfolding in front of him and gets a grip on his handlebars, but he's still flying, and he slews past the truck and flies into the path of the police car. Behind him, pedestrians wake up and start to scatter, but the trucker finally wrests control, stands on his brakes and sideswipes half a dozen parked cars before solidly coming to rest against a concrete lamp standard.

Meanwhile, the fleeing bank raider has crashed headlong onto the hood of the police car and is staring through the windshield at the astonished policewoman.

As Constable Wendy Martin leaps from her car and takes a step towards the stricken man, the cocked pistol slips from Joliffe's raincoat pocket and begins a slow glide down the hood. The *crack* of the shot when the gun hits the ground is smothered by the cacophony of sirens and the throb of the police helicopter hovering overhead, so much so that the woman police officer shares everyone's surprise when her right leg suddenly caves under her and she falls heavily to the ground.

chapter thirteen

Davin Bliss is pacing at Vancouver's downtown police station. He's anxious for members of the press to settle, and the conference to begin, when Peter Bryan gets through to him on Phillips's cell phone with news of Maurice Joliffe's escapade. It's still morning on the Pacific coast, and still raining, but it's six in the evening in soggy London, where the Friday rush hour is winding down and the snarl-up in Kensington High Road is gradually being straightened out.

Despite the continuing rain, a crowd of rubber-neckers hang around as a tow truck hooks up the last of the smashed vehicles; while accident investigators take measurements and insurance adjusters scour the area searching for loopholes amongst the wreckage.

Constable Wendy Martin is in the emergency room at St. Bartholomew's Hospital. She will recuperate, once the bullet has been removed from her thigh; however, the fate of Joliffe's vintage bicycle is less certain. The mangled machine will probably end up as a curio in the force museum, though for now it sits in the evidence room at Kensington police station, together with the gun and the bag of stolen money.

Maurice Joliffe is also something of a curio, and a parade of amused officers take it in turn to gawk at the hapless, patched-up villain while he sits in the interview room, not knowing whether to chuckle or cry, as he waits for the legal-aid lawyer.

"Good news, Dave," says Bryan, as Bliss prepares to support Trina's anxiety-drained husband at the press conference. "We may have a breakthrough in the suicide cases."

"Oh. That's good," says Bliss absently, without admitting that since Daphne's disappearance he has given little thought to the situation that had triggered the imbroglio.

"Yeah, some old geezer on a bike just pulled off a blagging at a bank in Kensington, then he plugged one of the uniformed grunts on his way out."

"Okay, Peter, but that's armed robbery and assault on police," replies Bliss tetchily. "What the hell has that got to do with a bunch of crumblies topping themselves?"

"I've no idea," says Bryan, "but the robbery squad just called and they reckoned we'd be interested. Anyway, I'm going to interview him. I'll call you back."

Bliss has a perplexed look as he hands the phone back to his Mountie friend, but the hubbub is dying down in the room — the press conference is about to get under way — and he switches his focus back to Trina's husband, who is being paraded in front of the cameras by a uniformed superintendent. Rick Button has the fearful look of a shell-shocked prisoner, and every flash of a camera makes him jump as he edges his way to his seat at the table.

"Take your time," advises the superintendent as the wall of reporters seem to crowd in on Button, and the sleep-deprived man suddenly takes in the scene as if he has been caught in his bathtub by a party of visiting nuns.

"Umm ... umm ..." he stutters, his eyes darting back and forth, looking for somewhere to run.

"Just send a message to Trina," suggests Bliss gently in Rick Button's ear, as he lays a hand on the distraught man's shoulder. "Let her know we've not given up."

Button wipes his eyes with the flat of his hand, forces himself higher in the chair and focuses into the middle-distance, like a drunkard trying to see through the fog of inebriation. "I ... I want whoever is holding my wife ... to let her go," he stumbles through his tears, and Bliss watches with growing irritation as media hangers-on and camera crews wander around in the background, nattering about baseball and laughing at corny jokes, in a world that is, for them, a playground of normality.

"Sir, why do you suspect that someone is holding the women?" queries a reporter, seizing on Rick's faltering diction to slip in an early question.

"I ... I don't ... know what to think anymore ..." mumbles Button and, as the distressed man's voice gradually becomes incoherent, Bliss snatches the microphone from under his nose.

"Look, there are two women missing," declares Bliss firmly, once he has introduced himself. "Two women who happen to mean a great deal to their friends and families — and to me personally. And while I realize it may be inconvenient for a certain government to acknowledge what's happened to them, it is time to let them go home."

The immediate hush is palpable as another reporter begins to ask the obvious. "Are you suggesting —" she begins, but Bliss chimes in, "Yes. We have every reason to believe they are being held against their will by the American authorities."

"Where?"

"At a clandestine government establishment south of the border," continues Bliss with such forthrightness that there is a collective intake of breath.

The chatting stops. Cameramen rush to finely refocus their lenses. Sound men check their audio levels. And in the so-called monastery, John Dawson smacks his head into his hands and mutters, "Oh, shit."

"Fuck!" spits Bumface, alongside Dawson, as Bliss continues, straight to the camera. "... And I want to warn those people who are holding them, whoever they are: I've made it my mission to expose your activities to the world."

"What activities?" is one question drowned out by a cacophony of scandal hungry pressmen.

"Those are mighty fighting words, Chief Inspector," booms a baritone voice above the hullabaloo, and the burly Canadian reporter holds the floor as he continues. "Sounds like you're declaring war on someone."

"Well, I'm not the first David to take on a Goliath," concedes Bliss. "But if that's the way they want to play it ..."

"Shuddup, you jerk," mumbles Dawson at his television set. "You've got no idea what you're dealing with."

"All I can say is that I suggest you look no further than the U.S. government if I have a nasty accident ..." Bliss continues, but leaves the sentence hanging as a *Seattle Times* reporter challenges him.

"That's taking it a bit far, isn't it, sir?"

"Well, they've tried spiked belts and machine guns to keep me out so far," carries on Bliss, leaving Dawson mumbling, "Jesus Christ! Will somebody please shut him up." But Bliss is on a roll. "Unless they release the women immediately, I will take whatever action I deem appropriate to rescue them."

"Are you seriously suggesting that the government of the United States of America is responsible for abducting them?" asks an incredulous television newsman, and Bliss stares open-faced at the bank of cameras to reply: "And you, sir, are seriously suggesting that America doesn't have a history of kidnapping and holding people against their will?"

A titter of accord rings around the room, but in Washington state, John Dawson is not laughing as he downs a couple of painkillers for his burgeoning headache and turns to Bumface.

"You'd better shut down the funding operation immediately. Get the phones out and tell the guys to take a hike."

"They'll want cash."

"Give it to 'em. Just remind 'em that they're looking at ten to fifteen apiece if they ever blab."

"Okay, John."

"And tell Buzzer not to do any more collections."

"He'd better pick up what's there already."

"You're right. Just today, and I guess tomorrow. But that's it."

"Sure," says Bumface, then he looks to the wall of surveillance screens. "What about all of *them?*" he says, pointing to the numerous patients in various states of recovery following surgery.

"Hey, it's a charitable hospital if anyone comes asking. Of course we have sick people here."

"And what about the new cases?"

"How many?"

"There's a couple due in Vancouver today, and a load more next Wednesday or Thursday."

"Make sure Buzzer picks up the two today, and freeze the rest till we sort this mess out," orders Dawson, then he taps the TV screen where the press conference is winding down, saying, "You'd better pray that no one upstairs has seen this."

However, prayers may be too late, and the shrill ringing of a telephone signals to Dawson that his hopes are about to be shattered.

Mike Phillips's phone has also been ringing, and he turns to Bliss with a pained expression as the press conference breaks up.

"Dave. I don't know how to tell you this, but I've just been yanked off the case."

"Why?"

"Somebody has put the bite on the brass in Ottawa."

"And we can guess from whence that shark comes," says Bliss, his mind set on the south.

"Word has it that they're also squeezing the Canadian immigration department to throw you out of the country."

"Well, I obviously struck a chord with someone," Bliss laughs sardonically. "Though I'll be totally stumped if they persuade the British government not to let me go back home."

"You can come and live wiz me in France," suggests Daisy, taking his hand, and Bliss brightens at the notion.

"I'm surprised you still want me," he says, conscious that after four nights in North America they have got no closer than a goodnight kiss, but the tightness of her grip demonstrates her determination to hang on whatever the circumstances.

Some prenuptial honeymoon this is turning out to be, he thinks, then he stops, peers into her nigrescent Mediterranean eyes, feels the warmth of the Provençal sun still radiating from her olive skin, and challenges the seriousness of his intentions. But with Daphne's disappearance weighing so heavily on his mind, he lets the moment go and turns to Phillips.

"They're not going to stop me, Mike. I don't know what the hell their game is, but I *will* find out — one way or another."

"Unofficially, Dave," says Phillips, quickly checking over his shoulder, "I'll do whatever it takes to help. Christ, this is personal for me, too — and if they don't like it they can stuff their job."

"You don't mean that, Mike."

"Not really. But now that I'm married to a millionaire, I can always dream of quitting — though God knows if I could take the boredom."

"That's what bothers me," admits Bliss, still deliberating over his plans to leave the force to write. "Anyway, I'd appreciate your help. By the way, what about that white fishmonger's van?"

Phillips shakes his head. "Sorry, Dave. Anybody would think it was a state secret."

"Can't help you, Inspector. It's not registered," the Seattle officer had claimed when Phillips had phoned, and despite the Mountie's insistence that he had personally seen the vehicle on a customs surveillance tape at the border, the officer had stuck to his story. Two hours, and a dozen calls, later, Phillips had got no further, though no one had been willing to explain how a falsely registered vehicle had been permitted to cross and recross the border.

However, deep in a CIA basement room three thousand miles away, at the organization's headquarters in Langley, Virginia, Phillips's enquiry has caused something of a stir and has set in motion a storm that is gathering strength as it sweeps back across the country to a certain pseudo-religious establishment in the state of Washington.

"Mr. Dawson?" queries a voice with an accent honed on the east coast near Harvard or Yale, if not actually within their august precincts.

"Umm, yes, sir," replies Dawson diffidently.

"I guess you've been watching the news channels this morning?"

"No, sir," tries Dawson, but the caller doesn't buy it and drops his accent in favour of Brooklyn or the Bronx.

"Don't lie to me, f'kin asshole. You're supposed to be head of security out there. So tell me, what the friggin' ding-dong is going on?"

There goes my pension, thinks Dawson, but it's likely lost whichever way he jumps, so he opts for a stalling tactic. "I'm aware of certain allegations," he admits cagily, "and I'm carrying out a full investigation, sir."

"Okay. Good man," says the caller, repolishing his tone. "So, why the hell didn't you say so before?"

"Sorry, sir, but there was a junior officer in the room. He's gone now."

"Oh. Right. Well, get back to me P.D.Q. I've got the president's press secretary on my heinie. I need answers."

"Will do, sir," says Dawson slumping back into his chair, then he throws the telephone at Bumface, yelling, "Get working, Steve! Get this damn place cleaned up."

"So. Where do we go from here?" asks Rick Button once the press have their scoop, and Bliss and Phillips look in unison at the flagging man and join forces to say, "Bed."

But Button is still fighting. "No. Not until I've got my Trina back," he insists, and Bliss has a lump in his throat as he lays a comforting arm around the man's shoulder.

"Why not let Daisy take you home and leave it to us for a few hours?" he suggests. "I promise we're doing everything we possibly can, and we'll call you the minute we have any news."

"No ..." starts Button again, but Daisy steps in, gripping his hand and saying, "Come. I take you," with such authority that he meekly allows her to lead him towards Trina's car.

Phillips and his English counterpart watch the broken man shuffle disconsolately away, and the Canadian officer waits until Rick Button is out of earshot before turning to Bliss. "I'd love to be able to assure him she'll show up," he says, his tone devoid of optimism. "Although in truth I suppose it's only been two full days since they were last seen."

"It seems like forever," sighs Bliss, equally pessimistically. "Anyway, we both know that the first twenty-four hours are the most crucial. Which reminds me," he carries on, checking his watch, "I suppose I should phone Peter and see what's happening in London. He was jumping up and down about a bank job earlier on, though God knows what it has to do with the suicides."

Peter Bryan is still unsure of any connection himself when Bliss calls, and is chagrined with the robbery squad for fouling up his Friday evening.

"I don't think the blagging gang knows what to do with him," he tells Bliss candidly, and briefly explains the comical circumstances of Joliffe's villainous escapade before saying, "Apparently, all the witnesses have gone soft. Even the girl he robbed reckoned she would take him home as a substitute granddad if she had a chance."

"Oh, that'll bring out the Kleenex in the jury box all right," says Bliss, and Bryan agrees.

"Quite. He's got as much chance of doing time as O.J. Simpson."

"And his connection with the suicides is?" questions Bliss with mounting impatience.

"Tenuous at best, Dave," says Bryan, explaining that he had only been consulted because the octogenarian raider had apparently been quite prepared to blow his own brains out if he hadn't been allowed out of the bank with the money. However, since his arrival at Kensington police station, and following a brief interview with a legal-aid lawyer, Maurice Joliffe has completely clammed up.

"Anyway," asks Peter Bryan, temporarily washing his hands of Joliffe, "did Edwards get hold of you?"

"Oh — yes," says Bliss. "I'm disappointed, though. I was expecting him to suspend me."

"He can't," laughs Bryan. "If he suspends you, he can't order you home."

"And he needs to order me home because …?"

"Because the Americans are treading heavily on the Home Secretary's nutmegs."

"Really?"

"Oh, boy. You've done it properly this time. In fact, they say the British Ambassador in Washington has been summoned to the State Department for a few words of advice on international police relations. Apparently you and your big gob have pooped in their soup — again."

"Again?" questions Bliss.

"Well, they seem to think that your dig at their hypocritical stance on sex, booze, gambling and drugs at the conference wasn't exactly cricket."

"Hah. I expected that, Peter," chuckles Bliss. "Though do I sound as though I care? Anyway, if our boys weren't such Nellies they'd be giving the White House shit for kidnapping the women."

"They absolutely insist that they didn't."

"It's most likely some government boot camp," carries on Bliss with his ears closed. "They're probably training counter-terrorists so they can lob a 747 into the middle of Mecca during the Hajj to get revenge for 9/11."

"What makes you think it's official?"

"How else would they know that I'd been thrown out of the country before?"

"And they knew?"

"The bigmouth at the gate did."

Dawson may have been belligerent when he dealt with Bliss at the monastery's gate, but now that he senses that the wheels are coming off his wagon, he is in a quandary.

"What the hell are we gonna do with them?" he pleads, as he and Bumface watch Daphne and Trina on the surveillance monitors.

Daphne sits, motionless, on the edge of her bed, focusing all her energy on a way to escape her predicament, while Trina, in a separate room, sleeps off the sedative that was shot into her after she'd snapped following her recapture.

Daphne also has her eyes closed, but she is mentally alert and is carefully thinking her way through her well-thumbed collection of novels by Conan Doyle, Christie, Carr and a host of other mystery writers, searching for scenarios involving escapes from sealed rooms. But every plot she conjures up requires some form of outside assistance, or a prepared room — other than those relying on implausible devices like tame rodents and hocus-pocus, which she dismisses without consideration.

The snooping eye of the surveillance camera creates the greatest obstacle to every escape scheme. It's an impediment that obviously didn't exist in the era of the classics, and she dismisses idea after idea until she is finally left with only one viable scenario: feigned death.

The camera is also a source of concern for Dawson, whose escalating anxiety is reaching screaming point.

"You realize we're gonna get a visit, don't you?" he says, once Bumface has made a couple of calls. "And we're finished, man. I'm telling you — we're finished with a capital fuckin' F. The moment someone finds the women, we're screwed — and what about Allan? What's he gonna say?"

"Nothing," says Bumface. "He ain't gonna say nothing. His ass is on the line as much as ours. And stop worrying about the damn women. There's two hundred freakin' people here. How are they gonna find a couple of dames unless they check every room?"

Dawson stabs meaningfully at the monitors. "All they've gotta do is come in here and look at *this*, for chrissakes."

"Okay," says Bumface, "I can fix that," and a few minutes later Daphne's eyes pop open in surprise. Something in her environment has just changed. The feeling is ethereal and she can't grasp its root, though she has the sensation that a weight has been lifted, and her gaze instinctively goes to the surveillance camera.

In Vancouver, Bliss is seeking inspiration in a large coffee in the police station cafeteria when Phillips sidles up to him. "Good news, Dave. The white van's back."

"How do you know?"

"I have my sources," he says, as if it's some well-preserved secret, and then he relents. "The customs officer

— the one at the border who checked the videotape with me — he spotted it coming back about ten minutes ago. Apparently it comes over most days."

"Okay. So where do we go from here?"

"Well, let's have a little chat with the driver, shall we?" says Phillips as he phones his control room to say that he's taking the rest of the day off. "My wife's not feeling too good," he explains, and Bliss teasingly "tut-tuts" before asking, "So how do we find him?"

"It shouldn't be too difficult," replies Phillips. "I guess there's a good chance he'll be buying stock from the trawler fleet at the fisherman's wharf. Let's go see."

Mike Phillips's supposition is correct — although this morning there is no fleet, just a solitary vessel heading shoreward from the fishing grounds. However, the flock of raucous herring gulls hovering expectantly over the Vancouver quayside will eventually be forced to scavenge lunch at the city's garbage dump — the cargo in the hold of Victor Kelly's trawler won't be of any interest to them.

In London, there is an equally raucous gathering in the foyer of Kensington police station when Peter Bryan arrives to interview Maurice Joliffe. Fuelled by the young bank clerk's speculation that the bicycle bandit appeared to be in his late eighties, or possibly even nineties, a crush of reporters is badgering the press officer for information and demanding an opportunity to question the elderly man.

Joliffe is still in the interview room — unaware of the hubbub in the lobby, unaware that he is already being pejoratively labelled "The Grandfather" and that news organizations from around the world are badgering their London correspondents for information and pictures. In truth, considering the gravity of the charges, he should be locked up in the remand wing of Wandsworth jail, but no one wants to risk turning him into a folk hero. Even Wendy Martin, in her hospital bed, can't help feeling compassion for the distressed senior who had tried so hard to help her to her feet after the shooting.

"I'm ever so sorry, luv," the little old man had repeated several times, close to tears. "I must've forgotten to put the safety on."

If Peter Bryan had been doubtful of a link between Joliffe and the rash of elderly suicides when he first heard of the case, by the time he has been briefed by the robbery squad commander he is convinced. He's also convinced that the robbery squad have lumbered him with the ancient marauder because they realize there is little mileage in prosecuting someone who'll probably get more public sympathy than a pill-popping pop star or a drunken footballer. Maurice Joliffe appears equally aware of the dilemma, pleading, "You ain't gonna send me to jail at my age, are ya?" as soon as Peter Bryan switches on the video recorder and begins the interview.

"Well," replies Bryan, trying to sound convincing, "armed robbery with a prohibited weapon is a very serious charge."

"Yeah, but I told the girl straight that I wouldn't hurt her, and I never pointed the gun at her — or the others."

"But you shot the police woman."

"No, I did not," protests Joliffe. "It were an accident. The bloomin' gun fell out'a my pocket. I told her I was sorry — but it were an accident, honest."

"Well," admits Bryan, "it doesn't look as though you've got any previous form —"

"Dang right I haven't," cuts in Joliffe adamantly. "I ain't never been in trouble before in my life."

"Then why do this?"

The competing thoughts in Joliffe's mind contort his wan parchment face with such passion that Bryan finds himself wondering if there is another person inside struggling to escape.

"Take your time," advises Bryan gently, concerned that the tension will cause a stroke or heart attack as the old man's eyes and jaws quiver in nervous motion.

"What'll happen if I tells you the truth?" asks Joliffe eventually, as he gets a grip on his situation.

"Well, it's your first conviction," admits Bryan, "and considering your age and the fact that no one was killed, you might get probation, although I can't promise anything."

The whirl of indecision continues to haunt Joliffe's face, and Peter Bryan sits back to take the pressure off the elderly man. But Joliffe has been in turmoil for nearly a week, and he fidgets in indecision for a minute before making up his mind to confess.

"All my life, I've wanted to leave something for the kiddies," he begins to explain. "An' not just enough for me funeral. I always had jobs — worked damned hard to put a crust on the table. But there wuz never enough to put any by. Then I ends up on old-age pension and it hardly pays the bloomin' rent."

"Well, ten grand wouldn't make a lot of difference," suggests Bryan.

However, the ten thousand pounds Joliffe had demanded when he robbed the bank was only a fraction of his actual goal. Still, he's reluctant to acknowledge his true motive without some degree of assurance, and he looks to Bryan for confirmation. "They ain't gonna send me to jail, are they?"

Bryan opens his hands wide and disclaims responsibility as he answers, "Maybe not. You might just get a fine."

"Oh, that don't matter," laughs Joliffe. "I can afford it now."

"You're not thinking of using the ten thousand quid you nicked from the bank, are you?" enquires Bryan hastily.

"No — 'course not," says Joliffe. "I'm a millionaire. Why would I do that?"

"A millionaire?" questions the detective, surveying the beat-up old man and beginning to wonder if the Mental Health Act might be more appropriate than the Theft Act.

"Oh, yeah," continues Joliffe, finally deciding to come clean, and he has a triumphant note in his voice as he announces: "O'course, I'll only get five million now instead of the ten. Hah — what's five million when you've struck it rich?"

Peter Bryan eyes the old man sceptically, wondering if it's the right time to summon the psychiatrist, but he opts for a final question. "What five million?" he asks. "You only tried to steal ten thousand. You'd have to do a couple of hundred banks to get that much."

After a moment's hesitation, Joliffe drops his guard and his face lights up as he explains: "It were late last Monday night when I got the call. It were gone ten. I was just watching the news — thinkin' about turning in — and I thought, 'Who the 'ell can that be at this time?' Well, it was some Yank — at least he sounded like a Yank, though I suppose he was a Canadian. Well, you won't believe this, but you are lookin' at the bloke who won the Canadian National Lottery. All ten million of it."

"What?"

"Yeah. It's true. I've won the lot. After strugglin' through life, saving a bit here and a bit there, going without to leave a little nest egg, there I am — a rich man."

"Then why on earth are you robbing banks?" asks Bryan incredulously.

"Red tape," explains Joliffe succinctly. "See, the way it works is that I have to pay ... what did he call it? ... a 'clearance bond' or something before I can get my winnings sent over from Canada. That's why I told the girl at the bank that I'd pay it back next week with interest. I weren't lying — honest."

Peter Bryan spends a few seconds digesting the information. Something smells, but the officer isn't sure if it's the sweaty old man in front of him or the tale he's telling.

"Why didn't you just explain that to the bank manager and ask for a loan?" asks the detective.

"I couldn't," says the old man as he pulls Bryan closer with a bony finger and whispers him into a conspiracy. "You see, it's not strictly kosher." Then, with a wary eye on the video camera, Joliffe continues to elucidate, "Because I ain't a Canadian citizen there's some problem with the taxes. And if they found out who I was, well, the bloomin' taxman over there would snap up half the bloomin' winnings."

"You do realize that you must never tell anyone that you've won this," the late-night caller had warned, once he had explained the taxation situation in detail, and Maurice had quickly agreed. "No, o'course I won't. Cross me bloomin' heart."

"You see," continues Joliffe to Bryan, "I promised I wouldn't say anything 'cos he was worried we might both end up in jail fer diddlin' the taxes. But the bloomin' guvverment's had enough out of me over the years and I was buggered if I was gonna give 'em five million dollars — that's ... well, that's a lot of dough. He didn't want me to take the risk. 'Not just for five million,' he said. 'Five million?' I said. 'You gotta be joking, my son. If I won it, I should have it. It's mine, ain't it?' 'Oh, you've won it all right,' he said. 'There ain't no doubt about it.'"

"Five million dollars?" breathes Bryan.

"No. Five million wuz the tax. I'd won ten all told, but I didn't wann'a risk getting him into trouble, did I?" Joliffe continues in explanation to Peter Bryan. "I mean — he sounded such a nice young man. And I could hear the others in the background. They wuz all so happy for me — clappin' and shoutin', they wuz."

It might have taken more than eighty years, but the little man who'd grown up in the slums around London's dockyards had finally won something, and he pauses while his face warms at the memory of the cheers and the applause.

"'Well done, Maurice,' they wuz shouting down the phone. 'You're a rich man, Maurice,'" he continues with a laugh, adding, "I guess I'll just have to make do with the five million. I expect it'll see me out all right."

Alarm bells have been ringing in Peter Bryan's mind for a few minutes — from the moment that the old man's eyes lit up to announce that he was a millionaire — and the detective questions, "So — when did you buy the ticket, Maurice?"

"That's the strangest thing," replies Joliffe with a laugh. "I didn't remember buying it at all — but they got all my information right, so I must have done."

"And what information was *that* exactly?" asks Bryan, now knowing that the day that had begun badly for Joliffe was about to get worse — much worse.

"Name, address and phone number …" he starts, then something in the tone of Bryan's question alerts him to a problem. "What?" he asks, looking up at the detective and finding Peter Bryan sadly shaking his head.

"Maurice — is that the information that's listed in the phone book?"

"I suppose so. Why?"

chapter fourteen

By midday Friday there is little sign that the cloud cover left behind by Thursday's depression is ever going to break. And as Bliss and Phillips sit in the muggy warmth of a quayside fish restaurant, the English detective wonders whether it will ever stop raining.

"I can hardly see a thing," he says, wiping a window in the condensation with a napkin and peering across the fog-shrouded harbour. But there is little to see, apart from a ghostly water bus that fades in and out of the haze as it glides to and from the islands that make up the Vancouver archipelago.

"Now I know how Rick feels," he carries on while staring at the plate of haddock and chips in front of him. "It just doesn't seem right to eat while we don't know what's happening to Daphne and the poor guy's wife."

"But what do you intend doing?" asks Phillips, knowing that he need not add, "If the women never show up."

Bliss finishes the sentence in his mind. "I can't just go home and pretend she never existed," he answers, then puts down his cutlery to stare out of the window into the gloom. "In fact, I don't see how I'll ever be able to leave. I'll be like that dog in Scotland that never left his master's grave. What was it called — Greyfriars hound or something? Hah! That's appropriate, isn't it? Greyfriars — a monastery."

"So what are your plans?" persists Phillips.

"I'm going back in there, of course," says Bliss determinedly. "I'll camp on their bloody doorstep if I have to, and I'll make such a damned racket that they'll have to give me some answers."

"Dave, you can't be serious. They really *will* throw you in jail."

"Only if they catch me," he declares, almost as if he's planning it that way. "Anyway, that'll give them an even bigger headache. Can you imagine the fun the British press will have with that?"

"Assuming the Americans admit that you're there," says Phillips ominously as Bliss catches sight of the white prow of a vessel nosing out of the mist.

"Is that a fishing boat?" he asks, picking up his fork and stabbing at the emerging craft with it. But as Phillips squints through the haze, the boat develops into a sleek motor cruiser and he dismisses the million-dollar bauble at a glance.

"No — not unless a fridge full of caviar and oysters count as catch."

"That place has to be pretty heavy-duty," continues Bliss, unable to keep his mind off the supposed monastery.

"You're absolutely certain they are there?"

"I'd stake my pension on it," says Bliss, as another boat edges gingerly through the fog.

"Look. *That's* a trawler," says Phillips, drawing Bliss's eyes to Kelly's chunky vessel as it approaches the quay.

"Oh, yes," says Bliss, and while the seventy-foot fishing vessel holds no particular significance for him, with nothing else to focus on in the murk he watches the boat manoeuvre alongside where an inspector from the fisheries department waits to examine the meagre haul.

"How did you make out, Vince?" calls the inspector cheerily as Kelly ties off his lines and cuts the engines.

"Mainly cat food," mutters the skipper, sweeping his hand across half a dozen fish-laden plastic tubs on the stern deck. "It'll be another few weeks before the sockeye come in — *if* they come in."

"The eggheads are predicting a good run this year," says the inspector, running his eye quickly over the motley assortment in the tubs while picking at it with little interest. But it's a story the skipper has heard before.

"I'll believe it when I see it."

"You just wait," laughs the inspector over his shoulder as he moseys back to the shelter of a harbourside coffee house.

A white Ford van being driven slowly along the quayside catches Phillips's eye, and he's just saying, "Hey, Dave, this could be him," when his cell phone interrupts.

"It's for you, Dave," he says, passing it over without taking his eyes off the van.

"Dave," calls Peter Bryan from London, his voice bouncing with excitement. "I think I've cracked the suicide job, and it's got a Canadian connection."

"Really?"

"He's stopping at that trawler," says Phillips, his eyes tight on Buzzer's van. "But I can't see the plates from here."

"Yeah. You'll never believe what happened to them," continues Bryan, and he is about to explain the modus operandi to Bliss when Phillips starts to rise.

"Dave," says Phillips, grabbing his raincoat and heading for the door, "there's something funny going on."

"What? Hold on — wait," says Bliss, talking to both men at the same time, then he shouts, "I'll call you back!" into the phone and takes off after Phillips.

But the detectives are too late. Buzzer's white van is already pulling away from the quayside as they emerge from the restaurant and sprint towards the trawler, leaving them with the glimpse of a crew member scurrying back aboard and the sight of the fish trays still on the deck.

"What happened?" asks Bliss breathlessly as they watch the departing vehicle and clearly see that it bears the familiar Washington licence plate.

"Come on," urges Phillips, dragging Bliss towards his BMW at the far end of the quay, but they have no chance of catching the fleeing vehicle and Bliss calls a halt, demanding, "What the hell did you see, Mike?"

"There were three of them," he starts, then quickly explains that the men, all bundled in luminescent waterproofs, had come ashore from the trawler, and he had watched, expecting them to start loading the trays of fish into the Ford van. One of the men, the tallest of the three, had opened the rear doors of the van while the other two stood back, then the first man had quickly checked around before ushering the two men inside. "I was just beginning to wonder what they were playing at," continues Phillips, "when the guy on the quayside slammed the door and the van took off."

"With the others still inside?"

"Yep."

"Trafficking," Bliss immediately surmises, getting a nod of agreement from the Mountie. "They've got a nerve," Phillips says. "Bringing them ashore right under our noses in the middle of the day."

"But why here?" Bliss wonders, though Phillips knows the answer to that.

"They wouldn't risk dropping them south of the border. The U.S. Coast Guard is really hot."

"Okay. So what do we do?" questions Bliss, knowing he's way off his own patch.

"I should really call it in," admits Phillips, but he questions the wisdom of doing so, considering he'd lied about his wife's sickness.

"We could always try to head them off at the border," suggests Bliss, and they are on the point of leaving when Daisy shows up.

"How's Rick?" they ask in unison.

"He is sleeping like zhe baby," says Daisy, though she doesn't mention that she had spiked his tea with a sleeping tablet.

Rick Button's wife has also been floored by a soporific and has slept soundly since her capture the previous evening. She wakes mid-afternoon with a mouthful of cotton wool and an empty stomach, but unlike Daphne she has no inkling that the surveillance camera might be inoperative, and she spends several minutes jumping up and down in front of it, calling, "Hey! Let me out … I'm hungry!" and, "Where's my friend?"

"Oh, for chrissakes," mutters Dawson as he hears the woman's feet pounding overhead and her shouts echoing through the corridors. But without the camera, he's blind to what's happening.

"Steve — Steve! Stop her, for God's sake!" he yells hysterically as he downs more painkillers. The stress-induced headache, which has maddened him since Bliss's televised rant, has reached screaming point and is about to be exacerbated by the shrill ring of the hotline from the main gate.

"I've got a couple of official visitors demanding admittance," the guard tells him when he answers.

"Shit," he breathes, sensing that his day is heading south faster than stock in a dodgy gold mine. "Official?" he queries.

"Head-office types."

"Okay, stall them. I'll be right there," he says, then turns back to Bumface. "I don't care what it takes, but you'd better keep those women quiet."

"Right, John."

"And keep Allan out of sight."

"Okay."

"Steve," says Dawson, calling him back with a warning look. "Make nice — okay? You don't need a murder rap on top of everything else."

The two men outside the gate are unfamiliar to Dawson, though Bliss would recognize them instantly. It's Brush-head and his muscular mate — the heavy-weights who'd first warned him off after his abortive attempt to storm the monastery on Wednesday evening.

Martin Montague, alias Brush-head, is the CIA's station chief in Seoul — even though his security pass at the embassy in the Korean capital says that he is a press secretary — and he is not only way off his patch, but he's also way out of line in demanding entry to Dawson's fiefdom.

"What do you want?" asks Dawson, once he has run his eye over their identification documents.

"Answers, Mr. Dawson," says Montague, starting forward, but Dawson stands his ground and shakes his head, demanding, "Who authorized you to come here?"

"I don't need authority ..." begins Montague, and his partner steps powerfully forward in support. But

Dawson has a uniformed gorilla with a machine gun on his own team and he refuses to budge.

"This place is off-limits to everyone apart from specifically authorized agents," Dawson carries on firmly, but Montague refuses to be cowed.

"Listen, shithead," he spits, "I'm not interested in you and your childish games, but when you step on my toes you're asking for trouble."

"You'd better check with your director," suggests Dawson with a degree of finality.

"I don't check with anyone," answers Montague, getting physical and pushing Dawson aside.

But a second guard has come to Dawson's aid, and Montague finds himself facing the spiteful end of a machine gun.

"Go ahead, punk," scowls Montague as he keeps walking. "We'll use your office, Mr. Dawson," he continues, now in the driver's seat, and Dawson signals the guard to lower his weapon.

"And have someone send in coffee and donuts; this may take a while."

Bliss and Phillips have been flying since the white van slipped out from under them at the harbourfront, and according to Phillips's contact in the customs service they've beaten their quarry to the border crossing south of Vancouver.

"He must have stopped somewhere else," suggests Officer Cranley as he looks back up the highway towards Vancouver. "He definitely hasn't crossed back into the States."

"Thanks, Roger," says Phillips, adding confidently, "Hang around. I think we're going to have some customers for you."

"What's with the dick from Scotland Yard?" asks CIA Chief Montague once he and Dawson are in the surveillance room. "Who stoked his boiler?"

"God knows," says Dawson, keeping a wary eye on Montague's gorilla, who has yet to grunt. His overtaxed mind spins even harder as he tries to work out what motives and connections the men might have.

"So — what's the score with these women that he's looking for? He seems to think they're here."

"We ain't seen no women," answers Dawson, deciding that his best option is to keep his cards off the table as much as possible.

"Oh come on, Dawson. That cop puts his ass on the line to get in here, and then he goes public. He must know something."

Dawson sits back and looks at his hand before tossing out a couple of low cards. "I reckon he's a bit of a loony. Just likes to shoot his mouth off."

Twenty years' experience dealing with crooks, double-dealers and political gerrymanderers warns Montague that Dawson is lying, but he lets it go and picks up another theme.

"So, what do you do here?"

"It's off the record."

"Don't start that crap again. We're supposed to be on the same side — remember? We're in the same Boy Scout troop."

"Research," is all Dawson will admit, sensing that he can't afford to play a loose game, asking, "Anyway, what's your interest?"

"I don't want to have to pull rank," Montague starts, sounding sympathetic to Dawson's predicament while making it perfectly clear that he's not. "But *I* get to ask the questions. Okay?"

Dawson rolls his eyes and inadvertently draws Montague's attention to the bank of surveillance screens. Realizing his mistake, he hits a switch. "That's classified," he says as the monitors go blank.

Montague eyes him fiercely. "Turn those screens back on, Mr. Dawson, or I'll nail your ass for insubordination."

Dawson hesitates a fraction of a second, trying to get a read on Montague's hand, but the senior man knows where he stands and shouts, "Turn them on!"

Dawson jumps as the words pound through his aching skull. He knows Montague holds a strong hand, so he bluffs. "Sorry — no can do. They're on a time delay — security."

"*Turn them on now!!*" screeches Montague, and his gorilla starts to loosen his shoulders. "Turn them on or I'll relieve you of duty."

Dawson stalls. "I told you. You need special clearance."

But Montague holds at least one ace. "Okay, give me the phone. Who's your director?"

"I don't think —" starts Dawson, so Montague gives him an option.

"Give me some paper then."

It only takes Montague a few seconds to scribble a few words, then he hands the paper back, saying, "There you are. One authorization duly signed by a station chief. Now turn on those screens or start packing."

Dawson folds, and images of the various buildings, hospital rooms and corridors slowly reappear.

Montague waves for his sidekick to back down and then drops his tone in conciliation. "See, that wasn't so difficult," he says as he scans the screens and flicks from camera to camera until he's apparently satisfied, then he focuses on a number of Asian men playing mah-jongg in a sitting room. "Now what's the story here, John?" he wants to know.

"I told you — it's a research centre."

"Well, let me tell you what bothers me, John," continues Montague, making it clear that he's done some homework. "I've been in the Boy Scouts since Jimmy Carter cleaned house in '77 — you remember, after the Firm went rogue and lurched from catastrophe to disaster and back again. Hah! 'CIA — Clowns In America,' they used to call us. Let's face it, we *were* a joke, John. I mean, there was the Bay of Pigs, Watergate, Chile, Colombia, Iran — liquidating the wrong people, supporting the wrong side. You name it, we screwed it up. So when I hear rumours from my friends in China and Korea that we're playing dirty again, I wann'a know what's going on."

Dawson's listening, but he's not talking. "I just look after security here," he claims, but Montague isn't paying attention and stops him with a hand before pointing to the mah-jongg players.

"Maybe I should ask *them* what they're doing here."

"You can't ..." starts Dawson, but Montague's expression says he can — and will.

A procession of a thousand white vans has filed slowly past Bliss and Phillips at the Pacific Highway border crossing since lunchtime, or so it appears to Bliss. "It's so bloody frustrating," he says, sensing that he's close to the women, yet seemingly can do nothing to find them. "It's the utter helplessness, Mike," he carries on with growing anger. "It must be like having cancer — knowing damn well that it's in there somewhere, growing, getting bigger and bigger, eating you alive — and all you really want to do is grab a knife and just rip it out. But you can't. All you can do is put on a smile and pretend you're not scared."

"I know what you mean," admits Phillips.

"I just hope I'm not too late ..." starts Bliss, and he is reminded that he hasn't called his son-in-law for news on the suicide cases. "Damn! I forgot to phone Peter," he muses, but it's nearing midnight in England, so he lets it go. "I'll call him in the morning."

"I still don't know what you're plotting," says Phillips, growing increasingly uneasy about Bliss's determination to return and infiltrate the monastery.

But Bliss has no intention of compromising his counterpart's position in the RCMP by involving him in his scheme. "Don't worry, Mike. I'll be all right," he ventures, in a tone he hopes is reassuring.

"I just don't see how you're gonna get back in without a visa."

Bliss has a plan for that as well, although he's relying on Daisy to provide the means, and he would be relieved to know that the bouncy Frenchwoman has rented a Toyota and is driving south on the Pacific Highway to rendezvous with him.

Just ahead of Daisy, though lost in the miasma of fog and road spray, is a white van with a dubious licence plate. Buzzer and his sidekick are nearing the U.S., and home, and have their minds set on a relaxing weekend in the bar — though since Bliss rammed through the gates ahead of them on Wednesday evening, the establishment has been tense with rumours.

"I still reckon you know what's going down," Reggie says, pressing Buzzer for information as they approach the border, but it's a song he's been singing all day and the driver sighs with boredom.

"Give it a rest, Reg. I told you: I dunno what's happenin'. And that's real fine with me. They only pay for my hands, not my head."

"Well, *something's* happenin', that's for sure."

"How long have you been in the service, Reggie?"

"Two years an' a bit."

"God knows why they call it a 'secret service' with people like you," snorts Buzzer as they slow to exit Canada. "You can't even fart without blabbin' about it."

The border is only a hundred metres ahead of them, and Buzzer has his foot ready on the accelerator, knowing that he'll sail through the checkpoint with a friendly wave.

"What the hell —" he says when a uniformed Canadian customs officer steps out in front of him. "We're leaving your freakin' country, jerk," he mutters under his breath as he is forced to slow, then he turns to Reggie. "Leave the talking to me, aw'right?"

"Your passports, please, gentlemen," requests Roger Cranley, as Bliss and Phillips slip out of their parked car and start to move in.

"CIA," says Buzzer, quietly sliding an identity card under the customs officer's nose without taking the vehicle out of gear.

"Just turn off the vehicle, would you, sir," orders Cranley.

"What do you want?" asks Buzzer, dropping into neutral and irritably pumping the throttle.

"I want to talk to you —" starts Cranley, but Buzzer drops back into gear and is inching forward.

"Sorry," he says, shaking his head. "No can do. I'm on official business."

"I said stop!" yells Cranley, and Mike Phillips begins to loosen the pistol from his shoulder holster and edge forward in support of the unarmed officer as the vehicle continues creeping.

"Look," says Buzzer, making no attempt to stop, and giving no hint of his intention to do so, "you have no right to interfere with this vehicle. It's the property of the United States Government."

"I'm not interfering. You're still in Canada, and I'm telling you to stop."

Buzzer starts raising the window and is considering slamming his foot to the floor when Phillips leaps forward and thrusts his gun into the American's face. "Police! Stop or I'll shoot."

Buzzer stops, but he grabs his cell phone and starts to make a call. Bliss rushes in, yanks open the passenger door, reaches past a stunned Reggie and snatches the phone out of Buzzer's hand.

"Get out," orders Phillips, with his gun still stuck in Buzzer's face. Although the driver starts to climb down, he's still relying on his badge for protection.

"Mister, you're making one hell of a big mistake," he says. "Interfering with a CIA operation is a felony."

"Not in Canada, it isn't," says Phillips. "Now open the back doors for this officer, please."

"You've no right to do this," protests Buzzer. "This is government property. I demand you call the American consul. I know my rights."

"You're kidding," says Phillips. "Open the doors or we'll jimmy them open."

"You're way out'a line, mister. I'm not entering the country — I'm leaving," Buzzer is still ranting as Bliss steps forward and rips the vehicle's keys from his hand.

"Methinks he doth protest too much," mutters the British officer as he leads Cranley to the rear and begins to unlock the door.

"You've no right to search my vehicle," shouts Buzzer.

"That's where you're wrong," says Phillips, still holding the men at gunpoint. "This vehicle isn't legally registered. So we assume it's stolen — unless you can prove otherwise."

"I told you. It's a government vehicle."

"Not *our* government," says Phillips, "and that's the only government I answer to, whether you like it or not."

"Salmon," muses Cranley, as the open doors expose a deep steel container filled with dead fish.

"Just salmon," echoes Bliss disappointedly.

"Where did you get these from?" asks Cranley, calling to the driver and his mate, but neither man answers.

"They must have picked them up from another trawler in Vancouver," suggests Bliss.

"No," says Cranley. "You're missing the point. These are *Atlantic* salmon."

"So?"

"Well, this is the Pacific coast. The only Atlantic salmon here are from the fish farms, not from a trawler. Anyway, they've been frozen. Look at their eyes."

Bliss peers into the dull sunken eyes of the salmon and finds no memory of life. "Come on, give me a hand," he says as he starts to scoop the slimy fish aside. "There should be two men in here somewhere."

chapter fifteen

"So, Mister," says Station Chief Montague, as if offering the junior man a choice, "are you ready to show me around this joint or what?"

"I'd better just check ..." starts Dawson, reaching for the phone to contact Bumface.

Three days of disasters instigated by his subordinate have left Dawson wary of the man's competence in dealing with Spotty Dick, Trina and Daphne, and he desperately wants some reassurance before venturing forth. But Montague is in a hurry and is quick to his feet. "Okay, then. I'll find my own way around."

Dawson drops the phone and is at the door in a flash, demanding a guarantee. "This is an order — right?"

"Yes, Mr. Dawson, this is an order. Now get out of the way."

Allan Wallace is someone else on the move, but unlike Montague he has no option.

"You'll be safe enough here if you keep your mouth shut," Bumface warns his erstwhile partner as he leads him into a dilapidated outhouse on the building's grounds and brings out a pair of handcuffs.

"Watch the wrist!" howls the injured man at the sight of the manacles. "What are you going to do with the women?" he demands as Bumface shackles him to a steel water pipe.

"You're too f'kin soft — that's your problem, you dick. You didn't really think you'd get 'em out of here, did you?"

"If you touch —" starts Wallace, but Bumface stops him. "Don't worry, Allan," he sneers. "John and me will take good care of them."

"You still haven't told me what this place is all about," Montague prods as Dawson tours him, together with his muscular mate, past operating and recovery rooms that wouldn't be out of place in a ritzy New York clinic.

"Like I said — I just handle security," claims Dawson, steering well clear of areas occupied by patients. "All I know is that it's kind'a sensitive."

"C'mon, Dawson. Have you got a nasty cold or something? I could smell this place all the way over in Seoul. My information is that people are lining up to get in here. What are you offering — immortality or something?"

"They don't tell me."

"*They?*" questions Montague. "Maybe I'm talking to the wrong person. Maybe I should be talking to *them* — whoever *they* are."

Dawson pulls up sharp and plays his trump. "Look, sir, I've already put my career on the line by letting you in. I'm doing my best here — I'm showing you around. I want you to see for yourself that this isn't Roswell. You won't find any little green men or flying saucers. But if any of the staff knew I'd broken protocol ..." he pauses to let his words settle, adding. "Well, I'm sure you understand."

Montague's raised eyebrows suggest otherwise, but he doesn't push the point. "Okay. But you'd better be levelling with me, Mister, 'cos this place still stinks at the moment. And it sure as hell stinks to that cop who reckons you've got his women here."

"I dunno what his problem is," sneers Dawson as he continues the tour past laboratories and X-ray rooms. "What the hell would we do with them?"

"That's what I'd like to know," complains Montague. "Exactly what would you do with women here?"

Bumface knows what he would do with Trina and Daphne, given a free hand, but he has been forced to put them back in the same room and promise them some undoped food. The reunification wasn't his idea. Trina yelling, "I'm gonna scream and keep screaming and screaming ..." had left him little choice.

"And one more peep out of either of you ..." he warns with a twitchy trigger finger as the two women joyfully embrace, but Daphne refuses to be browbeaten.

"And you'll do what?" she says, breaking away from Trina and using the strength of her voice to back him towards the door.

"Look, lady," he tries with a forced smile, "we're doing our best to sort things out. Just behave, and who knows — another day or so and we should have you out of here. Aw'right?"

"Oh, listen to Pinocchio," she laughs into his face, sensing that she has him on the run. "I seem to remember you saying that before."

"Look," he spits, "you just don't get it, do you? You're in America now — not some lefty, liberal, pot-smoking, pansy-loving democracy. We don't piss around here. So shut up."

"Well," says Daphne as the door closes behind him and the electronic lock clicks into place. "That's very interesting."

"What?"

"According to Spotty Dick, they were going to rub us out ... pull the plug ... deep-six us, or whatever he called it in their language. But I think someone's persuaded them that it wasn't such a clever idea."

"That's good —" starts Trina, but Daphne shushes her with a finger to her lips.

"I think the heat's on," she whispers, sounding more like a hoodlum than a greying spinster as she ushers Trina away from the eye of the surveillance camera and into the bathroom. "Let's see how long it takes them to find us," she adds, as she shuts the door and turns on the taps.

The next ten minutes pass with the slowness of a day on death row as the two women perch on the edge of the bath waiting for Dawson or Bumface to yell, "Come out of the bathroom, ladies." However, Daphne is less surprised than Trina when nothing happens.

"I knew it. They've switched off the camera," she says confidently, and she strolls into the bedroom to boldly confront the intrusive artefact.

Trina is more reticent. "What if they want us to try to escape so they can mow us down and claim they had no choice?"

"No," says Daphne, pulling up a chair and staring straight into the lens. "They've had several chances to do that already. My guess is that David found my hanky and he's kicking up a storm. He might even be at the gates with a search warrant right now."

Bliss isn't at the gates, nor does he have a warrant, but he is certainly planning on visiting the monastery in the very near future. Buzzer Busby and Reggie Jones, on the other hand, aren't going anywhere until they've explained the presence of a couple of confused Koreans in a concealed compartment under the fish tank in the back of their van. The attempted transportation of thirty-five thousand dollars in cash across the border is another matter they are being asked to explain.

"That's a crime, to start with," says Roger Cranley, although no one in the vehicle is putting his hands up to owning the stuffed leather cash bag that had been stashed under the fish. In fact, neither of the low-level CIA men is talking, and neither are the Koreans, although an interpreter is on her way from Vancouver.

The most perplexing issue to Cranley is the fact that the Asians have valid U.S. passports. "Our immigration people say they look legit," says Cranley. Then he flicks through the blank pages of the recently issued documents to make a point to Phillips and Bliss. "Look, no foreign stamps," he says. "They can't use these to get into the States without someone wanting to know why they weren't stamped by a foreign agency."

"But where have they been?" asks Bliss.

"I bet neither of them have ever been outside of Korea before," says Cranley knowingly. "It's my guess that someone in the U.S. immigration office in Seoul is selling citizenships with a complete set of documents to match."

"That would be pricey," mutters Phillips.

"You bet it would," agrees Cranley. "Of course, I may be wrong, but I'll get the Americans to run the reference numbers through their systems. They should be able to give us an answer straight away —"

"Wait a minute," cuts in Phillips. "What if Busby and Jones are genuine CIA, and these documents are straight? The monastery could be some kind of bona fide government operation."

"Finally, Mike!" exclaims Bliss, throwing his hands in the air in the background. "I've been trying to tell you that for the last three days."

"Then why smuggle people in via Canada?"

"Don't ask me," shrugs Bliss.

"And why risk exposing it by kidnapping the women?"

"Ditto."

"Okay," says Phillips. "So, where to now?"

The name LeBlanc means nothing to the American border officer as he checks Daisy's passport and visitor's visa thirty minutes later.

"May I ask the purpose of your visit to the United States, ma'am?" asks the unsuspecting man.

"*Oui.* I have to fly home from Seattle tomorrow morning," she says, flourishing her return ticket, and within seconds she is headed south towards Seattle. Behind her, Mike Phillips keeps his head down at the wheel of Buzzer's Ford van, and is relieved when the officer simply glances at the vehicle's registration plate and waves him through.

"Ah, the power of the CIA," muses Phillips.

"I really have to stop travelling this way," Bliss says ten minutes later, once the van has pulled off the highway and he has been hauled out of the hidden compartment by Phillips and Daisy. "I'll travel with you," he carries on, taking the Frenchwoman's hand and leading her towards her car. "It's our last day together."

"*Daavid?*" questions Daisy. "Don't you mean zhat it is our *first* day together?"

Bliss stops thoughtfully. "I am so sorry," he begins as he takes her in his arms and tries to kiss her, but she backs off with a grimace.

"Ugh, *Daavid*," she cuts in, turning up her nose at his jacket. "I zhink zhat I prefer zhe bananas."

"Oh. Fish!" he mutters, now wishing that he had slipped across the border in the trunk of Daisy's car as he'd originally planned. He is still trying to brush off salmon scales and slime when she hops into the rented car and locks the doors.

"I zhink maybe you should stay in zhe van," she laughs through a crack in the window, adding cheekily, "Unless you want me to take all of your clothes off."

"Now *that* sounds like an interesting proposition," sniggers Phillips as they get into the van, though Bliss is less sure.

"I'm beginning to wonder if it'll ever happen," he sighs dejectedly, realizing that he's hardly been out of his clothes all week. "She goes home tomorrow morning."

"Let's hope we get lucky today, then," says Phillips as they drive off, although he still has reservations about their plan, and it certainly wasn't an idea popular with Cranley.

"I can't let you do this," the Canadian customs officer had protested with a grave face when Phillips had outlined his intention to use the CIA vehicle to smuggle Bliss into the States and gatecrash the monastery. "That vehicle is evidence in a criminal case."

"Don't worry, Roger," Philips had replied. "I'll give you my personal guarantee that we'll bring it back in one piece."

"I don't know …" Cranley had wavered.

"Okay," Bliss had said, apparently giving in. "As long as you can live with the blood of two women on your hands."

"We could get twenty years apiece for doing this," Phillips continues as they head south with Daisy tailing them in the rented Toyota.

"Stop worrying, Mike. It's an unregistered vehicle," Bliss reminds him. "Anyway, think of the press coverage we'd get: two foreign cops riding to the rescue of a couple of defenceless women being held prisoner by the U.S. government."

"*If* they are ..." says Phillips, still not completely convinced.

While "prisoners" may correctly describe the women's status, "defenceless" is an epithet that could get Bliss into a lot of trouble were he to repeat it in their presence. And now that they are refreshed and reunited, it is a state of affairs Daphne and Trina are working to rectify.

"Maybe we should do an experiment," suggests Daphne, still with her eyes on the surveillance camera, and Trina jumps in enthusiastically.

"I know!" she says, and seconds later she has upended her bed and is making a flamboyant show of dismantling the metal frame using a table knife.

"I thought so," muses Daphne a few minutes later when there is no reaction from the guards. "Give me the knife," she says, and she makes her way to the door and starts sawing through the adjacent wall. "If we can get to the door-lock control panel we should be able to create a short circuit," she explains as she hacks away lumps of plasterboard.

"How do you know all this stuff?" asks Trina incredulously.

"I've been very lucky," Daphne laughs. "I've never had a husband." Then she turns to the younger woman. "You used to kick-box, didn't you?"

"Yes. I still do."

"Okay," says Daphne, already feeling a glow of victory as she digs deeper into the wall and strikes the electronic locking mechanism. "It's time we took the upper hand. This time we'll go out fighting."

"That's about it, sir," says Dawson, arriving back at the surveillance room after leading Station Chief Montague in an innocuous circle. Then the security head smiles as he adds in relief, "See, no little green men. Just like I told you."

"It's not the green ones I'm worried about, John," says Montague, refusing to be humoured, and he takes another thoughtful look at the patients on the surveillance monitors, wondering why he'd not bumped into any during his tour. "Just how many inmates do you have here, precisely?"

"You make them sound like prisoners," laughs Dawson. "Look at them," he adds, tapping a screen where the happy-faced mah-jongg players are bantering over their play. "They're all very willing volunteers."

"Then why all the razor wire and armed goons?"

"The place is like a concentration camp," Bliss warns his Canadian counterpart as they turn off the highway and drive the forested road into the foothills.

"Another reason why I still think we should ask the locals for help," answers Phillips.

"Mike!" exclaims Bliss in exasperation. "I already tried that — remember? — and all I got was the bum's rush. Anyway, now that we've nicked a CIA motor, Prudenski and his mob wouldn't need an excuse to bang us up."

"We've only borrowed it, Dave," Phillips reminds him. "But I still don't see how we're going to get in."

"We'll just have to keep our heads down," replies Bliss. However, he's praying that the transponder stuck to the windshield will open the gates and clear a path through the minefield of tire shredders and armed guards, although he does have an insurance policy. "Pull over there," he says to Phillips as he spots the bar where he'd met the amused woodsman the night the Kidneymobile disappeared.

"Give us exactly two hours," he tells Daisy as he settles her in the saloon with a coffee and he hands her a list of phone numbers headed by those of CNN, the CBC and the BBC that he'd had Phillips draw up before leaving the border. "If we're not back, call Roger Cranley and the television people first," he tells her. "Then call the British and Canadian embassies in Washington."

"*Daavid*," she says worriedly. "Please be careful."

"I will …" he starts, but she grabs his shirt and hauls him to her lips.

"*Daavid*," she whispers, barely breaking her kiss.

"Yes …" he sighs as he drinks in the sweet warmth of her breath.

"Please throw zhat jacket away."

Martin Montague is on his way out through the front doors, although he's still uneasy with the spotty information he's received and the fact that, despite his desire to talk to patients and staff, Dawson has managed to head him off with darkly worded admonitions about the need for secrecy.

"I hope for your sake that this place is on the level," Montague says in a final warning as Dawson begins to close the door on him. But then the visitor stops and peers downs a lengthy corridor lined with closed doors. "What's down there?" he questions. "You didn't take me down there."

"It's just patients' rooms," shrugs Dawson. "You saw them on the monitors."

"Show me," insists Montague, turning down the hallway.

"Sorry — I can't," explains Dawson, pointing to the security keypad by the side of each door. "I don't have the codes. And we could jeopardize an entire program if we introduced a virus."

"Yeah, right," says Montague, but he keeps walking anyway.

The true extent of Daphne Lovelace's electrical engineering experience may be the replacement of a blown fuse in the cupboard under the stairs of her tidy house in Westchester, but she is undaunted as she beavers away at the wallboard until she has exposed all of the wires.

"Now what?" whispers Tina as she leans over the elderly saboteur's shoulder and peers at the myriad of coloured strands snaking to and from the control unit to various locks and sensors.

"It's very interesting," says Daphne, as if she knows exactly what she's looking at and merely needs a moment to decide what action will best achieve the desired outcome.

"You *do* know about these things?" questions Trina, with a touch of concern.

"Oh, yes, of course," lies Daphne, then she confidently wriggles a bunch of the wires, adding, "I learnt how to defuse land mines and make fertilizer bombs during the war, you know."

"Wow!" says Trina, taking a step backwards as if expecting the panel to explode.

However, the computer-controlled electronic sensing and locking mechanism is a world away from the primitive devices Daphne had worked on during her training as a resistance fighter in 1942, and even with an instruction manual she would have difficulty sorting out the multitude of wires.

"When in doubt ..." she muses to herself, then firmly grasps half a dozen wires and calls to Trina, "Are you ready?"

"I think so," says the other woman, as she limbers up with a few high kicks.

"Okay," says Daphne with her eyes closed and her grip tightening. "Get ready."

The sound of a lock clicking open spins Montague towards the women's door. He turns just as the door flies open, and Trina lets out a scream as she kick-boxes her way into the corridor.

"What the —" starts Montague, but he is totally off-guard as Trina leaps into the air and slams a foot into his face.

"Oh, Christ," mutters Dawson as he bends to help his falling comrade, but Daphne is also in fighting mode. She rushes out of the room and slams him over the head with a chair.

"Run, Trina!" yells Daphne, but Montague's beefy henchman acts as a backstop and, with the element of surprise gone, the two women are powerless.

"Okay … So, shall we start again, Mr. Dawson?" says Montague with twists of blood-soaked Kleenex stopping up his nose.

Resigned, Dawson deflates into his chair in the surveillance room. "Yes. All right."

"What the hell were you planning on doing with them?"

"I don't know."

"You don't know?!" screeches Montague.

"All right — we were going to liquidate them," admits Dawson.

"Brilliant strategy," scoffs Montague. "No wonder half the world thinks we're a bunch of cowboys."

"Look, sir. We screwed up, okay? But we had it under control until that English cop slipped his leash and started mouthing off to the press."

"Anything can happen when an agent goes rogue," agrees Montague, though he has his eyes on Dawson, not Bliss.

"Maybe we could do a deal with them — get them to sign something and let them go," suggests Dawson, brightening.

"You might have been able to in the first few hours. You should have just put them in a car and driven them to a hotel."

"I know that *now*," cries Dawson. "The trouble was that the old bird caught on right away."

The shrill ringing of the hotline from the gatehouse alerts Dawson to the possibility of more bad news, and he is tempted to let it go, but Montague picks up the phone and hands it to him, then watches the junior man's reaction.

"Well?" asks Montague when Dawson has taken the brief call.

"It's nothing, sir," he says, controlling his face.

"Just one of our delivery drivers hasn't reported in on schedule, that's all. His van's probably broken down."

Buzzer's van appears to be working perfectly, though Bliss and Phillips are unaware of the radio protocol that the CIA operative would have followed had he still been with his vehicle.

"It's only about a mile from here," says Bliss as he pulls off the road into a clearing from whence they can finalize their assault. "I just hope that Daisy doesn't jump the gun."

"She seems pretty sensible," says Phillips, trying to ease the tension.

"The best I've ever met," admits Bliss. "And if I get out of this mess in one piece — well, who knows."

"So. How do we get out?" questions Phillips, hoping Bliss has a plan, but beyond slipping through the gates in Buzzer's guise, Bliss is as much in the dark as his colleague.

"We'll just have to play it by ear," he replies. "I'm just hoping that they rely on the perimeter defences for security. Once we're inside, we should be safe."

"Until we try to get out," adds Phillips ominously.

"Oh, well. Here goes," says Bliss, turning the key. But nothing happens.

"Shit!" he mutters, and both men immediately know the problem.

"It's got an ignition cut-out switch," suggests Phillips, and he's not at all surprised when, milliseconds later, a piercing security alarm sends a murder of raucous crows into the air above the surrounding forest.

Half an hour later the two detectives are still tinkering under the hood of the van, while, not far away, Daphne and Trina have been elevated to a new world. Dawson has squeezed a gathering of surgeons out of their private lounge, and, while Montague's right-hand man might be standing sentinel at the door, the station chief is, in his own words to the women, "determined to establish who is responsible for this unfortunate situation, and taking every possible step to bring it to a satisfactory conclusion as soon as circumstances permit."

"That was a mouthful," Daphne had muttered under her breath as Montague left.

"I wish I hadn't kicked him so hard now," says Trina as she tucks into a plate of smoked-salmon sandwiches. "He looked kind'a pathetic with that tissue stuck up his nose."

"Well, I wish I'd hit the other one a damn sight harder," confesses Daphne.

It may be nearing midnight Friday across the Atlantic in London, but Montague is high enough up the ladder to have yanked a U.S. Embassy cultural attaché out of a West End strip club. The man, a CIA plant with more connections than the Internet, had only taken minutes to report back.

"What do they know about her?" asks Dawson, once Montague has put down the phone.

"You're not going to like this," says Montague, and Dawson's headache worsens when he discovers that, thanks to Bliss's outburst at the morning press conference, Daphne has taken on celebrity status. "Apparently, she's some kind of hero."

"What?"

"Yeah, you idiot. That woman you and your clowns locked up has the Order of the British Empire for intelligence work."

"Christ! She must be at least eighty."

"Maybe nearer ninety, from what I hear. But don't knock it. She's the one who infiltrated your supposedly impenetrable establishment."

"Yeah, but —"

"And disabled a sophisticated security system."

"Okay. But who the hell is she?"

"She was some kind of special agent during the Cold War."

Dawson exhales a breath of deep understanding. "So that's how she got Allan eating out of her hand."

"Allan?" questions Montague, still ignorant of another agent's involvement.

"One of the guards," says Dawson, sloughing off his injured junior without explanation.

"Let's face it, John, the fact you were taken by a geriatric foreign agent is not gonna look good in your annual report."

However, his annual report is the least of Dawson's concerns. "Look, sir. Can't we keep this quiet?"

Montague gives Dawson a cagey look, and leads him sideways. "And how would you propose to do that, John?"

"There are drugs ..." he starts, and Montague plays along.

"Really?"

"Yeah. Just enough to screw their memories up. Then we could ditch them in the forest somewhere. What d'ye think?"

"I think you need some psychological adjustment, mister. Now, do they know what you're doing here?"

"They guessed —"

"No. You're not listening to me," warns Montague. "Do they know?"

"No ... not as far as I know. Not specifically."

"Good," says Montague, starting to rise. "In that case, have my man get my car. We'll take the ladies home."

"You can't —"

"Mr. Dawson, I don't have the authority to relieve you of duty ..." starts Montague, eyeing the junior man fiercely. "But I'm certainly authorized to shoot you as a dangerous lunatic. So I suggest you get my car."

"But they'll talk."

"Well, I'm gonna ask them real nice on behalf of the president not to. But then I'm coming back for a discussion with you. By which time, I'm sure you'll have some answers — *capisce?*"

"Got it," says Phillips, having rewired half of the van's ignition system, and the engine bursts into life as Bliss turns the key.

"Thank God for that," mutters Bliss, then he checks his watch. "We've still got nearly an hour before Daisy starts phoning."

"We'd better get moving, then," says Phillips as he slams the hood and leaps into the passenger seat. "Although I still think we must be crazy."

Bliss drops the van into gear but he doesn't pull away. "Mike," he says seriously, "this isn't really your problem. You can bail if you want to. I'd understand."

"No ..."

"Look. You've got a pregnant wife waiting for you —"

"Yeah. And you've got Daisy waiting for you," Phillips reminds him as he takes out his pistol and checks it over. "So put your damn foot on the gas and let's make some waves."

"I hope you won't need that," says Bliss, as the heavy van lumbers onto the road, and Phillips agrees.

"It won't do much good if they open up with machine guns again."

"Why would they?" asks Bliss. "It's *their* van. We'll be okay as long as we just drive in as though we own the place."

Less than a mile ahead of the two detectives, the gates are swinging open and a black Mercedes silently glides out onto the road.

"Steve!" yells a panicky Dawson into his cell phone as the gates close behind Montague's car. "They've gone. But they took the women."

"What? Okay, I'll get some wheels," says Bumface without a moment's hesitation. "Grab some artillery. We've gotta stop 'em."

"Steve … I don't know —"

"Shit! Are you crazy? It's perfect. We'll hit 'em on the freeway. With any luck they'll smack into a big rig. We can take 'em all out in one go."

"Are you comfortable, ladies?" asks Montague as he turns from the front passenger seat and smiles at the two women in the rear.

"Yes, thank you," says Daphne warily. "But who are you and where are we going?"

"We are taking you back to Canada —" he says, but Trina cuts him off.

"How do we know that? They've been promising to let us go since Wednesday."

"Please, Mrs. Button," continues Montague softly, "it was all a big mistake. Now just sit back and enjoy the ride. We'll soon have you home."

"Get ready," says Bliss as he prepares to round the final few bends before the entrance to the bogus monastery. "It'll be coming up on our — what the hell?" he exclaims as the Mercedes skims past in the other direction.

"What is it?" asks Phillips.

"That was Daphne," breathes Bliss, almost in disbelief, having caught a glimpse of the woman with her face earnestly glued to the side window as she tries to record landmarks.

"What?" demands Phillips in amazement.

"It was Daphne — in that car," Bliss shouts excitedly as he slams on the brakes.

"Are you sure?"

"Yes … no — I don't know," wavers Bliss as the van slews to a halt. "It was so fast and she was in the back."

"Quick, turn around. Let's check it out."

"Oh, shit. We've got trouble," mutters Montague a few minutes later as he spots the white van closing in from behind.

"What's up, boss?"

"I thought he'd pull a stunt like this," spits Montague. "Research, my ass. Put your foot down, Nick. There's a couple of heavies on your tail." Then he spins to the two women in the back seat. "You'd better get down, ladies. Get down as low as you can."

"They've spotted us," mutters Bliss as the Mercedes suddenly speeds away from them, then he sees the gun as Montague leans out of the window. "Oh, Christ! He's shooting!" he exclaims as the pistol recoils. Then he starts weaving erratically, hoping to dodge a bullet.

Phillips drops the passenger window and has his gun at the ready, but Bliss reaches over to pull him back.

"No, Mike," he yells. "They might crash."

The heavy van is no match for the Mercedes on the straight, but Bliss knows the twists and turns of the forest road better than Montague's driver and manages to keep the car within sight for a few miles. However, half a ton of wet salmon slopping from side to side has him constantly fighting the wheel as he broadsides around bend after bend. "We'll never keep up in this," he shouts, as he cuts a blind corner with a silent prayer, but Mike Phillips is on his cell phone checking out the registration of the fleeing car.

"You're right, Dave," he says after a few minutes. "It's registered to an import company that's a known cover for the CIA."

"They're moving them to a safer spot, Mike."

"Yeah. Your warning on TV worked," admits Phillips. "But it won't do us any good if they get away."

"I know that!" shouts Bliss as they near the bar where Daisy is waiting. "I'm gonna leap out and get the car," he adds. "Get ready to take over."

Daisy is staring anxiously out of the bar's window with one eye on her watch, though she's not expecting the reappearance of the van, and she's on her feet and at the door in a second as it slides to a halt in a hail of gravel.

"Hey. You haven't paid —" yells the barman as she heads for her car. "Jesus, what is it with these foreigners?" he mutters in disgust. "Don't they ever pay?"

"Keys!" yells Bliss to Daisy as Phillips scorches away in the van, and in seconds he is back on the trail of the Mercedes with the Frenchwoman beside him.

"What's happening?" she asks, but Bliss is focusing on the road.

"We've got to catch them," he says as he lunges the car through bend after bend until the van is in sight.

The large vehicle is swaying dangerously from side to side with the weight of wet fish as Phillips desperately tries to catch up to the fleeing Mercedes, but he's blocking Bliss's path.

"This is worse than England," moans Bliss as he jinks from side to side, seeking an opening. "Get out of the bloody way, Mike," he screams as he leans on the horn, and Phillips finally pulls over. Now, with a clear road, Bliss throws the car furiously at the bends, and he feels the tires sliding on the damp pavement as he slams his foot from throttle to brake and back again, but there is no sign of the Mercedes.

"We've got to catch them soon," he tells himself, knowing that he'll have only a fifty-fifty chance of choosing the right direction once they hit the freeway.

Buzzer's van quickly recedes in Bliss's mirror. It has taken a couple of hits from Montague's pistol and is beginning to falter, while behind it, Dawson and his henchman hustle to join the race.

"It's Buzzer," says Bumface in surprise as the two men find themselves balked by the meandering vehicle. "What the hell is he doing?"

"Get out of the way!" screeches Bumface, leaning out of the window.

"You can wait," mutters Phillips, and he ignores the flashing headlights and blaring horn of the trailing vehicle as he sticks to the crown of the road.

"I'll call him," suggests Bumface, but Buzzer isn't answering his cell phone this afternoon.

In the Mercedes, Station Chief Montague is also on the phone — he's spotted his persuers and is calling the police in Bellingham, giving a description of Bliss's car and asking for backup.

By the time they hit the main highway, Mike Phillips in the van is all but out of the race. Alarming noises from the engine compartment suggest that Montague's shells may have penetrated some vital organ, and the temperature gauge hit the top several miles ago. However, Bliss is still in the hunt. Daisy had spotted the Mercedes taking the ramp onto the freeway and they are hastening northwards with the fleeing car in sight.

"This thing won't go any faster," moans Bliss with his foot on the floor as he weaves through streams of traffic, and he is beginning to wonder if he'll ever catch up when the surrounding traffic begins to slow.

"It is zhe police," says Daisy, turning at the sound of sirens.

"Mike must have called them," says Bliss thankfully when he checks his mirrors and finds the flashing lights of three police cars fanned out across the highway behind him. Other cruisers are racing to catch up, and a loud throbbing in the air alerts him to the presence of a helicopter hovering overhead.

"Thank God for that!" whoops Bliss. "Good old Mike."

But after a moment's elation there is the dawning of unease in his mind as he looks ahead and sees that the car containing the captive women appears to be headed straight for the Canadian border.

"What is zhe matter, *Daavid?*" asks Daisy, sensing a problem as the line of cruisers catch up to them.

"This is the police. Pull over or we'll shoot," commands a voice through the loudhailer of the lead vehicle.

"What?" utters Bliss disbelievingly.

"Pull over or we'll shoot," repeats the officer as if hearing him.

Daisy's presence in the car dissuades Bliss from trying to outrun the officers, and with the border in sight, he's confident that the Mercedes will be stopped, so he brakes to a halt.

"Get out of the car with your hands in the air," commands the voice as officers leap from their vehicles and take up firing positions.

"This is bloody ridiculous," says Bliss, getting out but not complying.

"Put your hands on your head. Put your hands on your head!" screams the voice maniacally.

"Will you stop messing around?" shouts Bliss, unfazed by the fact that ten officers have their weapons trained on him. "I'm a police officer."

"Stop where you are. Get down on the ground," the orders continue with increasing insistence.

"Oh, give it a rest," says Bliss, strolling towards them with his empty hands spread wide.

"Hit the ground. Hit the ground," continues the stentorian voice, but then one of the officers slowly stands up and lowers his weapon.

"Oh, no. Not *you* again," sighs Captain Prudenski, and he waves for his officers to lower their weapons.

"Thank God," says Bliss, then he frantically points at the fleeing Mercedes. "But you're letting them get away with the women."

John Dawson and his henchman keep their heads down behind the cordon of police cruisers and the backed-up traffic, while Mike Phillips, with smoke belching from under the hood of Buzzer's van, drives along the hard shoulder, screeches to halt and races towards the officers with his RCMP badge in hand.

"Stop that Mercedes! Stop that Mercedes!" he is yelling, but the vehicle is already slowing for the border control.

"Take it easy, Mister," says Prudenski. "They're CIA officers."

"I know that," says Bliss. "Why the hell doesn't anyone listen to me? That place you call a monastery is an undercover CIA operation."

"Really?" says Prudenski, as if surprised.

"Don't tell me you didn't know."

"Not until fifteen minutes ago."

"The women were there, like I told you. Now you've let them get away. They're in that car."

"Yeah, I know that," admits Prudenski, making no attempt to chase after the vehicle.

"Well, why won't you stop them?"

"Because," he says with a smirk, "they're taking the women back to Canada."

"What?"

"And they thought that you were trying to stop them."

"We were ..." Bliss is admitting when a muffled explosion spins them around, and several officers hit the ground simultaneously.

"Oh, shit," mutters Phillips at the sight of Buzzer's white van engulfed in an inferno. "There goes Roger Cranley's evidence."

chapter sixteen

Daphne Lovelace looks more like an elderly aunt returning from an afternoon's mystery bus tour than someone who has just eluded the Grim Reaper as she and Trina step out of the Mercedes at the U.S. customs post.

"Hello, David," she calls with a smile and a wave, and the sun finally shines after three rainy days.

"Are you all right?" Bliss asks, leaping from Daisy's rented Toyota and dashing towards the woman.

"I lost my bloomin' hat," she moans, as if that is the most important issue. "But otherwise, yes, we're fine — aren't we, Trina?"

"Are you sure?"

"Yes, we're all right, David. They were just a bunch of amateurs."

"They didn't touch you, did they?" asks Phillips, running up to peer into Trina's eyes.

"Oh! No," shrieks Trina. "And Wilting Willy was quite nice really."

"Wilting Willy?" queries Mike Phillips.

"Of course, his real name was Spotty Dick," admits Trina conspiratorially, "but I thought he looked more like a Wilting Willy."

"Oh. I see …"

A large Buick with deeply tinted windows drives slowly up to the border. Bumface, in the passenger seat, has a sub-machine gun across his lap and he would happily wipe out the entire assembly, but the area is swarming with police and customs officers.

"I think it's time we got out of here," says Dawson as he sees the women relating their story, and he slowly turns the car and doubles back.

"I'd better phone my office and let them know that the women are safe," says Phillips, but Trina whips the cell phone out of his hand as he begins to call.

"Hey!" he protests, but he's wasting his time.

"I gotta call Rick," she says, as if she is entitled.

"Hey, Rob. It's me — your mom," she yells excitedly into the phone when her teenage son answers. "I'm back."

"Oh. Hi, Mom," Rob says cheerily, adding. "Hey — is Daisy with you?"

"Yeah …"

"Oh, great. She makes awesome sandwiches."

"It's definitely a hospital," Daphne is explaining to Bliss and Phillips. "I smelt it as soon as we arrived. And most of the people I saw were in wheelchairs or walking with sticks. But they were all Chinese."

"Or Korean?" questions Phillips.

"Perhaps. Although they might even have been Vietnamese or Cambodian."

"What were zhey in for?" asks Daisy as she hangs on to Bliss's arm.

Daphne shrugs. "I was more interested in getting us out of there, to be honest."

"Daphne was terrific," gushes Trina while she waits for someone on the other end of the phone to wake her husband. "I thought my guinea pig was good at escaping, but Daphne could winkle an elephant out of a mouse hole." She goes on to recount details of Daphne's various breakout bids as Montague hovers sheepishly in the shadows.

"Daphne Lovelace, you are absolutely amazing," says Bliss, gathering his elderly friend in his arms once Trina has finished.

"Oh, it was nothing, David," she says, brushing it off. "I once saved my life with a packet of chocolate digestive biscuits."

"I remember that," laughs Bliss, and he continues to warmly hug the old lady, saying, "All's well that ends well."

"But what about Minnie? And what about all the others who killed themselves?" asks Daphne, breaking free.

"Oh! I was supposed to call Peter," says Bliss, checking his watch. "He said he had a lead."

"Well?" queries Daphne.

"It's nearly two in the morning there," he says, making it clear that he won't be calling till later. Then he turns coldly to Montague. "There's obviously something very dodgy going on up at that monastery place."

"That's why I tried to warn you off the other day," admits Montague.

"Brilliant," says Bliss. "And I was supposed to know that?"

"Okay, point taken," says Montague. "But I didn't want to jeopardize the establishment's cover if it was an authorized operation."

"Well, is it?"

Montague hesitates, reluctant to disclose that he's not in the loop. "We're getting a fix on that," he says, giving nothing away.

"So what exactly are they doing?"

"Now, that would be classified."

"Even if it's a rogue operation?"

"*Especially* if it's a rogue operation," says Montague, adding with an embarrassed laugh, "Come on, Chief Inspector. You don't really expect me to admit that some of my colleagues may have gone off the rails a little, do you?"

"My guess is that it's probably a zealous bunch of CIA creeps with a scheme to circumvent inconvenient legislation," suggests Phillips as he pulls Bliss to one side.

"Would they do that?" questions Bliss.

"Hey, what won't rogue CIA types do? Ollie North sold missiles to Iran and got away with it. He even ended up running for the presidency."

"And what does that tell you about the so-called leadership of the free world?" Bliss wants to know.

"Nothing changes, Dave. Absolute power corrupts absolutely. You know that," says Phillips. "Christ, the CIA were involved in Watergate, Whitewater, Irangate and Monicagate in the last few years alone, so why should they be upfront about some dodgy enterprise just because a couple of inconvenient busybodies stumbled across it?"

"I'd love to know what they're playing at."

Station Chief Montague would also like some answers, and he has slipped into the customs office to report to his deputy director — the head of the Operations Directorate in Langley.

"Our involvement has to be kept out of this," the deputy director warns him sternly before he's had a chance to explain his findings.

"But you told me to look into it."

"And now I'm telling you to forget it, Martin. Just get back to your station ASAP and keep your head down, all right?"

"So the Firm *is* involved, then?"

"Martin, it's not under my purview. That's all I can tell you," says the deputy, while not admitting that, since Bliss's performance at the press conference, papers are being shredded and hard drives wiped throughout the CIA headquarters building.

"I'd still like to know what's going on," presses Montague. "It may not be our department, but it sure as hell affects our clients."

"Sorry — I'm not at liberty to tell you, Martin, although it's been put on the admin director's radar screen. He'll deny all knowledge of course, although God knows what he'll say if the White House starts asking."

"Is there a lid on it?" Montague wants to know.

"Man, there'd better be. Our credibility is still in the toilet after the Iraqi deal."

"Hey, that was nothing to do with my section," protests Montague.

"I know that. But the whole house stinks when someone shits on the floor."

"So what happens now?"

"I understand there's a team of cleaners going in as we speak."

The "cleaners" have been on the move since Bliss's early morning outburst. Four carloads of heavy men lugging giant sports bags — pro footballers en route to a game, perhaps — had flown into a quiet corner of Sea-Tac Airport in Learjets, well away from the throng of regular travellers. And if any of the air traffic controllers happen to comment on the sudden increase in hastily arranged flight plans, they will be firmly reminded of their responsibilities as federal officials.

Further south, in the fenced compound of an industrial warehouse near Portland, Oregon, a fleet of blank-sided removal trucks are being warmed up for an overnight excursion by drivers who don't have to be told of the need for secrecy.

Montague is also doing his best to quieten things down at the border, and he pulls Bliss aside and holds out a hand in reconciliation.

"I just want you to know that I'm sorry about the other day, Chief Inspector."

"No problem — water under the bridge and all that," says Bliss, though inwardly he's seething at his waste of three anxiety-filled days.

Montague senses the stiffness in the Englishman's hand and decides to sweeten the pot. "By the way," he says, drawing a chequebook from his pocket, "we'd like to pick up the tab for the damage to your rental car."

"Thanks ..."

"How much was it — five thousand?"

"Yes ..."

"And what say we add a little extra for all the inconvenience," he muses as he makes the cheque out to "Cash." "Now. Is there anything more I can do?" he continues as he hands it over.

"Actually, there is," replies Bliss, folding the cheque into his pocket without a glance, and five minutes later he's in possession of a three-month U.S. visitor's visa with a promise that it will be renewed as often, and for as long, as he requires.

"Please enjoy the hospitality of our wonderful country," says Montague with an expansive grin, but Bliss barely masks his sour thoughts as he sneers, "That's very kind of you, but my girlfriend goes back to France tomorrow morning, and I leave Sunday."

"Oh, well. Come back and visit any old time."

That's interesting, Bliss muses silently as he walks away, feeling odd that, in middle age, he is still referring to his current love interest as a girl.

The commotion on the southern side of the border has spilled northwards to Canada, drawing Roger Cranley and a few of his colleagues to investigate.

"I brought the van back, as promised," Mike Phillips tells Cranley as he points down the highway to where the fire department is dampening down the smouldering heap by the side of the road.

"Oh, great!"

"Don't blame me. It was friendly fire," Phillips steps in quickly, and he points to Montague as the villain. "By the way," he queries, "what's happening with the two CIA men?"

"Don't ask," sighs Cranley in exasperation, then explains. "We had to hand them over to their own people."

"What?"

"The U.S. was threatening to shut down the border and inflict various other unspecified punishments if we didn't."

"So, what's the story with the Koreans?"

"We don't know, and we've been ordered not to interview them."

"Who says?"

"Whoever's squeezing the prime minister's balls."

"CIA?" questions Phillips, and he gets a nod in response.

"It's almost certainly a case of trafficking; plus, we've got no idea where all the money came from."

"Maybe I should call Peter after all," says Bliss, recalling his son-in-law's mention of a Canadian connection.

"Christ, Dad, do you know what the bloody time is here?" moans Samantha a few seconds later.

"Yes. Sorry, love, but it's important."

"It's nearly three in the morning, Dave," moans Peter Bryan once his new wife has woken him.

"I didn't expect you to be asleep," jokes Bliss. "You've only been married a few weeks."

"Very funny, Dave. But what the hell have you been up to?"

"You wouldn't believe me if I told you," laughs Bliss, once he has explained that Daphne and Trina are back in the fold.

"Well, you won't believe this, either," says Bryan, then he summarizes Maurice Joliffe's bungled bank heist before explaining that the elderly man had planned on sending the money to Canada to free up his lottery winnings.

"Oh, my God ..." breathes Bliss, catching on immediately. "Minnie Dennon's round-the-world trip."

"Exactly, Dave. What's the betting that she also got a late-night transatlantic call — and why settle for half the winnings if all it took was her life savings and a small bank loan to secure the lot?"

"And the admonition to tell no one would make perfect sense," carries on Bliss. "After all, who needs a demand from the taxman or a pile of begging letters anyway?"

"I think that amounts to the same thing," agrees Bryan with a laugh.

"Hah! What a con," says Bliss, imagining the embarrassment the elderly woman would have suffered if she had been forced to admit to Daphne that, not only were they not going around the world, but for the rest of her life she wouldn't even be able to afford to take the bus to visit her friend. "No wonder the poor old soul killed herself."

"We think they've probably scammed hundreds — maybe thousands," carries on Bryan. "Although I'm guessing that many will be too mortified to admit they've been taken, and some can probably afford it. It's only the ones that can't that are ending up on the tracks or in the canal."

"And let me speculate," says Bliss. "Mr. Joliffe was supposed to send the money to —"

"CNL Distribution of Canada," says Bryan, beating him to the punchline.

"Peter's cracked the suicide problem, Mike," Bliss tells Phillips, once he's drawn the detective away from the rest of the group. "Daphne's friend, Minnie, won ten million dollars in the Canadian National Lottery."

"And then she killed herself?"

"Seems like it."

"What a strange thing to do — wait a minute ... there *is* no Canadian National Lottery."

"I guessed that," says Bliss, and he waits a moment for his colleague to catch on.

"Okay," says Phillips. "What's the scam?"

"It was still murder," insists Daphne, once Bliss has given her the news. "Whoever took Minnie's money threw her into the path of that train just as surely as young Ronnie Stapleton."

"If it was classed as murder we'd have the highest homicide rate in the world," replies Bliss. "Do you realize how many people get scammed and never report it because they are too humiliated?"

"Most of them don't kill themselves, though."

"True," admits Bliss, "though con artists never think about what happens to the mark when they're chasing a fast buck."

"Oh, David," laughs Daphne. "You're beginning to sound very American and you've only been here a week."

"Four days," he reminds her, "though it seems more like a month."

The past few days have also stretched to eternity for John Dawson, and as he and his partner take the road back to their cloister in the forest he is praying for some kind of salvation.

"We're finished if Montague or the women go public," he warns Bumface, as if he's just had a revelation.

"You should've let me drop 'em when I wanted to," replies the passenger without compassion.

"I wish I had."

"It's that cop who bothers me most," admits Bumface. "I can't see Montague saying anything — not outside of the Firm anyway — and who's gonna believe a couple of dozy women who got lost in a freakin' bathtub? But if Bliss keeps shooting his mouth off ..."

"Yeah, I know," starts Dawson, but the approach of a convoy of limousines in his mirror stops him.

"Don't look," he warns, and he slows and pulls to the side to let the cars speed past.

"Let's let Allan do the explaining, shall we?" says Bumface, reaching over to put his hand on the wheel and indicate that they should turn around.

"What about the cash?"

"I chucked about half a million in the trunk. It'll do us for a while, and we can always phone for more."

"Very clever," says Dawson, preparing to turn, though he has a wary eye on his colleague as he adds, "I hope you weren't thinking of taking off without me."

"John!" protests Bumface, though his apparent denial lacks conviction.

"I'd better get back to my wife," says Phillips, and he turns with a smile for Trina and Daphne. "Can I give you two ladies a ride to Vancouver?"

"What about you and Daisy?" Trina asks Bliss. "I've got a spare bedroom in the basement suite, if you'd like."

Bliss is holding firmly onto to Daisy's hand and he gives it a reassuring squeeze. "Thanks, Trina," he says, shaking his head, "but I expect we can manage in our little wooden shack in the forest just for tonight." Then he turns seriously to Daphne. "Perhaps you should come home with me on Sunday after what's happened."

"Hey, are you kiddin'?" she says with a passable American accent. "I was promised a holiday, and I'm going to make sure I get one. Anyway, Trina wants me to help plan the kidney marathon."

"You're not still going ahead with that, are you?" asks Bliss incredulously.

"Of course," says Trina. "People didn't stop needing kidneys just because we had a little problem. Anyway,

I've had this brilliant idea — though I'll be needing a lot of volunteers."

"Oh, I'm sure David would like to help — wouldn't you?" says Daphne, dragging Bliss into the spotlight.

"Well …"

"It's not until next summer."

"Go on, *Daavid*," encourages Daisy. "It is for a good cause."

"Maybe," he says warily. "You'll have to let me know what you would want me to do."

chapter seventeen

The warning shrieks of bald eagles electrify the tree-tops as they look down from their high perches in the foothills of Mount Baker and see an approaching car.

"Eagles!" calls Bliss excitedly, spying the piebald birds in the crimson blush of the setting sun as he and Daisy drive up the long track to their remote lodge.

"Zhis is so beautiful," whispers Daisy, craning to see into the canopy of the rainforest.

"I just hope they haven't re-let the place," Bliss laughs, only half-jokingly, as he pulls up to the door of the log cabin in the fading light, then scrabbles under a pot of geraniums for the key. But nothing has changed: the fresh smell of pine mingles with the smoky memory of a log fire; the evening light streaming through the west-facing window adds a comforting glow; the view from the balcony, across the valley to Puget Sound and the distant snow-capped peak of Mount Olympus, has not been marred by the days of stress. And, while the maid might have suspiciously eyed the unruffled bed and untouched

toiletries each morning, she had not informed the pro-
prietors of the lovebirds' apparent absence — after all, an
hour's pay is an hour's pay — so the luxurious cabin is as
neat and clean as it had been on their arrival.

"Oh, *Daavid,* zhis is so *romantique,*" says Daisy as
he makes a play of carrying her over the threshold into
the cozy nook.

"Finally," he says, kissing her gently, then laying her
on the settee in front of the fieldstone fireplace. "Now,
you just stay there," he tells her. "I'll light the fire, open
some champagne and get the food from the car."

The kindling catches quickly, although the room is
already warm from a few hours of evening sun. The
champagne, a Veuve Clicquot which has been cooling its
heels in the fridge since Monday, bursts exuberantly into
chilled glasses, and an assortment of Chinese goodies,
cooked up by a real Chinese chef in Seattle's Chinatown,
is being re-energized in the microwave.

"It'll only take a minute or so," says Bliss, slipping
into the living room to place chopsticks on the table as
an excuse for another kiss.

"Shall we eat on the balcony?" suggests Daisy,
reaffirming her Mediterranean preference for everything *en plein air*, and Bliss is quick to agree.

"I'll grab some candles," he says, bouncing joyfully
back to the kitchen.

The waning moon, still beneath the eastern horizon,
leaves the stage to the stars and, un-shadowed by city
lights, the heavens put on a show that takes the couple's
breath away.

"Orion, the Big Dipper, Mars, Jupiter ..." points
out Daisy as her finger traces the sky, then Bliss takes
hold and steers it to his favourite planet.

"Venus," he says softly before guiding the finger to his lips.

"Oh. *Daavid*," Daisy giggles, but she stops when the splash of headlights lazes through the forest from the road below. "Is zhat a car?"

"Probably another cottager," says Bliss, scanning the surrounding hillside for signs of occupation, though finding none. "Or someone who is lost."

Bliss is wrong. The car's occupants know exactly where they are going, though one of them, John Dawson, isn't convinced it's a good idea.

"I just wann'a few words with him, that's all," snarls Bumface in the driver's seat. "Make sure he keeps his freakin' mouth shut in future."

"And you're sure this is the right place?"

Bumface nods. "It's what he put on his visa application." But Dawson is still wary. "Look, Steve," he tries. "We've got some money. We're in the clear. Why screw it up?"

"C'mon, John. How long d'ye think it'll take 'em to find us?"

"South America's a big place, Steve. Anyway, we only did what we were told."

"Well, the lottery thing wasn't exactly kosher ..." carries on Bumface, tuning out his partner.

"Plausible deniability, they call it, Steve," mutters Dawson, also not listening. "As far as I was concerned, it was all okayed by the White House."

"It was fun though, wasn't it?" laughs Bumface, continuing his own conversation. "Congratulations, Bob — you greedy freakin' moron — you've just fallen for the oldest trick ..." he cackles with the same infectious enthusiasm he'd employed to scam Minnie, Joliffe and the dozens of other victims, then he turns to Dawson with a smile on his face. "Can you believe how freakin' happy they were, John?"

"So were the patients," Dawson reminds him, still on his own track.

"The one I liked best was the old bird who wanted to send an extra fifty bucks," laughs Bumface, without a thought to the carnage he has caused. "'Buy your kiddies a little prezzy from me, dear,' she told me, and she was bawling her eyes out, she was so freakin' happy."

"It kind'a gave you a good feeling, didn't it?" admits Dawson, recalling the times that he'd been whooping in the background, becoming so wrapped up in the joy of someone's apparent good fortune that he had overlooked the fact he was sending them down a black tunnel from which many might never escape. "That's why I reckon we should just cut and run," he continues. "We can set up anywhere and do it again."

"Not until I've had words, John," says the driver, his face set on the muddy lane winding through the woods to Bliss's cabin. "He screwed up the entire operation and I wann'a leave him with a little reminder."

"Hot and sour soup, sweet and sour prawns, and honey-garlic ribs," announces Bliss, as he lays the dishes on the rustic picnic table, while above him the crescent moon rises over the mountains and adds a warm glow to the cold starlight. But the chilly evening air is already sapping some of the heat out of the occasion, and Bliss's buoyant mood is sinking with the memories of the three anxious days and nights he had spent searching for the women.

"I thought I was going mad," he confesses as they start to eat. "I was beginning to wonder if it was just some crazy dream."

"It is over now," Daisy gently reminds him. "Everyone is all right."

But while Bliss is certainly grateful for the safe return of the women, he has a growing resentment over their treatment. "It's Daphne I'm thinking about. She can't afford to lose three days. It's not as though she's got that many left."

"Oh, I zhink zhat maybe it was a little exciting for her."

"Actually, I think you're right," admits Bliss with a laugh. "And Trina seemed to think it was just a lark. Although she thinks *everything* is a lark. Did you hear what she wanted me to do for her fundraising stunt?" he asks disbelievingly.

"Zhere is a car," Daisy says in surprise, hearing the sound of an engine closing in on them, though Bliss is still preoccupied with dark thoughts of Trina.

"I can't believe that woman at times."

"It is going to one of zhe other cabins, I expect," says Daisy, and her suspicion is apparently confirmed a few seconds later when the engine dies.

Beneath them, where the muddy lane from the cabin meets the road, two figures emerge from the parked car and meld into the cover of the trackside trees.

"I bet that Captain Prudenski was in on it from the beginning," Bliss is complaining, unfazed by the car's arrival. "All the time he and his men were so-called searching — I bet they knew exactly what was going on."

"Never mind, *Daavid*. You were right."

"I know, but it's very frustrating when everything you do fails. Sometimes I wonder why everyone else seems to slip so easily through life when I keep hitting the rough edges."

"But it is exciting?" suggests Daisy. "Zhat is what policemen do, is it not?"

"Maybe ... although I think I've had my fill of adventures," he says with a tone of finality. "That's why I was happy when they gave me a cushy number at Interpol. And look where that led me."

The dense forest absorbs the sound of movement as Dawson and his partner climb the hillside towards the cabin, but their progress is slow as they sneak carefully through the undergrowth and hide in the shadows. Then the five-gallon gas can in Bumface's hand clunks heavily against the stump of a felled tree as he stumbles in the twilight.

"Shush," warns Dawson, reaching out to stop his partner, and he uses his machine gun to point to an easier route.

"What gets me ..." Bliss continues, intending to whine about the blasé attitude of Montague as he pulls the CIA station chief's cheque from his pocket. Then he freezes in disbelief.

"Fifty-five thousand dollars," he breathes, and he quickly shoves the piece of paper under the candle for confirmation. "Oh my God! He's added fifty grand."

"What is zhat, David?"

"Hush money, Daisy. That's what it is," he fumes. "The bastard thinks he's bought me off."

"But zhat is a lot of money. What will you do?"

"First thing — I'm not cashing it," he carries on, angrily standing up and storming around. "They're not gonna buy my silence."

"*Daavid* — zhis is our last night together," Daisy reminds him.

"I'm sorry," he says, realizing that the worries of the past three days are scratching the gloss off his romantic plans, and he drops to his knees at her feet and peers into her eyes. "Daisy," he continues, "would you move to England if I asked you?"

"*Oui*. I zhink so."

"Thank you. Thank you very much," he says before kissing her again, then he leaps to his feet. "I won't be long. I've got something for you," he says, and he tops up their champagne glasses before bouncing back into the cabin and heading for the bedroom. He has an important question in his mind — a question he would have asked on Monday night, had he not fallen asleep; on Tuesday, had they not been tearing around in search of the Kidneymobile; on Wednesday, had they not been in different countries; and Thursday if he hadn't been so concerned about the fate of the missing women. But now it's Friday, and all the clouds have lifted. "So," he questions as he takes an antique diamond engagement ring from his suitcase and balances it in his palm, "what are you waiting for? Do you think she would prefer a new one?"

"That's the phone line," whispers Bumface, pointing to the terminal box at the base of a telegraph pole just below the cabin, and he quickly wrenches out the wires.

"Go for it," Bliss tells himself as he buffs the large diamond, but memories of Sarah, his ex-wife, glue his feet to the bedroom floor.

"You're never home — not when it matters," her voice echoes in his mind as he recalls her griping over his struggle to balance career and family.

I've changed, he tries telling himself, but he can't escape the way he's neglected his French friend since Monday. *That was different,* he protests.

"*Daavid* ..." calls Daisy, suddenly chilled by a rustling in the undergrowth beneath the balcony.

"Coming," he says, but he's still stalling as the woman in his thoughts accuses him of neglecting her in his quest to solve other people's problems — frequently slogging into the early hours, and throughout weekends and holidays.

"Most criminals don't work nine to five, Monday to Friday," he had often attempted to explain, but it had rarely mollified her.

"*Daavid*. Are you coming?" calls Daisy with a concerned edge to her voice, beginning to fear that it may be a cougar or a bear skulking in the bush.

Ten feet beneath her, in the dark shadow of the wooden decking, Bumface is carefully emptying the gas can into the brushwood. "Are ya ready?" he whispers to his associate as he ferrets in his pocket for a box of matches.

Dawson clicks off the safety of his machine gun. "Guess so," he says, with little enthusiasm.

"Get up there, then," Bumface continues in hushed tones as he nods up the wooded slope towards the front of the cabin. "And get ready to zap him."

"What have you got to lose?" muses Bliss, pushing himself towards the bedroom door, but Sarah still stands in his way, complaining about the amount of time he'd spent in the company of robbers, murderers and rapists. "It's my job," he had objected honestly, but now he is haunted by the recollection as he considers his future with Daisy.

"*Daavid …*"

"I'll be right there!" he calls with his hand on the door. "No going back," he warns himself as he takes the next step, then he pauses to worry. *What if she turns me down?* She said she'd move to England. *But what about her mother and grandmother? She's an only child — will she leave them?*

"*Daavid … I zhink I heard something …*" Daisy is saying when the *whoosh* of an inferno and an explosive burst of gunfire rip through the forest, sending Bliss hurtling out of the bedroom and through the living room towards the balcony.

"Daisy!" he yells, but the roar of the gasoline-fed firestorm overwhelms his voice, and a second volley of shells zips through the balcony, sending a cascade of splinters into the air.

"*Daavid …*" Daisy is pleading as he reaches the balcony door, but a wall of flame shooting up the side of the cabin traps him inside.

"I'll have to go 'round!" he shouts, and he heads back through the cabin towards the front door.

Outside, as golden flames burn a bright hole in the darkness, Dawson crouches in the shadow of Daisy's car with the cabin's front door in his sights.

"Get him," mutters Bumface maliciously, having scrabbled up the bank to join his colleague, and the fire is reflected in his eyes as he waits for Bliss to emerge.

"Just his legs," insists Dawson, aiming low as the door starts to open.

With his mind reeling with concern for Daisy, Bliss has no thought for his own safety as he rushes out. But the zinging of shells slaps him back inside. Chunks of wood splinter into the air as a trail of bullets zips across the door, and he slams the heavy bolt into place before backing off and rushing to the bathroom.

"Okay, that's enough. Let's go," says Dawson, standing and preparing to run, but Bumface raises his gun.

"Just a minute," he says, and he rakes a line of shells across the hood of Daisy's car. "Let's see how far they can walk."

A few seconds later, with a wet towel hastily wrapped around his face and a fire extinguisher gushing foam from his hands, Bliss crashes through the wall of fire onto the blazing balcony. "*Daisy!*" he yells as he stumbles blindly through the smoky darkness, but her chair is empty.

"*Daisy! Daisy* ..." he continues to yell as he attacks tongues of flame, but the smoke and steam from the rain-soaked wooden decking sting his eyes as he desperately searches for her in the gloom. Then the nearby sound of a vehicle rocketing off through the silent forest stops him in his tracks. "Oh my God," he gasps, and he is about to make a dash for Daisy's car when a thin voice breaks through the crackling of the burning timber and starts him breathing again.

"*Daavid,*" cries Daisy weakly from somewhere in the bushes beneath the deck, and Bliss feels his way to the edge, yelling, "I can't see! Where are you?"

"I'm down here," she calls, spying him ten feet above her, his hazy figure silhouetted against the moon. "I jumped."

"I zhink zhat *je me suis foulé la cheville,*" says Daisy once Bliss has scrabbled down the smouldering timber supports, but one look at the crazy angle of her foot in the moonlight tells him a gloomier tale. "I think it's a little more than a sprained ankle," he says. However, while the fuel may have exhausted itself in the initial explosion, hot spots of burning timber beg his attention. "You'll be safe here for a minute," he continues, and he breaks off a verdant cedar branch to flail at the burgeoning fires.

"Who are zhey, *Daavid?* Why did zhey do that?" Daisy wants to know, once he has beaten out the last of the flames.

"I don't know," he says darkly, although he has a few faces in the frame, but he pushes them to the back of his mind while worrying about her ankle. "Let's get you to a hospital," he starts, as he bends to lift her, but she screams at the pain.

"*Shhh,*" he warns, fearing that an attacker might have been left behind to clean up the evidence. "They could still be around."

"Sorry ..." she whispers in his ear, and she clutches him tightly as he scrambles up the slimy embankment with her cradled in his arms.

The laneway where the car is parked is more exposed, and Bliss hunkers low as he carries her. "It shouldn't take long to find a hospital," he reassures her as he opens the door and places her on the back seat. "I'll just get the keys," he adds as he heads for the cabin — then he has a sinking feeling. "Oh, no!" he sighs, realizing that the solid wooden front door, now perforated by a trail of bullets, is firmly bolted on the inside. Then he turns and spies the run of holes across the Toyota's hood.

"Bastards," he swears.

Bumface is still laughing as they hit the highway and head south. "*Whoosh!* It went up like a freakin' rocket!"

he roars, using his hands to demonstrate an explosion, but Dawson answers him coolly.

"It's over, Steve. Let's just forget it, okay?"

"I'd love to see his freakin' face when he tries to start the engine ..." he is continuing, when Dawson interjects nastily.

"I said, *forget* it."

"Don't worry. I'll call for an ambulance," Bliss says as he carries Daisy into the cabin a few minutes later. Then he places her on the settee and stokes the log fire before picking up the phone.

"Dead," he says worriedly, but hasn't time to explore the cause before Daisy shrieks at the sight of blood oozing through his trouser leg. "You've been shot!" she cries.

"Just a scratch," he claims, then confesses that, in his rush to put out the fire, he'd hardly noticed the flesh wound.

"Show me," she insists, and tears well in her eyes at the sight of the ragged gash.

"Don't worry," says Bliss, as he grabs a handful of tissues, slaps them over the injury, and applies pressure. "I'm a first-aider." And to prove his point, ten minutes and one ripped-up bed sheet later, Daisy's ankle is professionally splinted to a wooden cheeseboard, and his leg wound is neatly bandaged.

"Look at us. One good left leg and one right," he says lightly, hopping to the couch and slumping beside her. "We'd make a good pair ..."

A very good pair, he thinks to himself, then steps back twenty minutes and rummages through his pockets, knowing that he has some unfinished business.

"What is zhe matter?" asks Daisy, noticing him blanch.

"I'm worried they might come back," he stalls, but his mind is whirling with the sounds of gunfire and conflagration as he retraces his movements at the start of the attack. *Did I put it somewhere safe? Back in the suitcase, perhaps … No, it was in my pocket.*

"I'm just going to make sure they've gone," he says and struggles to the window. One glance into the darkness tells him that if the ring, bequeathed by his great-grandmother through his mother, has fallen in the scorched undergrowth or in the mud of the embankment, he'll probably never find it.

Is this just another sign? he wonders as he slumps back onto the settee, realizing that fate has been against him all week, from the very moment he'd first been delayed at the border and had shown up late to meet Daisy in Seattle. But if fate is taking a hand — whose side is it on?

"I'm sure they won't come back," he says, taking her into his arms and comforting her in the warmth of the log fire. "We'll be safe enough, and the maid will be here in the morning."

chapter eighteen

"I've a good mind to go back and get my bloomin' hat," muses Daphne at Trina's breakfast table early Saturday morning.

"Great idea!" exclaims Trina excitedly. "But I'd better not tell Rick. He worries about me. Though I don't know why."

"Don't be silly. I was only joking," laughs Daphne, but Trina has got her teeth into the scheme.

"No, I mean it," she enthuses. "It's not like they're going to do anything to us now."

"I don't think so …" Daphne is continuing, but Trina isn't listening. "We'll just drive up to the gate and tell them we want it," she explains confidently. "The worst they can do is to say no."

"I suppose we could …" says Daphne hesitantly.

"I'll make sure my cell phone is working, and we'll just ask nicely. We needn't even get out of the car."

"But what about your children? You've hardly seen them since Tuesday."

"I think Rob's still disappointed that Daisy didn't come back," laughs Trina, sounding unconcerned. "And Kylie's been telling her friends that she was adopted at birth since that picture of us in the paper in the Kidneymobile. Anyway, they're teenagers."

"So?"

"It's Saturday!" she explodes, as if Daphne should have figured it out. "They won't be up before lunch."

"And Rick?"

"Oh, he was happy enough to see me last night, but I expect he'll sleep for a week."

"Well … maybe," says Daphne, still equivocating.

"You could always check with David," suggests Trina, offering Daphne a phone.

"It's no good asking him," she chortles. "He's a policeman — he was born saying no. Anyway," she adds meaningfully, "I don't expect he'd be thrilled if I got him out of bed too early this morning."

"Oh, Daphne!" shrieks Trina.

However, bed has not been an option for Bliss. The heavy wooden bedstead that should have given him and Daisy a pleasurable night now barricades the splintered front door, while its king-size mattress blocks the light from the glazed balcony slider. Bliss wouldn't have bothered for himself — "They won't come back," he assured Daisy — but as the night wore on she became increasingly alarmed at the possibility. And now, despite the sun rising high over the mountains, they cuddle under a duvet in front of the log fire, dead to the world, pooped by a sleepless night of pain and discomfort.

The Saturday-morning officers at the U.S. border show little interest in Trina's Jetta as the two women join the throngs of families streaming to Washington for the weekend.

"We're only going to ask at the gate," Daphne reminds Trina resolutely as they take the highway south. "We're not going in."

"I agree."

"After all, it's only a bloomin' hat."

"I know that."

"I can easily make another one."

"Don't worry," says Trina, "we're not going in."

"Good. As long as we've got that straight."

"We have."

Steam rising off the treetops vapourizes into the clear blue sky above the Cascade Mountains as the VW turns off the highway, but while robins and chickadees twitter cheerfully in the forest, fresh memories of the ill-fated expedition in the Kidneymobile begin to weigh more heavily as the women drive the twisty road towards their goal. They drive in silence, neither of them admitting any apprehension. The road that had taken them several hours to navigate in the mechanical bathtub takes only fifteen minutes by car, and they arrive at the gates before they have a chance to change their minds.

"Here we are," says Trina in surprise as she slows in the shadow of the high gates, although she is momentarily confused when she sees that the mission's signboard has gone, replaced by a more sinister one that warns that the premises are the property of the federal government and that trespassers will be prosecuted. "Is this the place?" she asks, turning to Daphne.

"It looks like it," says Daphne releasing her seatbelt. "Pull in over there."

But a chill comes over Trina as she views the high fence topped with a roll of razor wire. "I'm not so sure about this …" she begins, and she readies to drive on.

"Don't worry. I'm not going in," repeats Daphne as she catches hold of the door handle. "They can bloomin' well bring it to the gate after all the trouble they've caused. You just keep the engine running and we'll take off at the first sign of trouble."

"You be careful …" cautions Trina as Daphne heads for the entryphone.

"Are you sure they've gone?" whispers Daisy as Bliss drags himself to the balcony's glass door and eases the mattress aside.

"Don't worry, love!" he calls. "It's broad daylight. The maid should be here soon …" Then he pauses. "Oh, no!" he sighs with the sudden realization that it is Saturday, the projected day of Daisy's departure, and he had declined cleaning services. "The maid might as well wait until I've left on Sunday," he had told the operator when booking.

"You are going to miss your flight," he tells Daisy as he checks the bandage on her swollen ankle, once he's explained the situation.

"*Maman* will worry."

"I'd better try to get to one of the other cottages and find a phone …" he starts, but Daisy stays his hand. "*Daavid*," she queries, with something that's been on her mind for several hours.

"Yes?"

"Last night. Before zhis happened. You said you had something for me."

Now what? he questions himself. *Admit that I lost the ring; admit that Sarah was probably right — that*

I did usually put the job before her; admit that I might do the same again with Daisy? "It'll keep," he says with the realization that his vacillations had kept him awake almost as much as the pain in his leg and his concern over the attackers' return.

Daphne stands at the gate with her finger on the entryphone's call button, but she turns and shrugs to Trina when there is no response.

"Come on, let's go," says Trina with growing uneasiness. But Daphne spots the surveillance camera and stares at it openly.

"Halloo," she trills. "Anyone there? I've come for my hat."

A flock of gulls takes off from garbage bins inside the compound, and their shrieks of alarm make her jump as they pierce the silence. But once the birds have flown, peace returns and she again yells, "Halloo ..."

"Daphne ..." calls Trina, but the older woman waves her to be quiet. "I think I heard someone," she says, but Trina is doubtful.

"Are you sure?"

"Listen," says Daphne, then she loudly shouts, "Halloo! Who's there?"

"Maybe I should call Mike," suggests Trina. "He's a policeman. He'll know what to do." But her face falls when she pulls out her cell phone. "No service," she says, dropping the car into drive. "We'd best go. I'll treat you to another hat."

"Trina," Daphne reminds her sternly, "I made that hat with my own hands."

"Sorry ..." starts Trina, but the other woman has set her sight on the fence. "Where are you going?" Trina demands as Daphne begins to kick a path through the undergrowth at the side of the gate.

"Don't worry," says Daphne, "I'm not going in. I just want to get a better view. I'm sure I heard something."

"Daphne ... Come back!"

"The place looks deserted," she calls over her shoulder as she peers into the grounds.

"We'd better go, then," advocates Trina, but Daphne is tugging speculatively at the wire.

"Have you got a towrope?" she asks roguishly.

"No," lies Trina, but she gets out of her car and calls. "Hey! Anybody there?"

"Another one bites the dust," muses Bliss as he and Daisy prop each other over the raised hood of Daisy's rental car. "The radiator's got a couple of holes, the air filter's punctured and some of the electrics look shot."

"Can you make it go?" asks Daisy hopefully.

"If we push it," laughs Bliss, then he looks down the track to the distant road and adds, speculatively, "although it *is* downhill most of the way."

"Keep going ... keep going ..." encourages Daphne a few minutes later as Trina inches the Jetta forward with her tow-hitch tied to the fence.

"Just get ready to run," Trina warns, still expecting half a dozen gun-toting guards to rush out and blast them, but Daphne isn't listening as she waits to slip through the gap.

"I'm only going to get what's rightfully mine," she calls, readying her defence.

"This is very dangerous," admits Bliss, at the wheel of the freewheeling Toyota as it gathers speed, in reverse, down the hillside towards the highway. "I just hope the brakes will hold without power."

"See. I told you there was no one here," says Daphne, strolling nonchalantly into the empty guardhouse and kicking at a few scraps of paper on the dusty wooden floor.

"Nothing ..." agrees Trina, pointing to frayed wiring where phones, cameras and lights had been forcefully ripped out.

"I bet they didn't leave my bloomin' hat," says Daphne despondently as they carry on through the compound towards the main building, but Trina is still wary, and she carries her useless cell phone ahead of her like a weapon.

"They were obviously up to no good," Daphne is saying, pointing to the deserted offices and living quarters, now stripped of every trace of habitation, when a metallic *bang* brings them up short.

"Run!" cries Trina, but Daphne grabs her hand.

"Who's there?" demands Daphne with the authority of a sentry, and as her words echo around the empty buildings, the gulls take off in fright again. But amongst the birds' raucous cries there is an unmistakeably human sound.

"Help ..." cries a weak voice from inside an old outhouse on the edge of the forest. "Help ..."

"Someone's here."

"I told you."

"Help ..."

"I didn't realize it was this steep," yells Bliss as he grapples with the wheel, one-handed, while he hangs onto the handbrake with the other. Behind him, Daisy grimaces as she is flung around by the bouncing car. "Hang on," he shrieks as he sees another looming pothole, but he's zooming backwards without power and can't avoid it.

"*Putain!*" screams Daisy as she flies off the seat and comes down heavily.

"Sorry," says Bliss, keeping up the pressure on the brake.

"I think it came from over there," whispers Trina, pointing to an old outhouse on the edge of the forest clearing, and they creep, hand in hand, towards the building. Then, after a moment's pause to look at each other, Daphne whips open the door.

"Willy — it's you!" cries Trina at the sight of the pitiable man chained to the steel pipe.

"Who?" asks Wallace.

"Oops — oh, sorry ... Spotty —" she starts, but Daphne kicks her.

"What's your name?" asks Daphne.

"I don't think I should ..." he begins, and Daphne starts to close the door.

"All right ... all right."

"Well?" questions Daphne.

"It's Wallace — Allan Wallace," says the pathetic-looking prisoner. "Can you get me out?"

"Yes —" starts Trina, but Daphne kicks her again.

"Possibly," says Daphne, as if giving it her fullest consideration.

"I helped you escape," he pleads, and Daphne seemingly relents.

"All right. But we want to know what was going on here first."

"I can't —" he starts, and the door begins to close again. "Okay, okay. I'll tell you."

"Hold tight!" yells Bliss, seeing the traffic on the highway approaching at speed, and he puts all his weight behind the brakes and prays.

By the time Bliss has brought the car to a stop and flagged down a passing motorist, Daphne and Trina have used a tire iron to jemmy Wallace from his makeshift cell. And as Bliss and Daisy ride to hospital in Seattle, the forlorn CIA officer is cadging a lift into Bellingham from his erstwhile prisoners.

"Wait a minute," says Daphne as they prepare to drive away. "I still I haven't got my bloomin' hat."

"Never mind," says Trina, happy to get away. "You've got plenty more at home."

"No," insists Daphne, "it's my favourite. And you never know; I might get invited to a wedding while I'm here."

chapter nineteen

"*Daavid*. It is *la Tour Eiffel!*" yells Daisy, pointing excitedly towards the replica of the famous structure as the white limousine sweeps them to the door of the Paris Hotel two days later.

"I know," says Bliss with his finger on a pictorial map. "I promised you a foreign holiday, and that's what you're getting. And look — over there is New York, and up there is Venice, Monte Carlo, Luxor, Mandalay ..."

"We got the whole damn world here, sir," drawls the Nevada driver as he opens the door for Daisy, and he's not entirely wrong. Samantha and Peter Bryan have arrived from England, Daisy's mother and an aunt are on their way from France, and a slew of people led by Trina and Daphne have flown down from Canada.

"Las Vegas?" Daphne had trilled disbelievingly when Trina had taken the call from Bliss on Saturday afternoon.

"Yeah," Trina had assured her excitedly. "And he wants us to fly down there on Monday. He says that his Uncle Sam is gonna pay."

"He's never mentioned an Uncle Sam to me," Daphne had said, scratching her head. "Let me speak to him." But Bliss had gone by the time she had taken the phone. "Where is he?" she'd asked, turning to Trina.

"He was on a pay phone somewhere," she'd replied, looking puzzled. "But he said he had to go, because Daisy's ankle was being operated on."

"Just remember," Daphne whispers as she and Trina watch Bliss pushing Daisy towards them in a wheelchair. "Don't mention that we went back to the monastery. He won't understand."

"Hello, Daphne," beams Bliss as he spies the two women in the hotel's Parisian-styled lobby, then his face clouds in confusion. "How on earth did you get your hat back?"

"Uh-oh!" exclaims Trina, and Daphne kicks her foot. "This one?" asks the Englishwoman, as if she is surprised to find it on her head.

"Yes," enquires Bliss. "Wasn't that the one you lost at the monastery place?"

"Similar ..." nods Daphne, then she uses the cast on Daisy's foot to get her out of the jam. "Oh, dear. What on earth has happened to you?"

"Hey, Mike!" calls Bliss, leaving Daisy to explain her injury as he spies his Canadian counterpart talking to Trina's husband. "Any sign of the baby?"

"Another week, they think. But what's been happening? I heard you'd been shot."

"Just a scratch," replies Bliss before briefly outlining the nighttime attack.

"You could've been killed," says Phillips, but Bliss shakes his head. "Just a friendly warning, I think; although I wouldn't mind catching them."

"Maybe you should hire Daphne and Trina to investigate for you," laughs Rick Button. "They're calling themselves 'Lovelace and Button — International Investigators,' and Trina has run up some fancy business cards on my computer."

"Really?"

"Yeah. They reckon they've cracked the secret of that monastery place."

"Seriously?" asks Bliss.

"Hi, Dad," interrupts Samantha as she and her husband approach. "What have you been up to now?"

"Upsetting the natives," he laughs.

"I've kept your seat warm for you, Dave," says Peter Bryan, smiling broadly as he holds out his hand, though Bliss can't help feeling that it will always be something of a hot seat with Chief Superintendent Edwards at the helm.

"Actually, I want to speak you about that, Peter," he starts. "But what's the outcome on the suicide situation?"

"It's pretty much resolved," says Bryan, "and the charges against young Ronnie Stapleton have been dropped."

"I was never really convinced that he'd shoved Minnie," admits Bliss. "I feel kind'a bad that he ended up in hospital."

"His father's gone public, demanding a gallantry award for him for attempting to save the old lady's life," says Bryan. "And he's pushing for a public enquiry."

"Talking of enquiry …" says Bliss, and he turns to Daphne. "Rick tells me that you've solved the monastic mystery."

"Oh. Didn't I tell you, David?"

"No. You know very well you didn't."

"Well, I thought you would have worked it out for yourself, to be honest," she teases, "now that you're a

Chief Inspector." Then she carries on relentlessly. "Especially as you're the great detective who discovered the identity of the man in the iron mask?"

"Yes, enough already," he laughs. "But I'm keeping that under my hat until my book is published."

"All right, then ..." says Daphne, starting to wander away.

"Whoa!" says Bliss, holding her back. "You haven't told me what they were doing at the monastery."

"No, I haven't," she says, straight-faced. "I'm keeping that under my hat — just in case I decide to write a book as well."

"Dad," asks Samantha petulantly, "when are you going to tell us why we are all here?"

"I'll tell you at dinner," he says. "But Daphne's going to spill the beans about the monastery first — aren't you?"

"Okay. I'll do a deal," Daphne relents. "I'll show you mine if you show me yours."

"Daphne Lovelace!" he exclaims. "I don't believe you said that."

"It was a government hospital for tourists," she finally explains, knowing that Bliss will jump to the wrong conclusion.

"So why the secrecy?" he asks, falling into the trap. "What were they — foreign dignitaries? Disgraced monarchs?"

"No — they were tourists with something to offer," she replies enigmatically, playing a guessing game. But Trina can't wait and jumps in with the answer.

"Kidneys," she says excitedly. "All the patients were each selling a kidney."

"Really?"

"That's right," says Daphne, then she recounts details of Wallace's confession.

"Do you realize that every time an American citizen goes to Korea or China to buy a kidney from a living donor it sucks seventy-five thousand dollars out of our economy?" the CIA officer had told them, repeating the mantra that had been used to sell him on the idea.

"And it goes into the pocket of some poverty-stricken peasant who is willing to risk his life to feed his wife and kids," Trina had suggested acerbically.

"Sometimes," Wallace had admitted. "Though more often than not they'll blow it on a new car, a satellite TV and a cell phone. Anyway, think of the health benefits of having the operation in a modern Western clinic compared to having your kidney whipped out in a backstreet butcher's shop in P'yongyang or Beijing."

"So you bring them here so that they can blow it on a shiny new Ford —" Trina had started, but Wallace had cut her off.

"No. They don't get paid. They get something much more valuable — a passport from the U.S. of A."

"Who told you all this, Daphne?" Bliss wants to know when he's heard her out.

"Chief Inspector!" she exclaims, apparently mortified. "I'm surprised you would expect me to reveal the source of confidential information."

"What source?"

"You're doing it again. Anyway, don't you want to know about the lottery scam?"

"Are you saying that was them, too?"

"Yup," says Trina. "And Daphne got Wilting Willy to confess that as well."

"Got who?" asks Bliss.

"Oops! Sorry," says Trina as Daphne kicks her again. "Me and my big mouth."

"His real name is Spotty Dick, if you must know," explains Daphne, confusing the issue. "And he was the one who tried to help us escape."

"So you let him go?" nods Bliss, catching on.

"Once I'd put the bite on him a little," admits Daphne as she leans into Bliss conspiratorially. "Anyway, he's a marked man."

"So, c'mon, Dad," says Samantha. "You didn't drag us all this way to discuss police business."

"You'll have to wait —" he is saying when Trina cuts in.

"Your dad's gonna help with the kidney marathon — aren't you, Dave?"

"No, I am not."

"Spoilsport," says Daphne.

"She only expects me to dress up as a giant condom and hand out free samples along the road," he explains in mock outrage.

"Oh, Dad ..." laughs Samantha, but Trina is serious.

"Sexually transmitted diseases are a primary cause of kidney failure," she says snottily. "I just thought you would want to help, that's all."

"I do," he says curtly. "I'll give you a hundred dollars."

"We need kidney donations, not money," snorts Trina. "I mean, look what was happening at the monastery. They were shipping poor Asians in so that some rich Yankee jerk who's spent his life abusing his kidneys could just buy himself another one. I bet they wouldn't give me one if I needed it."

"Your kidney patient committed suicide while he waited for a transplant, didn't he?" Daphne reminds her as an example, but Trina looks around sheepishly before admitting, "Actually, I got it wrong. When the office said Norman wouldn't need me anymore because he'd taken matters into his own hands — well, I just assumed he'd ... you know."

"And he hadn't?"

"No," she laughs. "He'd gone to China to get a kidney transplant. He's coming back next week; a new man."

"Okay," says Bliss as he starts pushing Daisy away in the wheelchair. "I've booked a table for us all at seven o'clock at Caesar's Palace. Now Daisy and I are going shopping."

"C'mon, Daphne," says Samantha, once her father is out of sight. "What's he planning?"

"I don't know. But I haven't seen him so happy for a long time."

"Amazing what a good woman does for you," says Peter Bryan putting his arms around his wife.

"Okay," says Daphne with her eyes on the casino. "This is Vegas. Let's hit the tables."

Daisy's mother's flight arrives mid-afternoon, to be met by Daisy, Bliss and a nattily dressed chauffeur. "See? I promised you I'd get her a limousine," Bliss had said when he'd ordered the smartest one in Vegas, and he has also ensured that the French woman will receive VIP treatment at the Paris Hotel upon her arrival.

"Zhat will make her very happy," Daisy had said, and Bliss had smiled at the prospect.

"*Maman!*" cries Daisy joyfully as she waits to greet her at the arrival's gate, but the elderly woman's face falls at the sight of the wheelchair. "*C'est rien* ... It is nothing," she says, and stands up shakily to prove her point.

Dianna LeBlanc has the same olive skin and raven hair as her daughter; however, age and stress have dulled her ebony eyes over the years. But as they ride to the hotel in the stretch limo, she soaks up some of the Las

Vegas glitz and continually repeats, "It is very beautiful
... It is very beautiful," in a heavy accent.

"Zhat is all *Maman* can say in English," Daisy con-
fides when Bliss asks if she enjoyed the flight, so he
switches to French.

Trina is bursting with excitement when Bliss, flanked by
Daisy's mother, pushes her daughter into the dining
room at Caesar's Palace.

"Daphne won five hundred bucks," Trina blurts as
Bliss helps Daisy into a chair.

"You lucky thing," he is saying, when Samantha
spots Daisy's diamond necklace.

"Is that a Tiffany?" she asks in awe.

"It is a present from your father," says Daisy with a
proud smile.

"Oh ... my ... God," screeches Trina, and the women
rise as one to fawn over Daisy while Mike Phillips and
Peter Bryan slap Bliss on the back.

"My mother says she would like to give you a
special present, *Daaavid*," says Daisy once the commotion has died down.

"What's that?"

"She says zhat she would now like you to write
your book."

"Really?"

"Yes. She says it is time for zhe truth to be known."

"Thank you very much," he says, before turning to
the assembly with an announcement. "Well. I guess you
all want to know why you are here," he says as if he has
no notion of the pent-up expectancy, and then he takes
a crumpled envelope from his pocket and hands it to
his son-in-law with a wink. "Here. Give this to the
commissioner, will you?"

"What is it?"

"It's my resignation, Peter, and that's why I wanted you all here — to celebrate this moment with me."

"You can't quit," bleats Peter Bryan.

"I just did."

"But what about Edwards?" Bryan continues in dismay. "You promised to nail him before you left."

"I know," says Bliss. "And I will, in my own way."

"What way?"

"I'm going to make him the villain in my book."

Time stretches. Eight pairs of eyes focus on Bliss. He knows what they want, but he's haunted by the warning he uttered at Samantha's wedding. *The poor sucker hasn't got a clue what he's taking on,* he is thinking when he realizes that no one is breathing. Then Samantha breaks the spell.

"Is that it, Dad?" she asks finally. "Your resignation?"

"Oh. No," he says, then pauses as if he has to give it some thought. "There's more," he continues, knowing that they are all waiting to hear the word "marriage," but instead he turns to Daphne and Trina, splits Montague's hush money, and announces that they have each been awarded ten thousand dollars' compensation by the U.S. government for their unlawful detention.

"That's terrific ..." starts Trina, and she grabs Daphne's hand. "Hey ... how 'bout you and me taking that world trip you were planning?"

"Are you serious?"

"Yeah. Of course. We can do it as a sort of tribute to Minnie."

"Well, I suppose she did pay for it in a way," admits Daphne, then she turns to Bliss. "But what on earth are you going to do with your time now you're quitting the police force?"

"Well," he says as he hangs on to Daisy. "I think you were right, Daphne. I think that you can reach a point where all you have to look forward to is the past. So, I've decided to start looking to the future. I'm going to live in France and write a book that will stand the literary world on its head."

"About the man in the iron mask?" she queries.

"Yes," says Bliss. "The true expose of a three-hundred-year-old mystery that involves political intrigue, government dishonesty and individual greed."

"That sounds very, very, familiar," says Phillips.

"Yes, Mike," agrees Bliss. "Absolutely nothing has changed."

"And ...?" questions Samantha, seeing the adoration in Daisy's eyes and hoping to push her father in that direction.

"And," he says after a moment's silence, "I shall call it, *The Truth behind the Mask*."

The End